LOVE'S A SHOT IN THE DARK...

Owen Daniels is a simple man. He has his friends, two thriving businesses, and a kick ass house he renovated himself. He also talks to his dead mom on a regular basis and can't get a certain curvy brown-eyed woman out of his head. Not to mention the fact that the former soldier and National Guardsman isn't quite the ladies' man his friends think he is. Okay, so maybe he isn't that simple after all.

Women's Three Gun Champion Caridad Mathews is back home in Del Rio, Texas, after leaving seven years ago with a vow to never return. But she's just inherited her abuela's house and lost her apartment in Dallas, so back home it is while she tries to get her life back together. The last thing she needs is a sexy ginger distracting her and trying to fight her battles for her.

But as Owen and Caridad unearth long-buried secrets, neither can deny the attraction that burns hot between them. Can Caridad learn that trust and vulnerability don't always lead to heartache and pain? And can Owen break down his own walls and accept that he can't save everybody?

By Aubrey Gross

Hair Trigger Heart

AUBREY GROSS

Copyright

Book layout © 2015 Indie Book Design
Book cover © 2015 by Indie Book Design

Hair Trigger Heart/Aubrey Gross -- 2nd ed.

Epub Edition August 2015 ISBN: 978-0-9962821-6-1

Print Edition ISBN: 978-0-9962821-7-8

To everyone who's ever survived.

"Without your wound where would your power be?"

Thornton Wilder

CHAPTER ONE

"Gunpowder and Lead" blared from the truck's speakers as Caridad Mathews sped down the farm to market road, her hair dancing in the breeze from the open windows. The weather had finally decided to cool down, with highs dropping from the nineties to the seventies overnight.

Gotta love west Texas in November.

A sign came up on her right. Devils Ranch. She slowed and turned left into the drive. Caliche bounced against the underside of the pickup as she pulled up to a closed gate. She rolled to a stop next to an intercom system, which had a sign above it directing her to press the green button and wait a few seconds.

Caridad sighed as she opened the truck door in order to actually reach the button—being short definitely had its drawbacks—and then followed directions. Moments later a masculine voice said, "Yes?"

The guy—whoever he was—may have sounded like a phone sex operator, but he also sounded rude. Caridad reigned in her temper.

"Yeah. I have a reservation for this weekend. Caridad Mathews?"

She heard a couple of clicks from what she assumed was a mouse, and then the phone sex operator spoke again. "You're a little early, so we don't have your room ready yet. That going to be a problem?"

She glanced at the clock on the dashboard. 12:23. Dammit. She was early. By an hour and a half.

"Not at all, just as long as there's a bathroom I can use." It had been a couple of hours since her last stop on the drive down from Dallas, and her bladder was letting her know it.

"Absolutely. Once you pull through the gate just follow the signs. The ranch house is about a quarter mile up the drive. Just pull up close to the house." Phone Sex Operator's voice quieted as the intercom clicked off.

The gate swung open and Caridad drove through, following the caliche road around a curve. In front of her the ranch house and out buildings sprawled, the stone and metal appearing to spring out of the earth.

The photos on their website did not do the place justice.

Transfixed by the rustic elegance of the main house, Caridad pulled to a stop and stared. Maybe this hadn't been such a bad idea after all.

Pulling her gaze away from the buildings, she reached over and grabbed her backpack off of the passenger seat before removing the keys from the ignition and opening the door. Placing one foot on the running board, she hopped out of the truck and closed the door behind her.

A cool breeze ruffled her hair and the sound of sotol fronds rubbing against each other greeted her ears. She'd traveled all over the country and seen some amazing sights, but there was still nothing like a fall day in west Texas.

The sound of gravel crunching under feet sounded on the other side of the truck, and Cari pulled herself from her musings as she rounded the hood. A stocky, well-built man walked towards her, a slight smile on his bearded face.

Holy hotness, Batman.

She'd never really been into gingers, but this one might make her change her mind. His hair was hidden under a ball cap with the Devils Ranch logo on it, but a few strands curled out from under the edges. His beard—also something she'd never particularly been into—was just between well-groomed and *Duck Dynasty,* giving him a look that screamed, "I don't care what you think." His eyes were hidden behind mirrored aviators, and she couldn't help but wonder what color they were. Green? Blue? Brown? Would they dance with laughter or would they smolder?

What in the world? She never got fanciful over a guy's eye color, much less used the word "smolder," but something about the sight of him had her brain going fuzzy. He just oozed sexuality, and her body was lighting up like the Fourth of July.

Also something that didn't happen often.

Or ever.

Certainly not recently, which was part of the reason why she'd decided to go through with this weekend in the first place.

Despite the fact that she was alone.

ℭℯ

Owen Daniels strode across the caliche drive towards the newer model F-150 and the woman standing in front of it. Backpack slung over one shoulder, wariness pulsed off of her in waves.

Weird. Women were never wary around him.

Then again, there had been a bit of snippiness in her tone when she'd buzzed over the intercom, which was probably his fault since he'd been distracted when he'd responded. He'd probably inadvertently come across as a little rude.

As he reached her—Caridad, she'd said—he sized her up. About five-two. Curvy—he knew better than to guess any woman's weight—and probably around a 38DD (that one he was more than happy to guess—and verify). Heart-shaped face. Button nose. Olive skin that he guaranteed did not come from a tanning bed. Straight black hair.

Her eyes were hidden behind a pair of dark-lensed sunglasses, but his gut told him they were brown. Something about her just screamed, "brown-eyed girl."

He reached the front of her truck and held out his hand. "Owen Daniels. Nice to meet you."

Her hand was small but the grip firm. "Caridad Mathews. Sorry I'm early."

He grinned. "No problem. It's not a big deal. Like I said over the intercom, we don't have your room quite ready, but you're more than welcome to go ahead and bring your things inside and grab a bite to eat."

She nodded, the movement almost stiff. "I'll just get the rest of my stuff, then."

She rounded the truck and opened the back door before pulling a wheeled carry-on out. A large purple and black range bag followed, which she strapped onto the carry-on. She then pulled out a hard-sided rifle case and shut the door.

"I can help you with that," Owen offered.

She shook her head. "No thanks. I've got it."

He sighed. Great. Looked like she was going to be one of those stubborn, independent types who thought an offer of help from a man was chauvinistic. Not that he had any problem with strong, independent women. His best friend Jenn was the very definition of strong and independent, even if she was shacking up with his friend and business partner Matt Roberts. And his friend Chase's fiancée, Jo, was also strong and independent, it was just that both women understood that a guy offering help didn't mean he thought less of her.

In his case, he'd had good southern manners drilled into his head since he was a boy.

Yes ma'am. No ma'am. Yes sir. No sir. Please. Thank you. Always hold the door open for a lady.

Even though both his grandmother and his mother were now gone, he could still hear their voices in his head on a daily basis, urging him to always do the right thing and be a good boy.

He turned on his heel and followed Caridad into the ranch house, and his gaze accidentally on purpose dropped down to her ass.

Sometimes it was really hard to be a good boy.

She could feel his gaze on her ass.

At least, she was pretty sure she could. To be fair, she wasn't entirely sure he was checking out her backside, but the hair on the back of her neck was standing up and she felt twitchy, like she was being watched. Once she was inside the ranch house, she stopped abruptly and turned towards him.

Crap. She'd forgotten about his sunglasses, so there really was no way to know if her suspicions were correct.

Owen stepped inside and closed the door behind her, gesturing towards the open space they'd stepped into before taking off those aviators. Unfortunately, the bill of his cap obscured her view of his eyes. *Seriously?* "As you can see, this is the primary gathering and living area. Very open floor plan. We have a chef who cooks meals for our guests during our busy season, but if you prefer to cook for yourself or want a snack or anything, feel free to use the kitchen and whatever's in the pantry and fridge."

Caridad stepped further into the house and pushed her sunglasses onto the top of her head. She wasn't really into cooking—her travel schedule meant she spent a lot of time in hotels—but even she knew quality appliances when she saw them. Stainless steel gleamed and the countertops were a spotless gray made out of some stone material—quartz or granite, she honestly wasn't sure. The cabinets were stained a dark brown, picking up the natural grain of the wood. There was a huge kitchen island with bar stools along one side, and over it hung a rack heavy with copper and stainless steel pots and pans. An open shelf on the end of the island held numerous cast iron skillets.

To her left was the living area, filled with large, comfortable-looking furniture; a couple of recliners, a couch with media seating and a smaller love seat that looked like a great place to curl up with a book. In front of the couch was a heavy wooden coffee table, the rustic piece matching the pine end tables and entertainment center that spanned the entire length of one wall. The doors on it were closed, but she imagined it held a television most men only dreamed of having (and let's face it, The Devils Ranch was definitely geared more towards men than women).

There was also a small dining area with a table that looked to hold about eight, but could probably hold more if necessary. Chandeliers fashioned out of antlers hung from the ceiling and provided light, surprisingly coming across as rustic and tasteful rather than tacky. The handful of mounted game made it clear this was a hunting lodge, but the walls weren't filled with taxidermy like she'd imagined they would be.

"It's really nice in here."

"You sound surprised by that." His tone sounded teasing rather than offended, but Caridad stole a glance at him anyway to make sure. A small grin tilted the right corner of his mouth up, and she finally managed to catch a glimpse of his eyes, even though she wasn't sure why it was so important to her to know what color they were.

Ends up, they were clear blue and almost burning with heat and life.

She felt that little grin, and the heat in his gaze traveled straight to her core.

Crap. That was inconvenient.

She shrugged and tried to school her features so he wouldn't know she was standing there thinking lustful thoughts about him. Because, hello, kind of creepy considering they'd met, oh, ten minutes ago.

"To be honest, when you hear the words 'hunting ranch' or 'hunting lodge' you kind of get this immediate picture of dead animals everywhere, muddy boots on cheap furniture and a bunch of old, fat dudes drinking beers and farting. You don't imagine something that feels upscale yet comfortable."

"'Upscale yet comfortable,' huh? I'm gonna have to pass

that one along to our website guy."

She snorted. "You know what I mean."

He nodded then walked into the kitchen and opened the fridge. "You want anything to drink? Even if this place does look 'upscale yet comfortable' we do have those aforementioned beers."

"Am I going to be handling firearms later?"

His gaze flicked down to the gun case she'd set at her feet. "Probably not, unless you want to use our indoor range to make sure your rifle's sighted in. Your hunt doesn't technically start until tomorrow morning."

He had her at 'indoor range.' "Is it as awesome as it looks on the website?"

He closed the refrigerator door and smiled, sending a sucker punch straight to her ovaries. "It's even better."

"Holy crap." Her voice was almost reverent as they stepped into the ranch's private indoor range.

The door closed behind them, locking all sound out and keeping all sound in. "I told you it was awesome."

Caridad stepped forward and set her range bag and rifle case on the floor in front of the shooting bench and propped her hands on her hips. "I've seen some nice ranges in my time, Mr. Daniels, but this one is right up there with the best of them."

Owen leaned against the wall and crossed his feet. Hands in his pockets, he said, "You can call me Owen, Ms. Mathews."

She nodded once. "Fine. And you can call me Caridad."

He fought a grin. Jesus, she was a mystery. One minute she was friendly and almost flirtatious, and the next it was like a total stranger had taken her place. Normally he wasn't the type for games or having his head messed with, but something about Caridad Mathews was piquing his curiosity.

She sighed and squatted so that she could open her range bag. Owen's gaze followed the motion. Okay, so he knew at least one thing that was piquing his curiosity. The woman had a very nice ass. As she pulled ammunition and shooting equipment out of her range bag, he fought to remain professional. It was hard, though, considering the way her jeans pulled across her butt and her cotton t-shirt stretched across her breasts.

They were kind of magnificent.

She stood and set a box of ammo on the shooting bench, followed by shooting glasses and what looked to be some expensive electronic in-ear noise protection. She stooped down again and opened the hard-sided gun case before removing an AR with a custom purple and teal paint job.

"What caliber is that in?" he asked.

She glanced up at him before grabbing the magazine that had been beside the rifle in the case. "Three-oh-eight. Why?"

"Just wanted to make sure it wasn't two-twenty-three. That can take a deer, but it's not the most humane way to do it."

She gave him some serious side eye before standing up and placing the rifle on the shooting stand. "Please. Just because I'm a woman that doesn't mean I don't know my ass from a hole in the ground."

"Never said you didn't. But you'd be surprised how many people think they're going to take a twelve-point, mature buck at two hundred yards with a round that's better suited to varmint hunting."

She snorted and pulled a baseball cap out of her range bag. He watched as she put her hair in a ponytail then threaded it through the back of the cap before settling it firmly in place on her head. "You got ear protection?"

He walked over to a cabinet where they stored things like ear muffs, shooting glasses and a trauma kit—just in case—and grabbed a pair of electronic ear muffs and glasses. He made sure the muffs were on and working before slipping the safety glasses onto his head. Caridad had already put her ears in and glasses on, and began loading the magazine when he was once again behind her.

He had to admit, he was fairly impressed so far with her gun safety skills. Unfortunately, he'd been around one too many people who didn't seem to understand that guns were not toys.

As was his usual MO when around someone he didn't know who was handling a firearm, he watched her like a hawk. Okay, so maybe the watching wasn't so bad, all things considered.

Come on, man, get your shit together. She's a client, not some chick you just met in a bar.

Annoyed with himself and his seemingly one-track mind, he forced himself to focus on Caridad's actions and his surroundings. He kept an eye out to make sure she kept her finger off the trigger, had the rifle pointed down range at all times, that the safety was on. The same things he made sure of with anyone.

The calm, efficient manner with which she loaded the magazine and the rifle, and then positioned herself at the shooting bench told him she was familiar with and comfortable around guns. She was safe—that was obvious—and she wasn't scared. If anything, she looked more relaxed with her cheek against the collapsible stock of her rifle than she had since she'd gotten here.

That thought did nothing to calm his mind. Instead, it worried him even more, mostly because women who knew their way around guns were hot. Seriously so.

And it wasn't the whole girls in bikinis holding guns thing, either. Honestly, that wasn't all that hot and was pretty demeaning towards women, like all they were good for was gun porn and, well, porn. It was more that confidence was sexy, more so than any amount of glistening cleavage featuring a Glock would ever be.

He knew there were some women who had started out as gun girls and had successfully transitioned from that into true shooting careers, and more power to them. There was something about a woman—okay, in this case Caridad—who just exuded a quiet competency and lack of fear that caught his attention.

His gaze dipped down to the curve of her ass in her jeans, and he quickly jerked it back up.

Okay, so more than her competency and confidence had caught his attention, but the whole package was definitely piquing his interest.

"Ready?" Caridad asked, pulling him from his thoughts.

Owen inhaled and mentally shook himself. "Ready!"

She flipped off the safety. He saw her inhalation and slow exhale just before she fired the first shot down range. In rapid succession she fired five rounds before flipping the safety back on and standing straight. She looked back through her rifle scope and nodded once before turning to him and asking, "Mind if I fire off a few magazines? It's been a stressful week."

Her smile was kind of crooked, almost apologetic. Owen felt it like a kick to the chest. Understanding that sometimes the best kind of therapy involved lead and a paper target, he smiled and said, "Sure. Have at it."

She smiled back at him, fuller now, before repositioning herself behind the bench.

Caridad could feel Owen's gaze on her as she readied herself behind the shooting bench. He'd watched her the entire time they'd been in here, his eyes and mind making note of every single one of her movements.

As if she would ever handle a gun improperly.

But again, he wouldn't know that.

Because he didn't seem to know who she was.

She was grateful for the anonymity right now, that he didn't know who she was. Too often when she was around other gun enthusiasts—and Owen definitely came across as a gun enthusiast—they only wanted to bitch about politics and talk about legal stuff or competitions.

All she wanted to do was shoot her guns, compete, drink some beer afterwards and maybe enjoy a good cheeseburger on occasion. Was that really so much to ask?

Not that she wasn't glad for her success. She'd worked her ass off to get to where she was as the reigning Women's American 3-Gun Champion, had trained long hours and competed even when she didn't feel like it. There were days, though, when the minor celebrity that came along with the title grated on her nerves.

The biggest was that people sometimes treated her differently. Women would look at her either in awe or like she was an alien. Men who weren't previously interested in her sometimes looked at her in a completely different and highly sexual sort of way. Sure, there were always the folks who respected her and acknowledged the achievement and were more interested in asking for training tips or what it was like to compete at that level, and luckily those people really did outweigh the bad.

The problem was that there had been so much of the bad stuff here lately.

Just one more reason why getting out of Dallas for the weekend had probably been a good idea.

Caridad pushed her thoughts to the back of her mind and focused on the rifle in her hands and the target down range. She took a couple of slow, even breaths before flipping the safety off.

Once she'd acquired a good cheek meld and centered the target in the crosshairs of her scope, she curled her finger around the trigger.

Breathe in.

Breathe out, just a little.

Squeeze.

Exhale.

She regained her sight picture, briefly noted that the shot had been almost dead center, just as her first six shots had been. Breathed in. Breathed out, just a little. Squeezed the trigger. Exhaled.

She fired off the rest of the rounds in rapid, efficient fashion, ejected the magazine and flipped the safety back on before stepping back. Silently—which was how she liked to work—she reloaded the magazine and repositioned herself behind the bench.

Three magazines later (she was really glad she'd brought a few boxes of ammo), she felt lighter and her head clearer than it had in days, if not weeks.

It really had been too long since she'd gotten in any range time.

After ejecting the final magazine and flipping the safety back to the ON position, she bent down and grabbed a spotting scope out of her range bag, which she handed to Owen. "So do I pass the test?"

He quirked up a golden red eyebrow. "What test?"

She rolled her eyes. "The test I've been taking ever since we stepped in here."

He snorted and took the spotting scope from her, put it up to his eye and said, "Wow, that's impressive."

She shrugged. "Eh, I've had better days."

He handed the scope back to her. "Better days? You completely obliterated the center of the target and there isn't a stray bullet hole anywhere on paper. I'm a pretty damned good shot, and even I can't shoot that accurately."

His matter of fact praise warmed her a lot more than it should have, all things considered.

You don't even know the guy.

"Nice Armalite, by the way."

She walked back to the bench and placed the scope back in her range bag. As she packed up her gear, she said, "Thanks. It was actually a gift—custom paint job and all—and I've barely gotten to shoot it since I got it. I figured now was as good a time as any, right?"

"That's a pretty nice gift."

"I agree. Although the person who gave me this accidentally dropped the fact that they were going to get me a LaRue, but decided not to because of the backlog." For some reason, she didn't quite want to share that the gift giver was someone he might know—her sometimes agent who also happened to be one of the owners of the Devils Ranch, and most likely Owen's boss. This weekend had also been Darrin's idea, his way of telling her to get out of the city because she'd been driving him nuts.

"Wait. So the person who gave you this actually let it spill that they were going to get you a LaRue instead? No offense to Armalite—because they have some seriously nice guns—but that's like telling someone they won a Lamborghini then giving them a Corvette."

"I know, right? Believe me when I say I gave him hell about that for weeks, because, seriously, LaRue. But ultimately it's the thought that counts, right? And the custom paint job really was a nice touch."

And it had been. Her favorite colors were teal and purple, so Darrin had had the custom paint job done before giving it to her after she'd won the national championship. Even better was the fact that the pattern wasn't camo—instead, it was this cool, almost abstract splatter design—and it wasn't pink. She was all for getting more women interested in the shooting sports, but there was definitely a pink camo apocalypse going on right now.

It wasn't pretty.

She zipped up her range bag and grabbed her rifle, which she returned to its case. She quickly cleaned up her brass, and once that was done, she stood and grabbed both her range bag and rifle case. "Thanks for letting me use this. It's a pretty good indoor range."

Owen shrugged before returning his ear muffs and glasses. "No problem. We enjoy it, and like that we can sight in rifles or shoot handguns during deer season. We eventually want to add on, take it out to five hundred yards or so."

She raised an eyebrow as they exited the range and walked

across the patio area between it and the main house. "We?"

He shoved his hands into the back pockets of his jeans, making the edge of his t-shirt ride up just slightly in the front. She almost stumbled at the sight of that little strip of taut, male stomach.

Eyes up ahead. Eyes up ahead.

"My partners and me."

"Partners…?" she asked.

"The other three guys who own this place."

Her little anonymity bubble suddenly burst at the knowledge that he did know Darrin, apparently pretty well if they were freaking business partners. She didn't know why it mattered that Owen didn't know who she was, but for some reason it did. "Oh. So you're one of the owners, then?"

"Yup, guess I forgot to mention that earlier," he said as they reached the house and he opened the door for her. She stepped inside and he followed, the door quietly closing behind them.

Caridad set her rifle and range bag down next to her suitcase and changed the subject. "Do you think my room's ready by now?"

Owen glanced at the watch on his wrist. "It should be. Let me check for you."

He pulled out his phone and typed something into it. Seconds later he glanced up at her and said, "It's ready. Let me show you the way."

Part of her wanted to tell him it was okay, that she could find the way herself, simply because she was feeling an antsy need to get away from him. Why, she wasn't sure.

Okay, if she was being honest with herself, she did know why she was feeling antsy; she was attracted to him and shouldn't be. Plus, the fact that he knew Darrin was bothering her a lot more than it should have.

That was all moot, though, considering she didn't know which room was hers to begin with.

Yeah, slight problem, that.

Caridad shouldered her laptop bag and moved to pick up her range bag, but Owen beat her to it. "I get the impression you're fully capable of taking care of yourself, and you've got that whole independent woman thing going on, but you're a guest. I've got this."

His expression clearly said he wasn't going to budge, and Caridad shrugged. "If it makes you feel better to roll my carry-on, be my guest. I've got the rifle, though."

He smirked. "As if I would have even attempted to carry that for you. I'm all about customer service, but not at the expense of my balls."

A snort laugh escaped before she could stop it. "Glad we've come to an understanding."

As she followed him through the living area and to a long hallway—trying not to stare at his ass—she asked, "So are there any other guests this weekend?"

"Nope. You're our only one."

Darrin must have pulled some strings. "Any reason why?"

He shrugged and then stopped at an open bedroom door before turning to her and casually saying, "Darrin said you needed the time to yourself, that you needed to 'get away,' if I recall correctly. Anyway, here's your room."

She walked past him, being sure not to brush against him, and into the room. It was spacious, decorated like the rest of the house in a classy yet rustic style. A king-size bed with a wooden frame dominated the space. There were fresh flowers on the dresser, a bowl of Twix on the nightstand. "Darrin put you up to the candy, didn't he?"

Owen wheeled her carry-on inside and placed it beside the dresser. "Yup."

Caridad set her stuff down at the foot of the bed and turned towards him. "Well, thanks for going to all the trouble."

He nodded once and turned to leave.

"Oh! What's the schedule for the rest of the weekend like?"

He stopped just inside the door, turned back towards her

and leaned against the door frame. He scratched his beard and said, "Supper's usually around seven. We'll probably try to get out to one of the blinds by five-thirty in the morning, so we'll meet in the living area around five. If you want to take coffee with you, feel free to do so; we have a ton of Thermoses and a Keurig with just about any type of coffee you can imagine. If you prefer frou frou drinks, we have an espresso machine that makes lattes, too. We'll spend however much time you want out in the blind, so if you want to stay out all day until after sundown, we can. If you want to come back here for breakfast and then go back out in the afternoon we can do that, too. It's pretty much your call."

"You keep saying 'we.' Does that mean you're my guide?"

His smile didn't quite reach his eyes. "Yes, ma'am."

With that, he left her standing alone at the foot of the bed and feeling all kinds of emotions she didn't know how to process. She was kind of irritated with Darrin for essentially booking her a private weekend that had to have cost him—and the ranch itself—an arm and a leg. Not that he couldn't afford it, but still. He wasn't even her full-time agent; it definitely wasn't his job to give her gifts and take care of her, even though he seemed to think it was. She was kind of irritated with herself for being attracted to Owen when she shouldn't be. And she was definitely irritated that he was her private guide for the entire weekend.

It was one thing to be mildly attracted with the thought that she could maybe avoid him most of the weekend by simply staying away from the main house. It was another thing entirely to be told she'd be spending many hours in very close quarters with Hottie McGinger himself.

"Ugh," she groaned as she sank onto the bed. The relaxing weekend Darrin had convinced her to take was looking more and more like it was going to be exactly the opposite.

CHAPTER TWO

OWEN GLANCED AT CARIDAD OUT OF THE CORNER OF HIS EYE as they bounced down the sendero in one of the ranch's utility vehicles. She was even quieter this morning than she had been yesterday and last night. He got the distinct impression that she wasn't happy about something, and he had a sneaking suspicion that something was him.

What he'd done, he didn't know, but he'd long ago resigned himself to never being able to fully understand the complexities of the female mind.

He didn't know much about her, just that she was a friend of Darrin's and that the past few months had been up and down for her. He hadn't asked questions, and had instead been grateful for the opportunity to get out of town for the weekend and spend some time communing with nature.

The fact that he apparently wanted to spend some time communing with his client was a bit inconvenient, though.

The Polaris Ranger's lights cut through the pitch black of night and illuminated the deer blind he'd decided to bring them to this morning, close to the Devils River State Natural Area, which was managed by Texas Parks and Wildlife. This side of the ranch wasn't fenced, allowing wildlife to come and go between the two properties as they pleased, which meant a higher volume of white tails this time of year.

He cut the engine and whispered, "This is it."

They exited the UTV, both of them with rifles in hand. Caridad slung a Camelbak over her shoulder before grabbing her Thermos of coffee. Owen slung his own Camelbak over his shoulder before pulling a small flashlight out of his jeans pocket and turning it on. As quietly as they could they made their way to the ladder of the box blind. Owen climbed up first and opened the door, checking inside for critters—wasps, snakes and ringtails liked to hide out in the dark space—before whispering to Caridad that it was okay for her to climb up, too.

Without speaking they situated themselves in the two chairs. Owen took a box magazine out of his pocket and popped it into his rifle while Caridad removed her magazine from a pocket in her Camelbak before seating it. They both chambered a round and flipped on their safeties, then Owen set his rifle in the corner closest to him—easy to reach but out of the way. Caridad did the same.

He pulled a pair of binoculars out of his Camelbak and set the backpack on the ground at his feet, knowing it would be easy enough to access the tube to the bladder when he needed a drink. Caridad set hers on the floor beside her, up against the wall on her left and took a sip of her coffee.

"Wanna help me lower the windows so we can see out?" he asked quietly.

"Sure." Her voice was barely more than a whisper.

He showed her how to lower the blackout coverings and then the windows, which was really pretty simple, but he'd been surprised before by how many people couldn't seem to figure it out. Caridad, however, caught on quickly and helped him lower the windows so that soon they could see out, but they also had a little bit of air flow.

Owen turned off the flashlight and put it back in his pocket.

"This blind is pretty close to the state-owned area, so we get a lot of four-legged traffic through here, including some monster bucks. The direction we're facing, there's a pretty good draw that seems to be a popular path for the deer to use, too. There's no feeder, but despite that this seems to be one of our prime locations," he whispered.

"I'm fine with that." She whispered before taking a sip of her coffee. "By the way, what are we looking for today?"

He glanced at her dark profile, a bit confused. "What do you mean?"

"Are there any culls you need to be harvested?"

"You'd be willing to take a cull?" He didn't even try to hide his skepticism.

A cull was a genetically inferior or injured buck, usually one with an under-developed rack. While the trophy bucks were nice, Owen was always more than happy to let one walk if he was young; it was important to make sure good genes were passed on during the rut.

"Sure. Antlers don't put meat on the table."

Her statement was so matter-of-fact Owen couldn't help but smile. Despite her obvious unease around him—which he really didn't understand—it was also obvious that they had at least a couple of common interests and beliefs. "I wish more people had that attitude."

"I'm guessing you get a lot of guys who are more concerned with the trophy for the wall than meat in the freezer or the health of the herd?"

"Yup. I mean, I can't blame them, considering how much a weekend out here costs. Might as well get your money's worth, y'know? But I've had guys get trigger happy over some really young, promising bucks, and it's not always easy to talk them down and convince them to wait for an older one."

"Do you manage to talk them down?"

"Most of the time. Then again, I don't guide the hunts very often, either."

"So why are you this weekend?"

He shrugged. "Darrin asked me to. It's the slow season

right now in my full time job, so taking an extra day or two off isn't a big deal."

"Isn't the boss allowed to take off whenever he wants to, anyway?"

"How'd you know I was the boss?"

"You have that whole authoritative thing going on."

"What 'authoritative thing?'"

She waved her hand in the air, which he felt more than saw considering the darkness. "You just…have this vibe, that's all. Like you're used to being in charge."

A variety of responses floated through his mind and on the tip of his tongue, none of which were remotely appropriate.

Instead of saying any of those wildly inappropriate things, he said, "Yeah, I'm the boss. And yes, I can technically take off whenever I want to, but I don't. Like I said, it's slow right now, so I had some free time anyway."

"So you own your own company?"

"Yes."

"Out of Del Rio?"

He glanced at her out of the corner of his eye. "Yes."

She sipped her coffee. "Sorry. I can be nosy sometimes."

"No worries. Back to our original subject, if you're willing to take a cull rather than a trophy, we have a few we've been tracking on the game cams for the past few months, and God knows that come opening morning the deer you'd been seeing will hide and suddenly you'll see a bunch that just came out of the woodwork."

"I remember that from hunting when I was a kid, except we didn't have all the technology back then that exists today. I don't think game cams were even a thing back then."

"You hunted as a kid?"

She got quiet for a few seconds and then whispered, "Yeah. My dad would sometimes take me."

"Why'd you stop?"

For a long time he thought she wasn't going to answer, the sound of sotol fronds rubbing against each other in the breeze and their breaths the only sounds. Then she surprised him. "I reached that age when girls start thinking about makeup and boys, and my mom figured hunting wasn't very girly."

"You obviously changed your mind at some point."

She snorted. "The hunting thing right now is purely at Darrin's suggestion. No, insistence. He pretty much insisted I come down here for the weekend."

Owen shifted in his chair, debating asking the question on the tip of his tongue. Aw, to hell with it. "So you and Darrin…"

"Are just friends."

He was way more relieved that he should have been. "Sorry. I guess I can be kind of nosy, too."

"I obviously get that." She took another sip of coffee. "By the way, should we really be talking so much? Isn't that breaking some sort of cardinal rule of hunting or something?"

"Eh, I've found it doesn't really seem to matter, as long as you're quiet. Hell, this one time last season I had a young buck come up to a feeder I was sitting at. It was close to sunset, and he was obviously one to let walk since he was young with an excellent rack. I kept waiting for him to leave so I could get out of the blind—I try not to let them see me, y'know—and he just kept standing there munching away on hay. Finally, I got tired of waiting for him so I started making noise in the blind. He looked up then went right back to eating that frickin' hay. So I pulled out my phone and started playing music. Loud. He looked up, looked around, went back to eating hay. Finally I gave up, turned the music off and said 'screw it' and just climbed out of the damned blind. It wasn't until I was starting up the Ranger that the stupid thing finally figured out there was a human less than a hundred yards away from him, and even then he didn't exactly run away screaming, just looked at me then calmly sauntered off. So, no, it doesn't seem to matter too much, as long as you're quiet when you talk."

Her body shook with silent laughter. "Oh my God. That's hilarious. You should have shot him just for being stupid. Darwinism and all that."

"I seriously considered it, but then thought about it and realized I didn't really feel like field dressing him that night."

"Lazy." Was she actually teasing him?

"That evening, yes."

"Still, though, that's a doozy of a story."

"I have more where that came from."

"What else do we have to do while we wait for the sun to come up? Tell me more, Mr. Daniels."

⚮

As they sat side by side in the blind, enveloped by darkness with Owen telling hunting stories, Caridad tried to calm her mind and body down.

He had no idea how sexy he was.

And since when did hunting stories turn her on?

Since when do you get turned on by men who aren't your boyfriend?

Touché.

Therein lie the problem, and the real reason behind this entire weekend getaway fiasco Darrin had put her up to. Her boyfriend.

Brian.

Brian, who was a good guy. Who'd done nothing to deserve her recent feelings of animosity. The animosity wasn't even directed at him, not really. It was more directed towards herself, for feeling like she was broken in some way.

She couldn't even love the guy she'd been living with for the past few years.

Oh, she'd thought she'd been in love with him. But loving someone and being in love with someone were two completely different things, or so she suspected. Because what she felt for Brian? Yeah, it didn't make her heart skip or butterflies dance in her stomach. She didn't feel like her world would end if he wasn't a part of it. She didn't have to be with him, didn't need him in that way she often heard associated with being in love with someone.

Once upon a time she'd been attracted to him. Kind of.

Looking back she could recognize the fact that it hadn't been love or even lust that had gotten her into a relationship with Brian. No, that had purely been nothing more than her fucked up psyche talking.

Because she was fucked up.

Witness: being attracted to a man who wasn't her boyfriend, even though she wasn't attracted to her boyfriend and wasn't in love with her boyfriend and probably should have broken up with her boyfriend months if not years ago, so really was it so bad that she was attracted to Owen?

She took another sip of her coffee.

Jesus, her thoughts were confusing. Her feelings were even more confusing.

Owen continued to tell her hunting stories, like he was some sort of deer whisperer or something. The thought almost made her laugh out loud.

Deer whisperer.

Caridad whisperer.

Same difference.

No, Caridad, not "same difference." He shouldn't be whisperer anything to you. Because, boyfriend.

Ugh.

She was officially a screwed up, hot mess.

The face of Owen's watch lit up briefly before he whispered, "Okay, we should probably be quiet now. Sunrise is officially in forty-five minutes, which means we can start hunting in fifteen."

They sat, silent, the only sound their soft breaths every now and then. She looked out the window in front of her and sipped her coffee, hoping the caffeine buzz would drown out the attraction buzz.

Unfortunately, the only thing it was doing for her was making her feel like she needed to pee. That was so not happening out here in the middle of nowhere with Hottie McGinger *right there.*

Yeah, let's not and say we did.

She was far too aware of him, though, her body warmer than it should have been considering the temperature outside was hovering somewhere around fifty degrees. Hardly a blizzard, but in southwest Texas that was downright chilly.

She, however, was not chilly. No, she was burning up over here in her little swivel chair. Going up in flames. Before you knew it—poof!—she'd be gone. Nothing but ashes.

Holy shit she was losing her mind.

Disgusted with herself, she shook her head and took another sip of coffee. Hunting. Boyfriend. Focus, Caridad.

Ugh.

She continued to stare out the window, willing the sun to just rise already so that she would no longer be sitting here in the dark with a man she felt like she was beginning to obsess over. Because, seriously. She barely knew the guy.

This was just good, old-fashioned lust talking. The kind that flared up, burned hot and bright before crashing and going up in flames.

Again with the fire analogies.

Maybe she needed to schedule an appointment with her therapist. It *had* been a while. Y'know, to make sure she wasn't suddenly developing pyrotechnic tendencies. Or something.

As her thoughts turned into crazy pretzels, the sky began to lighten, the darkness not quite as pressing as it had been just moments before. The black turned into dark purple, then dark blue. Soon, the dark blue was tinged with orange and pink on the horizon and all around them birds began to wake up, their chirping like a sudden cacophony. Then there was the sound of wings beating against the air, followed by the caw of a crow.

"Holy shit. How close was that thing?" she turned her head and whispered.

Owen grinned, causing his cheek to crease. Dimples, too? Life was so unfair. "Pretty close. They'll fly low like that a lot.

It's even cooler when you're in an open air blind, up higher, and can see them."

"I don't know if that would be cool or scare me."

"One too many viewings of *The Birds?*"

"Something like that."

She once again turned her attention to the scene out of her window rather than the one in the blind. The sun was beginning to peek over the horizon now, bathing the draw in front of them with soft light and shadow. Owen hadn't been kidding—they had a great view from up here.

Birds twittered all around them, and she heard the call of what she thought was a bobwhite quail.

"Do you hear the quail?" Owen whispered.

"I thought that's what that was. I haven't heard one since I was a kid."

"Yeah, they're starting to make a comeback, thank God. I love listening to them."

She knew from talking to her dad that the quail population had dwindled dramatically, to the point where it was almost impossible to find them at times. Part of that had been the recent historic drought the state had been in, and part of that had been due to urban sprawl and their natural habitat being taken away. Hunters and conservationists had been doing every thing they could to help boost the population, mostly by limiting quail hunts all together. Thanks to limited hunting and what ended up being a wet spring and summer, the population had begun to rebound slightly.

"They're kind of cute to look at, too."

"Seriously? Cute?"

"They are! They're these fat little birds with these cute little tufts on their heads. They almost waddle sometimes."

"Okay, so you know what they look like, I'll give you that."

"But you won't give me the fact that they're cute?"

"Nope. Not a chance."

She huffed out a laugh. "You just don't want to admit

they're cute."

"I'm a guy. We don't generally describe birds as being 'cute.'"

"I am well aware that you're a guy, Owen." Oh, hell. That had come out way more flirtatious than she'd intended. "I mean. Obviously. Look at you. Dude."

Oh, God. Kill her now.

"Exactly. And dudes don't usually use words like 'cute.' Just sayin'."

Apparently he'd decided to ignore her awkwardness that had almost sounded like flirting.

"And you are very obviously a woman. I mean, look at you. Chick." He sounded like he was teasing, but there was a stillness to his body that indicated otherwise.

Ooooo-kay. Time to change the subject. "So, yeah."

"Yeah."

Because that wasn't awkward.

She sighed and stared out the window, her arms crossed over her chest. Owen's posture said he was relaxed, but she could feel the tension rolling off of him in waves.

Or maybe that was just her crazy she was detecting.

Ugh. This wasn't like her. She didn't do the whole guy-crazy thing.

Not anymore.

And wasn't that just the story of her life? It seemed like there were so many things she didn't do anymore, things she'd once enjoyed. Instead of doing those things she played it safe. Insulated herself, really. Stayed in a relationship with a man who was more friend than boyfriend. Had infrequent, unsatisfying, vanilla sex. Had two people she considered friends and a ton of acquaintances who thought they were her friends. One of those two people was her agent.

Her freaking agent.

Her same agent who'd been the only one to realize that she was in a serious funk and needed to snap out of it.

The other friend was the guy she was supposed to be in

love with but was never around enough to realize she was in a serious funk and needed to snap out of it.

Oh, holy crap beans her life was beyond a hot mess. It was like a hot mess multiplied by a bajillion, topped with some warmed over horse shit.

Now there was a mental image.

Lost in her thoughts, she didn't see or hear anything until Owen nudged her with his elbow.

It was the first time he'd touched her since they'd shaken hands yesterday, and just like then she felt warmth spread through her body, radiating from her arm and throughout.

This attraction really was inconvenient.

"What. What's up?" she whispered.

"About fifty yards to our left. There's a doe with her fawn."

She turned her head slightly and saw them. The doe was beautiful, her coat a gorgeous cinnamon color, her eyes ringed with white fur, almost like eyeliner. The fawn still had its spots, its legs still almost gangly.

"It's November. Shouldn't the spots be gone by now?"

"Usually, yes, but sometimes they drop their fawns late, or the rut's late, or the fawn just holds on to its spots for longer. If you look closely, you can tell they're starting to fade."

She looked again and saw that, yes, the fawn's spots were starting to fade. She and Owen sat in companionable silence as the doe and her baby picked their way down into the draw. The doe stopped to munch on some sotol, and the fawn nuzzled her stomach.

"Oh wow. Is it nursing?" she whispered.

"Looks like it," he whispered back.

"That is so freaking cool." She couldn't keep the awe from her voice.

"You certainly don't get this from a textbook or a television set, that's for sure."

"Or YouTube."

"Well, you might on YouTube."

"But it wouldn't be the same as seeing it live and in person.

Kind of like seeing your favorite band live, y'know. Watching a live performance on video is nothing like being in the seats and singing along at the top of your lungs."

"What kind of music do you like?"

"Mostly girl power stuff. Miranda Lambert. Kelly Clarkson. Pink. Heart with some Fleetwood Mac thrown in."

"Girl power stuff, huh?"

"Yeah. Songs that are all like 'I am woman, hear me roar' and 'I'm not taking any shit off of this dude.' Those kinds of songs."

She felt his gaze on her and somehow resisted the urge to turn her head. "Yeah, I can see you as a 'Gunpowder and Lead' sort of woman."

He had no idea. "It's one of my favorites."

The fawn and doe continued to wander away from them, the doe stopping occasionally to munch on browse or nudge her baby along. "She looks like she's a good mom."

"Most of them are. Every now and then you'll find one that just isn't for whatever reason, but luckily does tend to stick together in family units and take care of each other and the fawns. We have a couple of family units we've been watching for the past few years, ranging from a few fawns to some does that are probably around four and a half to five and a half years old."

"Do y'all just let the does walk and focus only on bucks?"

"God, no. Part of herd management is keeping the buck to doe ratio healthy, which means harvesting the older does as they stop reproducing. Every now and then we'll take a younger one if she's showing signs of being aggressive or if she hasn't bred in her first couple of ruts."

"How in the world do you keep track of them all?"

"Game cams, census. We'll do spotlight counts, stand counts, aerial counts. There's even some pretty cool new software out there that lets you take your game cam photos and it'll tag deer with the same features, which is great since the bucks can look different from year to year. We work closely with a wildlife biologist to make sure our population numbers don't get out of control."

"So what you're saying is that this is a lot more involved than just point and shoot."

"So much more involved."

"You seem to be pretty passionate about this. Why don't you do it full time?"

She'd given up all pretense of looking for deer and had turned so that she was watching him. Owen turned in his chair and shrugged. "Because I love it. I don't want doing this full time to diminish my love of simply being outdoors and enjoying nature. It's about so much more than meat, although venison's nice, too. I don't know. I guess I just feel closer to God out here than I do anywhere else."

Their gazes caught and held. Jesus, he had beautiful eyes. Clear, piercing blue, almost like he could see right through her to the very bottom of her soul.

She took a sip of her now tepid coffee, not caring because her throat was suddenly dry and needed some sort of liquid, stat. "I get what you're saying. I feel like that whenever I stand in the ocean."

"Closer to God?"

"Yeah. The rest of the time I wonder if He's abandoned me."

Owen's eyes filled with something—pity, she feared—and she looked away. "Anyway. That was completely uncalled for. Sorry."

"You shouldn't apologize for being honest."

"I don't want or need your pity, Owen."

"Good. Because I don't pity you."

Lying liar who lies. She'd seen the pity all across his handsome face. "Whatever. Don't lie to me."

"Caridad—"

"Don't even 'Caridad' me. I said something I shouldn't have, and I saw the pity written all over your face. So just don't, Owen."

They'd at some point given up all pretense of whispering, and she looked out the window. "Something tells me we might have scared off the deer this morning."

"Probably."

"I think maybe we should head back."

He sighed, and she could feel his gaze on her face. "Yeah."

CHAPTER THREE

Chase: So how goes it with Darrin's special client?
Owen: It goes.
Chase: Uh oh. That doesn't sound too positive.
Owen: It just means that it's going. She's a little prickly.
A little standoffish.
Chase: You mean Darrin's special client is a she?
Owen: Yes. As in very much a woman.
Chase: Well that's interesting. You think he's interested
in her or something?
Owen: No. I get the feeling they're friends kind of like
you and I are friends with Jenn.
Chase: I didn't realize Darrin had female friends. That
dude attracts more women than you and Matt combined.
Owen: It probably doesn't hurt that players deflect wom-
en on to him.
Chase: True that. Anyway. Jo's calling. Later.

OWEN SIGHED AS HE TOSSED HIS PHONE ONTO THE BED IN what
he thought of as his room at the ranch. How goes it with Caridad?

Not at all.

He couldn't figure her out, and he wanted to. She was like
a puzzle and he was quickly becoming obsessed.

Way too quickly for his own peace of mind, that was for sure, considering he'd known her for less than an entire week-end.

He thought back over the past two days and groaned. It had been hell. Every single second had been hell. Mostly because every time he was anywhere near Caridad he was automatically at half mast and nearly cross-eyed with lust. It was making him stupid, and he didn't like feeling stupid.

The fact of the matter was, she was leaving tomorrow. She'd taken a cull spike this afternoon when they'd gone out, and had even surprised him by helping field dress it. She'd been very matter of fact about the whole thing, almost to the point of being standoffish.

He had a feeling it was more a defense mechanism than anything else, especially since in those rare moments in which she'd let her guard down, he'd gotten a glimpse at a lonely woman with more emotions than she apparently knew what to do with.

A part of him just wanted to hold her, be her friend, offer some sort of comfort. The other part? Well, that other part wasn't thinking sweet, wholesome thoughts, that was for sure.

She's leaving in the morning, Daniels. And she's a client. Not to mention Darrin's friend. So just stop it.

Unfortunately he was afraid he wouldn't be able to.

♋

Caridad stepped out of the shower before toweling off and putting on her robe. She wrapped it around her body and tied the belt before grabbing her iPad and opening the bathroom door. She stepped out into the hallway, looked down at the tablet to pause the music she'd been listening to, and ran head first into a solid wall that smelled a lot like gunpowder, Old Spice deodorant and laundry detergent.

Her ovaries knew who it was before she even gained a full sight picture.

Owen reached out, placing his hands on her shoulders to

steady her as her head snapped up. "Sorry, I wasn't paying attention to where I was going."

Caridad felt cool air on her left breast, looked down and realized her robe had come partially open so that the purple cotton barely kept her nipple hidden.

A nipple that instantly hardened when Owen also glanced down.

The air around them thickened, and as if in a dream she vaguely realized that she hadn't managed to pause iTunes, and Heart's "All I Wanna Do Is Make Love to You" was playing.

Fitting.

Wildly inappropriate, but fitting.

Owen slowly looked up and their gazes caught and held, his blue eyes filled with a heat and longing that made her breath catch in her chest while her belly dipped and danced like a spasmatic butterfly. Her feet felt rooted to the spot, her limbs heavy and uncoordinated. Almost in slow motion, one of his hands came up and lightly, gently touched her face.

She wanted to close her eyes, tilt her cheek into his hand like a cat.

Instead, she stood there, still as a stone statue, torn between longing and loyalty.

Slowly, he moved closer, so that their bodies were touching from chest to toes, the simple act lighting up her world. Goosebumps skittered across her arms, chest and legs. Her nipples tightened to the point of almost pain, and every time she took even the slightest, shallowest breath the friction against her terrycloth robe shot sparks from her breasts to her core.

Look away. Look away. Break the spell and run.

She couldn't. She was caught and held, trapped like a fly in a spider's web. Her brain screamed at her to high tail it out of there, but her body. Oh, her body burned.

He dragged a thumb across her bottom lip. The callused tip made her wonder what it would feel like to have his hands on her breasts. Her belly. Between her legs.

He lowered his head, his pupils dilated. He paused, his mouth mere millimeters from hers as his eyes searched hers, almost as if he were waiting for permission.

What would it be like to kiss Owen?

Like fire and thunderstorms and the first time you won a competition.

That callused thumb caught the edge of her mouth, dragged her lower lip down slightly in a gesture that was simple and demanding and wholly erotic. She closed her eyes against the sensation and the gaze that held her captive.

She felt his body shift slightly, and then his lips were on hers. Gentle. Light. They brushed against hers once, twice before he caught her lower lip between his teeth and lightly nipped.

Her body went up in flames.

No, no, no. This is wrong.

But it feels so right.

But it was wrong, and Caridad jerked herself away, her bottom lip stinging slightly. She ran her tongue over it to ease the ache, and caught the faint taste of him on her tongue.

Oh, hell.

She so wanted more, but she couldn't have more.

Caridad pressed a hand to Owen's—very firm—chest and stepped away. He rocked back on his heels, confusion pinching the corners of his mouth together.

"I have a boyfriend," she blurted out.

Smooth.

"Fair enough. I apologize," he said before abruptly turning and walking down the hallway towards the great room. Seconds later she heard a door open and close.

Probably an accurate statement regarding her life if ever there was one. She closed her eyes and breathed deeply, struggling for calm. Her heart felt like it was going to pound right out of her chest, and her stomach was still on a roller coaster ride. Her nipples were still hard and her lips felt like they'd been stung by bees. All from one little nip and brush of a callused finger.

Brian had never made her feel like this.

The thought should have given her pause, or at least made her feel something other than regret. Regret for playing it safe, for being with someone for so long who she loved as a friend but not as a lover. And to be fair, even though they lived together and occasionally had sex, they really were nothing more than roommates who happened to sleep in the same bed a couple nights a month.

And wasn't that just a sad state of affairs?

Caridad made her way back to her room, her thoughts spinning the entire time. She closed the door behind her and sat on the bed, iPad clutched to her chest.

She could try to blame the state of their relationship on their hectic schedules, but that was really nothing more than a convenient excuse. Sure, they both traveled a lot, but if they really wanted to make it work they could have. Instead, they'd stayed together simply because it was easier than breaking up.

Ultimately, it was a lot like that Delta Rae song, "If I Loved You;" Brian was a great guy and she kind of wished she was in love with him, but she wasn't. It was a little sad, but she also had a feeling she wasn't the only one wishing for things that weren't.

With a sigh, Caridad got up, set the iPad aside and pulled on her pajamas. As she tried to fall asleep, instead of focusing on what she needed to do once she got back to Dallas, all she could see was Owen's gaze burning with disappointment.

ↂ

She had a boyfriend. Of course she did. And he'd tried to freaking kiss her.

Ugh.

Disgusted with himself, Owen walked out to the fire pit and plopped into an Adirondack chair, not even bothering with starting a fire. He sighed and rubbed his hands over his face, head tilted back.

He gazed up at the stars, contemplating the swirling mass of light within the dark. Usually, the sight calmed him. There was just something about realizing how small you were in the grand scheme of things that had a way of altering your perspective.

Tonight, though? Tonight he just felt confused and a little bit angry with himself and with Caridad. He wasn't the type to cheat or assist in cheating; that shit sucked. And Caridad? Dammit, he knew he hadn't misread the chemistry, and she'd wanted to kiss him just as badly in the hallway just now. He felt a little bit led on and a tiny bit lied to, even if she had stomped on the brakes before they crossed the point of no return.

Dammit. Why did she have to have a boyfriend?

The logical part of his brain realized that if she was madly in love with this mystery guy she probably wouldn't have come so close to kissing him. Then again, attraction did work in mysterious ways. There was also the fact that she had stopped him and pushed him away, which meant her sense of right and wrong was more powerful than lust.

Owen scratched at his beard and fought to push the anger and *shoulda, woulda, couldas* to the back of his mind and focus on the here and now. His brain slowly quieted as he gazed up at the twinkling lights of the galaxy.

Yesterday he'd told Caridad that being out in a deer blind was a lot like being close to God. He'd been telling the truth, but right now he would be willing to amend that statement.

"So I almost just kissed a woman who has a boyfriend. I didn't know she has a boyfriend, but still, I feel pretty bad for that one."

The stars twinkled back at him.

"I've only known her a couple of days, but she's got me all twisted up inside. I'm not sure I like it."

He found the star he was looking for, the one just to the right of the moon, and focused on it.

"Even worse? She's a client. And Darrin's friend. This

shouldn't be so complicated."

The star sparkled, almost as if it was moving. Owen sighed, fighting back the ache of loss.

"I know, Mom. Love you too."

༄

"I can't do this anymore," Caridad said two days later.

Brian blinked at her and lowered himself to the edge of the bed. "I'm guessing by 'this' you really mean 'us?'"

Caridad nodded and sat down beside him. "Yeah, I do," she said softly.

"Okay."

"Okay?"

He shrugged. "Yeah, okay. I have to admit, I've seen this one coming for a while now."

"You have?"

"Yeah. We barely see each other, we haven't had sex in…" he rubbed his nose, "…two months? Three? Heck, I don't even remember. And I know you love me, but I don't know that you're in love with me."

Caridad leaned against him and put her head on his shoulder. "So you're not mad?"

"Not really, no. If I'm being completely honest, I don't know that I'm necessarily in love with you, either. I mean, I love you, but more like a friend I live with and have had sex with a few times."

She snorted. "I feel like I should be slightly insulted by that, but I'm not. Instead, I'm just a little bit relieved."

"Me too."

They sat in silence, the weight of their words heavy in the air.

"I'm moving out."

"You don't have to do that."

Caridad sighed. "Yeah, I kind of do. I feel like I've been in a holding pattern for the past year or so, and the only thing that's been keeping me going is competing. It's like everything I do in between waking up and falling asleep is gun related."

"But I thought you loved it."

"I do. But it shouldn't be my life, y'know."

Brian nodded. "So where will you go?"

She drew in a deep breath. "I'm thinking it might be time for me to go back home."

"Home? As in home to Del Rio?"

"The one and only."

It was time. Time to go back home, maybe face down the demons she'd been running from for what seemed like forever, and possibly have a shot of leading a normal, somewhat happy existence.

"You're sure that's what you want?"

She inhaled sharply through her nose. While she and Brian may not have worked out very well as a couple, she really was grateful for his friendship. "I'm not sure it's what I want, but I kind of feel like it's what I need."

CHAPTER FOUR

CARIDAD PULLED UP TO THE OLD FARMHOUSE AND KILLED the engine. She sat there for long moments, just staring into nothingness as memories floated through her mind.

Some of them were good. Some of them, not so much.

She was crazy, coming back here. Back here to the place where some of her best—and worst—memories lived. They were like ghosts, those memories.

Hopefully she wouldn't need to call in anyone for an exorcism.

Slowly, deliberately, she removed the keys from the ignition, grabbed her purse off the passenger seat and opened the door. Her Converse met gravel, and she swallowed before shutting the door and taking a step towards the house. Her keys bit into the palm of her hand.

She forced her feet to move. One step. Two. Left. Right. Left. Right. Like an out of sync marching band, herky jerky and uncoordinated.

Too soon she was at the bottom step, looking up onto the front porch.

Over there. In the corner. That was her abuela's favorite rocking chair. The rocking chair her grandmother had sat in day in and day out, observing the world around her as her gnarled hands snapped beans, knitted afghans, or brushed away Caridad's tears.

Instead of going to the front door and unlocking it with the key her mom had mailed her after Abuela had passed away, she instead slowly made her way to that rocking chair and sat. Fists clenched tight in her lap, she took a deep, fortifying breath and exhaled. Memories flooded her mind, overwhelming her. She swallowed past the lump in her throat, her nose and eyes stinging.

She sat back in the chair and pushed against the floor of the porch with her toes, setting the rocking chair into motion. Caridad stared over the porch railing at the big, old oak tree in the front yard, her gaze focused inward as she finally allowed herself to feel the grief she'd kept locked up for the past couple of months.

Sitting in Abuela's chair, it was almost like she could feel the older woman's comforting presence, could feel her arms around her shoulders and a reassuring pat on the back.

A couple of tears escaped, followed by a few more. She didn't bother to brush them away, remembering the words her therapist had said to her just yesterday: "It's okay to let yourself feel. Honor those emotions, Caridad. They mean something. You mean something."

It was hard to just let go, to allow herself to feel the things she'd bottled up. Abuela had passed the weekend of the national championship, but no one had told her until afterwards because they hadn't wanted to throw her off her game and potentially cause her to lose.

As if a silly shooting competition was more important than her grandmother.

She'd come home for the funeral, and had been so angry at her family that she'd driven back up to Dallas that same day. Then she'd been flung into promo spots for her sponsors, and she'd just stuffed everything down deep in order to get through it all.

The day had turned into the week which had turned into a month, until Darrin had finally taken her out for drinks one night and told her he'd booked a weekend getaway for her at the hunting ranch he owned with four other guys. And then, as they'd left, he'd pulled a rifle case out of his car and handed it to her.

Two weeks later she'd been at the Devils Ranch, almost kissing Hottie McGinger and feeling more emotions than she'd allowed herself to feel in months if not years. That had been last weekend and now here she was, not even a week later, back in southwest Texas.

To stay.

Which she'd sworn she wouldn't do when she'd left town at the age of twenty-one.

She stopped rocking and stood, brushing tears off of her cheeks as she did so. Enough of this maudlin, honoring her feelings crap. It was time to find out what kind of shape Abuela's—no, her— house was in.

Two hours later, Caridad gave up and decided to call in the cavalry. Pulling up her brother's number, she hit the phone icon and waited for him to answer.

"Hola. What's up?"

Caridad rolled her eyes but couldn't help but smile. "Dude, you're like the whitest half Mexican I know, which makes this sudden penchant for speaking in Spanish a bit disturbing."

Mikey snorted. "Whatever. Just because I'm not full Mexican like you doesn't mean I can't use the language of our mother land."

Caridad laughed. She adored Mikey, and he was an awesome little brother, but sometimes he was just too much. "I'm pretty sure your mother land is America. Just sayin'. Anyway. I'm at Abuela's and this place is a freaking mess. Think you could help a big sister out and come over, help me sort through this crap?"

"Dude, it's a Friday night. How do you know I don't have a hot date?"

"If you had a hot date you wouldn't have answered your phone."

"You know me too well. I'll be there in an hour."

"Thank you. You're a life saver."

"Whatever. See you later."

"Oh, hey!"

"Yeah?"

"You might want to pick up some pizza or something. I haven't gone grocery shopping and I doubt we could get delivery out here."

Mikey sighed. "Fine. But I get to pick the toppings."

"Whatever. Just get your ass out here. This place is scary."

"Adios," Mikey said before the line went dead.

Caridad shook her head and stared at the mess around her. Apparently, Abuela had been a hoarder. Fantastic.

"Holy shit. Who knew your grandmother was such a hoarder?" Mikey said as he set the pizza box on the coffee table Caridad had managed to clean off.

"I know, right? I mean, I realize it had been a year or so since I'd been over here last, but it was never this bad. I talked to her every week, and she never mentioned being sick or anything, never sounded like she was starting to slip mentally. This place was always in great shape as a kid. But this? Holy crap beans, Batman. I can't even."

Mikey gave her some serious side eye as he sat on the couch and opened up the pizza box. "Dude, you've been spending way too much time on the Internet."

Caridad shrugged before grabbing a roll of paper towels off the coffee table and handing them to him. "Hardly."

"How many hours a day do you spend blogging, or on Facebook or Twitter? And then there are those YouTube videos you've been posting for the past six months or so. Instagram. Pinterest. With all of the marketing and PR you do, how do you even have time to actually do your job?"

Caridad reached into the box and grabbed a slice of pizza. Mmm. Pineapple and Canadian bacon. Her favorite. Also Mikey's favorite, but that was beside the point. "What, exactly, do you think my job is?"

"To shoot stuff?"

Caridad took a bite of her pizza and considered her little brother's assessment of her job. On one hand, he was correct. On the other, her job was so much more than shooting stuff, considering shooting stuff didn't exactly pay all the bills.

"That's part of it. I go to matches and compete, and if I do well enough I make some money while doing it. But what really pays my salary is endorsements, speaking engagements, appearances, freelance writing, that sort of thing. So social media plays a role in that—the more visible I am, the more visible my sponsors are. Plus, the added attention can help me get new sponsors, which means more money. Or new speaking engagements or appearances, which also pay money. Not to mention, all that social media stuff I've been doing can also lead to more writing gigs and sponsors, which will also help add some income."

Mikey chewed, a thoughtful look on his face, and swallowed before responding. "So what you're saying is that you don't just shoot things for a living?"

"It's not just shooting things."

"Well, that's a little disappointing, so while I'm trying to process the fact that my sister's fairly normal like the rest of us, I'm just gonna sit here and eat this pizza and silently laugh at the sorry state this house is in."

Caridad nudged Mikey's shoulder with her own and smiled. "Te amo, hermanito."

"Love you too, sis."

ॐ

Three hours later, Caridad heard Mikey yell from one of the bedrooms, "I don't know why I do this shit for you! This place is a fucking mess."

Caridad rolled her eyes as she continued to pull random items from the kitchen cabinets. Standing on a stool so that she could actually see inside the upper cabinets, she'd found an interesting collection of dust-covered tequila bottles (most of which were empty), mismatched glasses, a crap ton of Fiestaware that she was pretty sure was the old school stuff with lead in it, and various plates and bowls that all seemed to come from different eras.

All of it looked like it hadn't been touched in years.

"I know it's a mess. That's why I called you, dipshit," she yelled back.

Seconds later she heard footsteps, and then Mikey was in the kitchen. She turned her head and looked over her shoulder. "What's up?"

He was holding what looked like a photo album in his hands, and he opened the cover and turned to the first page before holding it up for her to see. "Is that your dad?"

She sighed and stepped down off the stool before walking towards him and looking more closely at the photo he'd turned to.

"You know who my dad is. Same as yours."

He sighed. "You know what I mean, Caridad. Your birth father. The guy who's sperm joined with Mom's egg to create baby you."

"Dude, you are so effing weird. But yes, that's my father."

"You kind of look like him."

Caridad peered at the photo again. She'd seen pictures of her father over the years, obviously. Hell, she had a vague, very fuzzy image in her mind of what he looked like, could remember being happy every time she heard his voice. And of course, her abuela had shown her photos over the years, seeing as she felt that Caridad needed to have some sense of who she'd come from.

"Yeah, I guess I do. I look a little like Mom, too, though."

Mikey flipped the page and pointed to a photograph of their mom and her father together. Their arms were wrapped around each other as they gazed into one another's faces, completely oblivious to the world around them. They were wearing formal wear, and a huge corsage was wrapped around her mother's wrist. She slipped the photo out and flipped it over.

April 20, 1987. Del Rio High School Senior Prom.

She flipped the photo back over and glanced once more at the happy faces of her parents before sliding the photo back into its protective pocket. "What you're looking at right there, hermanito, is a photo of two people just hours before they conceived a baby."

Mikey made a choking sound. Caridad thumped him on his back. "You okay there?"

"Jesus, Caridad, give a guy some warning before dropping a bombshell like that."

She laughed. "Wait. You don't know that story?"

He looked at her out of the corner of his eye. "Uh, no."

She flipped through the photo album and said, "So Mom and my father were high school sweethearts and had started dating when they were in like the ninth grade or something. Of course they went to prom together their senior year, and we all know what happens after prom."

"You were conceived in a skeevy hotel room while classmates puked their brains out in the bathroom down the hall?"

"Dude, what kind of after-prom parties did you go to?"

"You don't want to know."

"Probably not. Anyway. That's not entirely how it went down. No pun intended."

Mikey groaned.

"They apparently got hot and heavy in the backseat of my father's car before he took her home. Six weeks later they graduated and Mom got a positive pregnancy test as a graduation present."

"Why do you even know that? I mean, you realize it's pretty weird to know the story about how you were conceived, right?"

She shrugged. "I know it's weird, but I was curious and I asked. Mom told me the story, with pretty much that level of detail."

He looked down at the photo album as Caridad flipped the pages. "I'm sorry you lost your father, but at the same time I'm glad Mom met Dad, got married and had me. I kind of like being alive, y'know."

Caridad snorted. "I'm glad you're alive, too. Besides, everything happens for a reason."

As she continued to flip through photos, she saw her mom's pregnancy chronicled, along with pictures she'd never seen before of her dad. She had a handful of photos of him that her mom and grandmother had given her over the years, but for some reason Abuela had never pulled out this particular photo album and shared it with her.

She'd loved her grandmother, but the woman had had her secrets. Apparently this photo album was one of them.

She turned the page and stopped on a photo of her mom and father in the hospital, her father beaming as he held a tiny pink bundle in his arms. Caridad grinned at the memory of her dad's smile, how it could make her feel like the most special girl in the world.

Caridad resumed flipping through the pages of the photo album, seeing photos of herself as a baby, toddler and child that she'd never seen before. There she was with her favorite teddy bear. On her daddy's shoulders, laughing. At Christmas unwrapping presents. Blowing out four candles on a birthday cake.

And then the photos stopped.

Just as abruptly as her dad's life had ended, so did the photos.

Caridad's breath hitched and she handed the album back to Mikey before turning away, back to the cabinets and a mess she could fix rather than the broken memories held in those photos.

"You okay?"

She stared blindly at the dishes in front of her and nodded. "I'm fine."

"Are you sure?"

No.

"Yeah, I'll be fine. It's just been a long day, and there are a lot of memories in this old house."

"Obviously. Anyway. I guess I'll go back to the bedroom. Call me if you need me."

Caridad nodded again, but in her mind she was once again four years old with her world falling apart around her.

CHAPTER FIVE

OWEN GRABBED THE BOTTLE OF WINE OFF THE KITCHEN counter and headed out the door. He'd noticed yesterday that a new neighbor had moved in—well, as much of a neighbor as you can get when your houses were all situated on five acres or more—and figured he would go introduce himself, see what the new person was all about and be, well, neighborly.

It was what his Mama and Grandma would have told him to do, at least, and somehow twelve years in the Army and then the National Guard hadn't managed to drum that out of him. If anything, his time spent serving had only reinforced his tendency towards social niceties and general politeness.

As he drove over to meet his new neighbor, Owen wondered when the place had been sold. He hadn't noticed any real estate signs, but he'd also been a bit busy over the past month or so since Mrs. Garcia—the sole inhabitant—had passed away.

A few minutes later he was pulling to a stop in the drive that ended just beside the terra-cotta colored house. He grabbed the bottle of wine before getting out of the truck, the walk to the front door short. He knocked and waited.

"I'm coming. Just a second."

Owen drew his brows together. That voice sounded oddly familiar.

Before he could place it, though, the door swung open.

He almost dropped the bottle of wine.

Caridad.

The woman he'd been obsessing over for the past week. The client he'd almost kissed. The client who'd starred in one too many sexy dreams.

The woman who was currently staring back at him, her eyes wide and her throat working as she swallowed.

"Owen. Um. This is unexpected. What are you doing here?"

Yeah, because randomly showing up on her doorstep couldn't possibly come across as creepy.

"Well this is awkward." He gestured with the bottle in his hand. "I noticed someone had moved in and figured I would be a good neighbor and bring over a housewarming gift."

She probably thought he was a pansy.

"Oh." She glanced away, and Owen couldn't resist getting a good look at her. Yoga pants. Clingy tank top. His dick began to stir. *Not the time, dude.* He looked back up at her face, noted the indecision clearly etched all across it.

"I'm sorry. If I'd known it was you, I…" Hell, what was he supposed to say here? He wouldn't have bothered? Yeah, right. He so would have bothered, just to see her again up close and personal, to see if the chemistry had been all in his imagination or if it had been as real as it had felt.

"Don't even try to say you wouldn't have acted as a one-man welcoming committee, because I'm pretty sure you would have anyway. You're too nice not to."

Nice. In other words, "You're a great guy but you're a pussy."

He almost groaned. He kind of wanted to show her how not nice he could be. Instead, he just shrugged a shoulder. "Probably. But if I'd known it was you I probably would have brought you ammo instead."

That got a chuckle out of her, at least. She crossed her arms and leaned against the door frame. "Why ammo?"

Owen shifted the bottle of wine from one hand to the other. "You seemed like you like to shoot, is all."

She didn't need to know he'd Facebook stalked her almost as soon as she'd left. Nope nope nope.

She snorted. "Just admit you Facebook stalked me and get it over with."

He widened his eyes, trying to look innocent. She laughed.

"Okay, you got me. I was curious. We get female hunters out at the ranch, and some of them are pretty damned good shots, but I've never seen anyone who shot as well as you do. Plus, there was the Darrin connection. So, yeah, I got curious and may or may not have Googled your name."

He wasn't going to mention that he'd also just wanted to see her face because he hadn't been able to get her out of his mind. There were lines, and he was pretty sure that was one that did not need to be crossed. She was wary enough as it was.

"And what did you find, Owen Daniels?"

"A very impressive resume. Congrats, by the way."

She nodded her head. "Thanks."

He looked down at the bottle in his hands. "So, uh, welcome to the neighborhood."

"Thanks."

He handed her the bottle of wine. She was careful not to let their fingers touch, he noted. Good to know she wasn't as unaffected as she was trying to appear.

"So, do you, uh, live around here? I figured you lived up at the ranch."

He stuffed his hands into his jeans pockets. "Nope. Just own it. Well, partially. Like I explained, it's me and three other guys. Including Darrin. Who I'm guessing is your agent. I actually live next house over." *You can shut up and stop sounding like an idiot now.*

"Oh. Which one?"

"The blue and gray one just before this one, on the right."

"The blue and gray one?" Her eyebrows knitted together.

"Wait. The only blue and gray one is a barn. You live in a barn? Like, literally, a barn?"

He smiled. "Kind of. It used to be a barn, but I converted it into a shared space. One half is a garage and workshop, the other is living quarters."

"Oh. Like a barndominium."

"A what?"

"A barndominium. Barn. Condominium. Throw the two into a blender and see what you get. They're all over the Internet these days."

"Ah. If you want to call it that, whatever. It's just an old building I renovated and slapped some paint on."

"So you own a ranch with three other guys, live in a renovated barn, and bring new neighbors bottles of wine."

"Pretty much."

Their gazes caught and held, electricity sparking in the cool early November air. Caridad's tongue darted out and wet her lips.

"I broke up with my boyfriend." The words were spoken quietly but rushed, almost as if they escaped against her will. Her eyes went wide and she slapped a hand over her mouth. "Oh, I did not just say that," she mumbled.

Owen grinned. "You just said that. The question is why did you say it?"

She shook her head. "I have no idea."

He stepped towards her, closing the distance between them, watching her for the first sign of bolting. "I think you do."

She dropped her hand. "I really don't know why."

He stepped closer, until he could feel her body heat just an inch away. Tentatively, he pushed her hair behind her ear, leaned in and whispered, "If I touch you now, Caridad, if I kiss you now, will you let me?"

Her swallow was audible, but she didn't answer.

He hovered there by her ear, then down the curve of her cheek, her throat, his lips just millimeters from her skin. She drew in a ragged breath, but didn't pull away.

"I haven't been able to get you off of my damned mind, Cari. Your scent. Your smile. Your voice."

She sighed.

"I wanted to kiss you that night so damned bad, to know your taste, to feel your skin under my hands. It killed me to walk away, but I would never be party to cheating, even if the relationship is on the rocks. And you're standing here now, telling me you broke up with your boyfriend while goosebumps race across your skin and I'm finding it real hard to think of reasons why I shouldn't do what we both wanted me to do that night."

She turned her head, brought her lips to his ear and whispered, "Then don't."

⚭

No sooner were the words "then don't" out of her mouth than Owen's lips were on hers. Finally.

Oh, Dios mio, finally.

Caridad moaned and gripped the bottle of wine in her hand tighter, as her mouth opened to his and his tongue snuck inside. He curled a hand around her hip as he kissed her, his lips and tongue wreaking havoc on her entire nervous system. She was hot and cold all at once, her skin covered in goosebumps yet feeling as if it were on fire.

She grabbed his shirt with her free hand, the soft flannel twisting in her fingers as she lifted her hips to his, pressing against him while what she wanted to do was climb him like a freaking tree. His fingers dug into her hip and he backed her into the door frame, his body hard and hot against hers.

Oh, holy erection Batman.

She rubbed against him like a cat, wishing they were skin to skin rather than cotton to cotton. She let go of his shirt so she could slip her hands underneath it and feel all that male skin under her palms. His stomach muscles rippled as her fingers skimmed along the edge of his jeans, and then up his side and back down. Her hand slipped under the waistband of his jeans, just above the curve of his ass, and she squeezed.

Owen moaned before breaking the kiss, panting as he looked down at her, his clear blue eyes blazing like the flame on a match. Or a forest fire. Either or.

"I never did ask you what you're doing here in Mrs. Garcia's house. Or in Del Rio, period."

She squeezed his ass again. "Afraid to get burned, Mr. Daniels?"

"Not really the type to have sex against the door jamb, Miss Mathews."

"Should we take this inside, then?"

He groaned before reaching back and extracting her hand from his pants and stepping away. Her hand fell to her side.

"I obviously want you, but no. We probably shouldn't."

Rejection hit her like a sucker punch to the gut. "Was I too forward for you, Owen? Too unladylike? Or did you just not like what you felt once you had your hands on me?"

Red crept up his cheeks from underneath his beard. "First, that last statement?" He shook his head. "Jesus, woman. I can't fucking stop thinking about you, and considering how we were grinding against each other just now you know I want you. So just cut the crap, okay?"

She sucked in a sharp breath.

"And second, it's not that you were too forward or unladylike. I like that you're assertive. But we barely know each other, and I'm generally not into anonymous sex."

"Is it really anonymous when you know each other's last names and occupations? Well, kind of. All I know is that you own a ranch and another business."

He nodded. "Construction. Mostly residential."

Of course he owned a construction company. He had that whole rugged, masculine thing going on along with faded blue jeans and scuffed up work boots that had definitely seen better days. There was something about his whole look that just got to her, which was weird because she'd never been into the rugged, outdoorsy, do-stuff-with-his-hands type. Which was really weird when you thought about it, considering her chosen industry and the fact that she wasn't the most feminine woman on the planet.

She shook her head to clear it of her wayward thoughts.

"Are you trying to tell me I don't own a construction company?"

She sighed. "No. Sorry. My thoughts just got away from me. They tend to do that."

"I never would have guessed," he said dryly.

"Smart ass. Anyway. So back to my question—is it really anonymous sex if we know each other's last names and each other's occupations, not to mention where the other one lives?"

"Not completely anonymous, no. But that's beside the point."

"How so? You're the one who said you weren't into 'anonymous sex.'"

"Are you always this argumentative?"

"Only when I'm trying to get my way."

"Well, you're not getting your way on this one."

She pushed him out onto the porch and then moved further inside her house. "Fine, then. Be that way. I'll just take this bottle of wine inside, draw a bubble bath and take care of things myself."

Caridad could have sworn Owen's eyes smoldered as she slammed the door in his face.

Owen stared at the door that had just been slammed in his face and thought about Caridad's parting words and what had just happened between them.

Holy crap that had escalated quickly.

It was like some invisible leash had just snapped when she told him she'd broken up with her boyfriend. He hadn't stopped to think about whether or not she was potentially heartbroken (she hadn't looked heartbroken, though, now that he thought about it) or if it was too soon, or anything, really. His brain had simply short-circuited and all he'd been able to think about was her mouth and finding out what she'd tasted like.

And then things had gotten a little out of hand.

He shook his head as he turned and walked back to his truck and made the quick drive back to his house.

He wasn't usually the type to move fast. And he'd been honest about the anonymous sex thing. He liked women— loved them, in fact—and the way they smelled and tasted, the way their skin was so much softer than his. But he'd seen the aftermath of casual hookups and one-night stands, both in society and his personal life.

It wasn't always pretty.

So he dated. A lot. And enjoyed the company of women, but if his friends knew the actual number of women he'd been with they'd probably laugh and call him a liar. Well, Jenn and Jo would maybe say he was sweet once they got over their disbelief. Matt and Chase, however, would probably find numerous ways to rib him about it.

He wasn't about to explain the complicated mess in his head where sex and women were concerned. It was probably screwed up enough that most people would tell him he needed a shrink.

Or that he had daddy issues.

Or mommy issues.

Whatever.

He just looked at it as doing the right thing, even if his head was a bit messed up at times. So sue him.

Back home, Owen looked around his house, at the space he'd completely renovated into living quarters. *Home.*

Right now, though, home didn't feel as comforting as it usually did.

Restless and suddenly full of pent-up energy, Owen pulled his phone out of his back pocket and shot out a group text to

Chase and Matt.

Owen: Y'all up for April's tonight?

April's was their favorite bar and weekend hangout, kind of like Cheers had been for Norm, Cliff and Frasier. The place usually had a great selection of Texas country, with some pop, rock and hip hop thrown in on Friday nights. Great pool tables. Huge beers. Popular yet not so popular that it was impossible to find a table or get good service.

Chase: Not tonight. Jo's in town for the weekend.

Matt: Jenn's still having to take it easy. Not tonight, man.

Owen frowned and pocketed his phone. Well, it looked like April's was out of the question since he generally wasn't into drinking alone. He could always call up Michelle, a girl he'd gone on a few dates with back in October. Except he was having a hard time seeing anyone's face but Caridad's.

Shit.

He had it bad.

With a groan he headed back towards the garage. Maybe a drive would help clear his head.

CHAPTER SIX

A WEEK LATER, CARIDAD FOUND HERSELF SITTING IN HER OLD chair at her parents' dining room table. The scents of her mom's chicken and sour cream enchiladas, refried beans and rice made her mouth water, as did the thought of her mom's fluffy, hand-made tortillas. The supper selection was rounded out by homemade guacamole and pico de gallo—with extra cilantro, please—along with tortilla chips.

While there had definitely been things about Del Rio she hadn't missed, her mom's cooking wasn't one of them.

Hell, the thought of the sopapillas that were sure to be served for dessert almost made her weep with joy.

"It's so good to have you back home, Cari."

Cari. The nickname made her think of Owen, the way it sounded rolling off his tongue. Like a lover's caress.

She shook herself, not wanting to go down that particular road in front of her parents and Mikey. No, thank you.

She looked at the man she'd thought of as Dad since he'd adopted her at six years old and smiled. "I'm honestly still trying to figure out if it's good to be home or not, but so far things are going well."

"Well I, for one, am glad you're back," Bruce said.

And that was the hell of it. She knew her parents and brother were glad to have her back home, but she still wasn't sure if she was glad to be back or not. Considering she'd left town with a trail of dust and exhaust behind her, middle finger out the window, she was just as surprised as anyone that she'd decided to move into her grandmother's house.

"You need to heal, Caridad, so that you can truly move forward with your life," her therapist had said to her just before she'd left Dallas.

And Dr. Tracy was probably right—God knew the woman was always right—but Caridad was still trying to figure out how to go about that healing.

There really wasn't a blueprint for forgiving your psychotic, stalker, abusive ex. Sure, there were plenty of self-help books, but she'd found those to be sleep-inducing at best. Talking about her experience had helped a decent amount, but most of the time she felt like picking up a pistol and taking her first defensive handgun course had helped the most.

Being able to defend herself should the psycho, stalker ex reappear had helped soothe her most of all.

"So did you have fun at that ranch you went to a couple weeks ago?" her mom asked as she pulled a casserole dish out of the oven.

Gloria Mathews was a short, voluptuous woman with black hair woven with strands of gray. She was also the best damned cook this side of the Rio Grande as far as Caridad was concerned. Even if certain parts of their relationship were still rocky after all these years, she knew one thing for sure— her mom was an amazing cook who would always have an open spot at the dinner table for her.

"Yeah. It was nice to get away." An image of Owen popped into her head and she quickly stuffed it back down.

No sense going there, considering how things had ended last weekend.

Ugh.

"You get anything?"

Caridad turned to her dad. "Yeah. I took a mature cull that happened to wander out in front of us. The meat should be ready for me to pick up any day now."

Bruce nodded. "I've heard things here and there about that place—what is it, Devils Ranch or something like that?"

She nodded.

"Is it as nice as rumors have it?"

She laughed. "Probably nicer. The main house is absolutely gorgeous, all limestone and wood. Mom would love the kitchen—and the chef, probably. The food was amazing. And they have an indoor gun range. A really kick ass indoor gun range."

"And what about your guide?" Mikey asked, mischief gleaming in his eyes and a smirk across his face.

Caridad barely resisted the urge to glare at him. She so should not have told him about Owen last weekend.

"What about him?"

Mikey leaned back as Gloria set the casserole dish in the middle of the table. His grin was pure little bother mischief. "What was he like? Was he any good?"

She was so going to kill him. "He was a wonderful guide."

Hell. She sounded fake even to her own ears.

Gloria shook her head. "Mikey, stop giving your sister a hard time."

"But it's so much fun, Mom."

Gloria sat down and gave him a pointed look. "No more harassing at the dinner table. Bruce, honey, would you say the prayer?"

Just like that Gloria had shushed a potentially sensitive subject.

Some things never changed.

⚭

Caridad managed to escape her parents' house without killing her brother—and more importantly, without being snarky towards her mom.

Since the drama with the psycho stalker ex, she and her mom had clashed, to say the least. Gloria hadn't understood why Caridad decided to pick up a gun and learn how to defend herself, much less why she even needed to in the first place.

Despite the bruises she'd had on her arms from where he'd grabbed her and thrown her across the room that last time. Despite the concussion from where she'd hit the wall. Despite the threats and the stalking after she'd left his sorry ass and filed a police report. Despite the fact that he'd completely ignored the restraining order she'd taken out against him.

Up until that night when he threw her against the wall, no one else had seen the abuse. Hell, it had taken Caridad years to see it herself.

They'd been high school sweethearts, and while he'd always been a little possessive he'd never been abusive or mean. Or so she'd thought. It wasn't until afterward—and through therapy—that she'd realized that the abuse had started long before he'd ever laid a hand on her.

Unfortunately, he'd done such a good job covering his tracks and acting like the nice guy that everyone believed he really was a nice guy. Even after she'd gone to the hospital and the police, it had still been hard for her mom to see anything other than the nice boy she'd loved like a son.

Her mom's refusal—or maybe it was just sheer inability—to see what he'd done to her daughter had been the last straw for Caridad. Tired of defending her choice of, well, defense, she'd packed up and moved away not long after the psycho abusive stalker ex had been thrown in jail.

She'd basically tossed all her clothes in a couple of suitcases, grabbed her Glock and ammo, and left town without much of a goodbye.

It had taken her years to come to a place of almost peace with the fact that her mom would probably never accept what had happened to her. She wanted to say she was okay with that, but she wasn't, and being around her mom again was reminding her of all the reasons she'd left.

The woman could not handle emotionally tough subject

matter.

Then again, she never had been able to, so Caridad wasn't sure why she suddenly expected that to change.

Sighing, she pulled herself out of her maudlin thoughts and logged on to Facebook and then Twitter. It was late, but she had posts she needed to schedule for tomorrow.

Besides, she had a feeling she wasn't going to be able to fall asleep any time soon—conversations with Gloria always hyped her up.

Once she'd gotten the posts out of the way, she pulled out a pen and a notebook to write out some notes on a YouTube video she was thinking about filming. She'd been scribbling away, jotting down thoughts for almost thirty minutes when her phone dinged with an incoming text message.

Darrin: I know it's late, but I just had a very interesting conversation that I think you might want to know about.

Curiosity piqued, she texted back: What's up?

Seconds later her phone rang.

"Hey there. What's going on?"

"So I was at CBD Provisions having dinner with a client tonight. Afterward we went over to Joule for drinks at the bar, and I ran into someone who was very interested in learning all about you."

Caridad drew her brows together. "Who?"

"Harold Murchison."

"Am I supposed to know who that is?"

Darrin sighed, and Caridad could almost see him shaking his head. "Harold Murchison, Caridad. The president of Outdoor TV."

"Outdoor TV?" she parroted.

"You know, the channel with all of the hunting and fishing shows. Outdoorsy stuff."

"I know what it is, I just don't see how any of this pertains to me."

"Apparently Murchison has been pushing to expand the channel's offerings beyond hunting and fishing shows while staying true to the values of Outdoor TV viewers and employees."

"Still not following."

"You're taking all the fun out of this."

Caridad snorted. "Sorry to burst your bubble."

Darrin laughed. "No worries. At any rate, since you're Miss Impatient tonight, they've been talking about filming a few shows that feature shooting outside of hunting. One idea they have is a reality show like *Top Shot* that was on The History Channel a while back. They have a few others, but the one he was most interested in talking about tonight was a show targeted directly towards female viewers."

"Well, that would make sense considering women are the fastest growing segment of gun owners and hunters in America."

"Right. Specifically, though, he was very interested in you for this show."

She didn't even have to think about it. "I would love to be a guest if it gets off the ground."

"Not as a guest, Caridad."

She stared down at her notepad, her thoughts racing. "What do you mean 'not as a guest?'"

"I mean he wants to film a show centered around you, following you to meets, talks, trade shows, etcetera."

"But why? I'm boring."

"You have more YouTube subscribers and views than any other female in the industry. Your Facebook and Twitter followings are growing daily it seems like, and I'm not sure what your website traffic is like but I'm willing to guess it's pretty heavy. You're not boring."

"I think you're full of it, but whatever. So this Murchison guy wants to film a show that's all about me?"

Darrin chuckled. "More or less, yes."

"I think he's crazy."

"I think he's on to something. I know you need some time to think about this, but I wanted to give you a heads up. We had a two-hour conversation about nothing but you, and I get the feeling he's willing to—no pun intended—pull the trigger as soon as you give him the green light."

Caridad looked up and around her grandmother's dining room, her eyes seeing but not focusing on anything. "I don't know, Darrin. I'm still nervous about how much I've put myself out there already, all things considered."

"I know. You don't have to make any decisions right now. He hasn't even made a formal proposal or anything. This just sounds like something that could end up moving really fast."

She took a deep breath. "Got it. Total change of subject here, but apparently your friend Owen and I are next door neighbors."

Where that had come from, she had no idea.

Yeah, you do.

"Really? That's a little bit of a small world. He's a good guy. Has a little bit of a reputation from what I understand, but I've never heard a woman say anything bad about him. It probably wouldn't hurt you to get to know him a little bit, make a couple of friends down there."

A little bit of a reputation? What the hell did that mean? Especially coming from mister "I don't do casual sex."

"Eh, I'll think about it. Right now I'm kind of busy cleaning out Abuela's house. Ends up, she was a bit of a hoarder later on in life."

"That's what cleaning companies are for."

"As if I would spend my hard-earned money on a cleaning company. You know better than that."

"One day, I will convince you that it's worth it. Anyway, I've got another call beeping in. Think about the TV show, okay?"

"Will do. Later."

"Adios," he said before hanging up.

Well, that had been an interesting conversation.

A conversation she had no idea how to process.

CHAPTER SEVEN

THE DAY AFTER THANKSGIVING, OWEN, CHASE, AND MATT
stood gathered around a pool table at April's, The Turnpike
Troubadours' "Gin, Smoke, Lies" thumping over the sound
system. As Matt and Chase teased each other in the way that
only brothers can, Owen chalked up his cue stick and thought
back over the past six months or so.

It had been kind of crazy, considering both brothers had
ended up going through their own scares—Chase, with his
slowly failing kidneys and Matt getting hit in the head by a
line drive, which had caused his brain to bleed. There had
been a time when Owen had wondered if either of them was
going to make it through their respective shit sandwiches with
any shred of sanity left. Hell, he couldn't have blamed them
if they hadn't.

In the end, though, Matt and Chase had both gotten lucky
and found someone to help guide them through those rough
transition periods in their lives. Matt with his injury, recov-
ery and retirement from baseball—all within a span of a few
months. And Chase with his updated diagnosis and increasingly failing health.

The brothers were cut from the same cloth—stubborn
and independent—and both seemed to realize just how lucky
they'd been to find Jenn and Jo. Well, re-find. Re-connect.

Whatever.

Here he was, though, feeling more and more often like a fifth wheel despite his friends' reassurances that he wasn't.

If he were being honest with himself, he would acknowledge the fact that the time of year had a lot to do with his melancholy feelings. His mom had loved Christmas. The day after Thanksgiving had been her favorite—not because of Black Friday sales, but because that was the day she put up the Christmas tree. Even though she'd been gone for three years now, it still hit him in the heart when he woke up on Black Friday and realized he wouldn't be going over to help her put lights up outside or drag the heavy Christmas boxes out of the attic.

Hell, he hadn't even been able to put up his own tree since she'd passed. And didn't that just smack of being some sort of pansy-ass Mama's boy?

Owen rubbed a hand over his face and tried to shake the maudlin thoughts. It was just that there were times when he felt, well, lonely. And even though he was in a bar surrounded by people—including Chase and Matt—he still felt that way.

The truth of the matter was that they were all at a crossroads, in some sort of transition period. Always. It was called life.

Sure, he'd had his fair share of transitioning over the past few years, too. First, with Mom getting sick then dying, second with leaving the National Guard.

Not to mention the fact that his best friends had coupled-up over the past six months, making him officially the odd guy out.

Ugh.

What was up with the pity party tonight?

Especially since he was supposed to be enjoying a game of pool with Matt and Chase—not feeling like a guest on Dr. Phil.

"You okay, man? You seem kind of out of it," Matt said as he racked the balls.

Owen thought about plastering a fake smile on his face. But hell, if you couldn't be real with your friends, who could you be real with? "Just feeling some old-fashioned holiday blues, my friend."

"Dude, it's the day after Thanksgiving," Matt said.

Owen shrugged and took a drink of his beer. "And Christmas shit's been out since before Halloween. Your point is?"

The former major league pitcher shook his head. "Fair enough."

Chase grabbed a pool stick and asked, "Missing your mom?"

Owen lifted a shoulder. "Yeah. You know how she was about the day after Thanksgiving."

"I take it this is one more of those things I missed while I was gone?" Matt asked.

"Yeah. My mom's favorite holiday was Christmas, and the day after Thanksgiving was always her big day to put up decorations, hang lights, and trim the tree. Because it was just her, my grandma, and me, it was a big family thing every year."

"I feel like I should have known about that," Matt muttered before saying, "I'm sorry, man."

Owen waved it off. "You've been pretty out of the loop the past ten years. It's okay."

"Not really, but I can't change the past."

Owen knew that Matt still held a lot of regret over his ten-year absence. Well, absence wasn't really the right word, more like withdrawal. Owen hadn't been around when Matt first bailed on everyone since he hadn't moved back to Del Rio until the next year, but it hadn't taken him long to put the pieces together. He learned that Matt had definitely withdrawn from his friends and family shortly after making it to the Bigs, and up until a couple of months ago nobody had known why.

Imagine the entire group's surprise when they'd found out Matt and Jenn had had a one-night stand ten years ago. Then multiply that surprise by a thousand when they found out Jenn had gotten pregnant, miscarried, and never told anyone.

The only non-surprise had been their officially coming out of the dating closet in September. And now they were living together and Jenn was pregnant. Again.

Speaking of Jenn… "Where are Jo and Jenn? I figured they'd be with you two."

Both brothers rolled their eyes. "Wedding dress shopping in San Antonio," Chase said.

"You sound thrilled," Owen deadpanned. "And wait, I thought Jenn was on bed rest or something?" All he knew was that because of the prior miscarriage, she was having to see a specialist and had to have a circle something or other done a couple of weeks prior and had been put on bed rest. He didn't know what the procedure was, but it had sounded painful—and he didn't even have a cervix.

Matt answered first. "Her doctor said she was doing fine and lifted the bed rest a couple of days ago. Just told her to take it easy. I'm not sure how wedding dress shopping is taking it easy, but Jenn knows her body and her limits, so I have to trust her."

Owen almost laughed at the pinched look on Matt's face, like he'd just swallowed a lemon or something. "I take it you're not too happy about her going with Jo to San Antonio?"

Matt shrugged. "I'm not, but I know better than to tell her what to do. Besides, Jo's with her and her fetal specialist is in San Antonio, so I'm trying to relax."

"You're not doing a very good job of that, bro."

Matt looked at Chase. "This coming from the man who sounds absolutely thrilled about his fiancée wedding dress shopping."

"Oh, I am. I can't wait to marry Jo. I just hate seeing her so stressed out."

"Dude, she's getting married in something like four months, not to mention getting her house ready to put on the market so she can move here after the semester's over. Oh, and there's that little thing called your kidney failure," Matt said.

"Hey. I'm not in kidney failure yet."

Matt glared at his younger brother. "The operative word being 'yet.' But you can't tell me you haven't been feeling worse here lately."

Chase ran a hand through his hair and sighed. "I still don't understand this brotherly thing you've suddenly got going on, but yeah, I've been feeling worse."

"Has there been any change in your levels or anything?" Owen asked.

"Don't know yet. I actually have labs next week and an appointment with my nephrologist the week after, so we'll see."

"Good luck, man."

"Thanks." Chase took a drink of water. "Anyway. How did we even get on this subject? Weren't we talking about what's wrong with you?"

Owen re-chalked the tip of his pool stick. "Nothing's wrong with me other than my usual holiday blues."

"Bullshit. You've been out of sorts for weeks."

He shrugged. "Who's breaking?"

"You can," Chase said. "Seriously, man. How long as it been since you got laid?"

"Too damn," Owen gave his usual, off-hand answer as he lined up his shot.

"I'm pretty sure I have an office manager who would be willing to help you out with that."

"I am so not going there with Kim."

"Here's what I can't figure out: does she really hate you or is the hate a mask for something else? Kind of like Jenn with Matt."

"I'm pretty sure she hates me."

"But why? Women love you."

"It's kind of sickening," Matt said.

"Like you're one to talk," Owen said to Matt.

"Okay. Fair enough. Aesthetically speaking we're three successful, reasonably attractive guys who generally don't have trouble garnering female attention."

"Dude. Seriously? You're my brother."

"I said 'aesthetically speaking'."

"Still, though. Kind of weird."

"Whatever. You're missing the point, which is that while you and I are having sex on a frequent basis Owen here appears not to be."

"I do not need to know how often you and Jenn have sex," Owen said. "She's like a sister to me."

Matt shrugged. "Point taken. Let it be said, though, that there are definite advantages to pregnancy hormones, especially since the sex moratorium has been lifted by her doctor."

Owen stuck his fingers in his ears. "La la la. I can't hear any more."

"Anyway. What's up with the lack of dates here lately?" Chase asked as Owen removed his fingers from his ears.

He was a serial dater. Everyone knew that. And everyone assumed he was having sex with all of those serial dates. They were wrong.

Quite wrong.

"I just haven't really been interested in anyone."

Lies. It was all lies.

"Anyway, are we gonna play pool or stand around gossiping like a bunch of women?"

"Studies have shown that men actually gossip more. Just sayin'."

Chase and Owen both stared at Matt.

"Weirdest. Brother. Ever."

ॐ

"So that's the guy that's had you tied up in knots?"

Caridad glanced at her little brother and sighed. "Yeah, that's him."

"Dios mio, chica. That dude is hot."

"You think?" She wasn't going to mention that Owen was also an awesome kisser, especially since he hadn't made any more neighborly visits since that evening a couple of weeks ago.

They were at April's, a bar she'd heard good things about, mostly that it was laid-back and not a meat market. Funny how as soon as she and Mikey had stepped in the door she'd spotted Owen.

"I'm pretty sure he's the type of guy Buzzfeed would do a lumbersexual pictorial feature on, and deservedly so. You should go say hi to him."

"Uh, I don't think so." And Owen's hotness went so far beyond lumbersexual it wasn't even funny. Plus, there was a distinct absence of man bun.

He gave her some serious side eye. "You've done lost your mind."

She shrugged. "Let's just say things didn't end so well the last time we saw each other."

Mikey raised an eyebrow. "So there's more to this story that you're not telling me."

Resistance was futile, apparently. "He kinda sorta kissed me, things got pretty heated, and when I invited him in to finish what he started he…um…declined."

Mikey's eyes rounded in shock. "What? What's wrong with him?"

"He said he wasn't into anonymous sex. Apparently he's one of those rare men who wants to know a woman before he sleeps with her."

"So you're saying he's a unicorn?"

"Pretty much. Yes."

"Then you should go forth and talk. Communicate. Get to know that fine ginger-haired specimen of a man and then ride that unicorn's horn."

"Really?" she deadpanned.

"Absolutely."

"I am not going over there and talking to him. A—he's

playing pool and therefore busy. B—I don't want him to think I'm stalking him." Besides, she could tell he was there with friends—even if she hadn't gotten a good look at those friends—and she really wasn't up for that whole new level of awkward.

Mikey rolled his eyes. "You think too much. Adios. Vamoose. Get to know the guy."

Caridad fiddled with the label on her beer bottle. "Mikey, I'm not interested in getting to know anyone. I just got out of a relationship for crying out loud."

Mikey snorted. "A relationship that was over before it really began. Don't even try to act like you're all broken-hearted because you're not."

Dammit, he was right.

"And you can't keep putting men at arm's length and punishing all of them for the sins of one. You're not that girl anymore. You're stronger now." He grinned. "Not to mention much better armed."

"True that."

"So, seriously. Go talk to the guy. Get to know him a bit. Then screw his brains out and give me all the details."

"You really are weird, you know that? Most brothers wouldn't want to know anything about their sister's sex life."

"Yes, well, lucky for you I'm one of a kind."

Caridad rolled her eyes. "You're something. Anyway, I'm going to go to the ladies' room real quick."

"Chicken."

She slid off of her barstool, turned back to Mikey and said, "bok bok" before walking away.

ॐ

Owen glanced up for the fifty-ninth time that night and noticed that Caridad was walking towards the restroom. Perfect.

He set his pool cue to the side and said to Matt and Chase, "Hey, guys, I'll be right back. I'm gonna go grab another beer.

Need anything?"

"Nope, I'm good. Who's the woman?" Chase asked.

Owen turned his head so quickly he felt a slight twinge. "What woman?"

"The one who's had your attention for the past twenty minutes. I haven't gotten a good look at her, but I know you, and you've definitely been distracted by something. My guess is that that something has breasts."

Did she ever.

He tried to act casual and shrugged a shoulder. "Maybe. Maybe not. Be back in a few."

Matt made a sound like a whip being cracked as he walked out of the pool room, and Owen shook his head. He loved those guys like they were his brothers, but damn were they pains in the ass sometimes.

Instead of heading towards the bar he made his way towards the bathrooms in the back, needing a Caridad fix like a junkie needed his next hit.

God, he had it bad.

He'd just made it to the men's restroom door when the women's door opened and Caridad came out, her head down and glued to her phone. Obviously not paying attention to her surroundings, she plowed right into him.

Perfect. He couldn't have set that up better if he'd tried.

The force of their impact caused her to stumble backwards, and Owen reached out and gently grabbed her arms to steady her. Without warning, her head whipped up and into his as her hand wrapped around one of his wrists. Rubbing his head with his free hand, he said, "Caridad. It's me, Owen. It's okay."

Her gaze snapped up to his, and he noticed her eyes looked unfocused, as if she wasn't one hundred percent present. Slowly, her gaze sharpened and focused, and she dropped his wrist like a hot potato. She took a quick step back, and then bent to pick up the phone that had fallen to the floor during their...whatever it was that had just happened.

Without looking back at him, she mumbled, "Sorry about that."

Slowly, he reached out and rubbed her arm. She flinched, and he dropped his hand. What the hell was going on here?

"It's okay. Or, rather, I'm okay, although I might have a bit of a bruise in the morning. Care to tell me what that was all about?"

Her gaze ping ponged around the dimly lit corridor, landing on everything but him. "Owen, I'm a single woman who lives on her own and who has pervy guys constantly commenting on her Facebook and YouTube accounts about how much they'd like to 'meet' me, among other things. I didn't see you, and when you grabbed my arms I went into self-defense mode."

"So what you're saying is that I should be glad we're in a bar which means you're not carrying?" he teased.

She smirked, but at least she finally looked at him, too. What he saw on her face was more than a fear of pervy fans, though. "Yeah, that's probably a good thing. I really don't want to have my title stripped from me or be put under any lengthy police investigations. Could really hurt my reputation, y'know."

"Have you forgotten the industry you're in? A story about a good girl taking out a bad guy with a gun would get you so much press you'd probably be fending off interviewers and advertising offers for months."

She barked out a laugh. "God, that is so true, and I honestly have enough on my plate to worry about."

He smiled. "Well, then, I'm glad you didn't have the chance to shoot me, especially considering I'm not a bad guy."

She shook her head. "I don't know you well enough yet to know if you're a good guy or a bad guy."

"But?"

She rolled her eyes. "But, my gut tells me you're not one of the bad ones."

"What else does your gut tell you?"

"That if I don't get back to the bar my little brother's going to come looking for me."

"You have a brother?"

"Yes. And he thinks you're hot, just FYI."

Owen laughed. "Fair enough. And what do you think?"

"I think you already know what I think," she said, her tone flirtatious now rather than weary.

Owen tentatively took a step forward. When she didn't move, flinch, or tell him to back off, he took another, and then another until he'd crowded her up against the wall next to the bathroom door. "I honestly don't know for sure what you think, Cari."

She looked up at him. "Does it matter what I think?"

"Absolutely."

"And what do you think, Owen?"

He moved in just a little closer, so that his chest and her breasts brushed against each other with every rise and fall of their breaths. He caressed her cheek with the pad of his thumb and watched as her eyes darkened and a flush stained her skin. "I think that I can't stop thinking about you. About what your mouth tasted like. About the way you felt pressed up against me and the little sounds you made in the back of your throat. I think I want to get to know you better, to know what makes you tick. I want to know your hopes and dreams and goals. I think about driving over to your house and asking you out on a date, so that maybe we can do this the right way and get to know each other. I think—no, I know—that I want you, and that you're the first person to ever make me remotely think about tossing my morals to the side if it means knowing what it feels like to kiss you, to touch you, to be inside of you."

She shivered and closed her eyes, her chest rising and falling rapidly. The feeling of her breasts against his chest—and her obviously hard nipples—had him rock hard and ready to go. Right here against the wall.

Inside a bar.

Just as Caridad swayed into him reality crashed down.

Hard. Suddenly he was aware of the sounds of people laughing and talking, the faint sound of balls clacking against one another in one of the pool rooms, and Whiskey Myers' "Broken Window Serenade" blaring through the sound system.

He was losing his damned mind.

Slightly shaken, Owen took a slight step backward and raked a hand through his hair. "That's what I think, Cari. If you're interested, you know where to find me." He turned away, his motions abrupt and jerky, like someone else had temporarily inhabited his body.

Hell, it was the only logical explanation for what had just happened, because he didn't do almost sex in a bar with a woman he barely knew.

No matter how much he wanted to.

Caridad slowly rested her back against the wall, willing her heart rate to slow down and her girly parts to get their collective act together. She closed her eyes and tried to convince herself that hadn't just happened.

Oh, it so just happened.

She breathed in through her nose and exhaled through her mouth, wishing she either had a beer or a Xanax right now. Something to calm her down.

I want you.

He'd really said that, hadn't he?

I can't stop thinking about you.

Yeah, join the club, buddy.

She shook her head at the war going on inside of her brain. This was getting ridiculous. He was just a guy. A hot guy, sure, but just a guy nonetheless.

He's so much more than "just a guy" and you know it.

Okay, he was just a man.

A man who'd made her body come alive with nothing more than some admittedly sexy words and a simple brush of his chest against hers.

Frustrated with herself—she didn't let men get the upper hand anymore—she pushed away from the wall and headed back towards the bar and her brother.

And got waylaid by the last person she'd expected to see.

"Caridad Mathews! Holy shit. What are you doing here?"

"Matt? I could ask you the same thing."

The former Texas Wranglers pitcher and future hall-of-famer pulled her in for a quick hug.

"Seriously, though, what are you doing here?" Matt asked as they stepped away from each other.

"Here as in April's or here as in Del Rio?"

"Both."

"Well, I'm here in Del Rio because my grandmother passed away a couple of months ago and left me her house and I decided to move back home. I'm in April's because I needed to get away from all the clutter and enjoy a beer without looking at stacks of random crap. Now what about you?"

"How is it we've known each other for as long as we have and I never realized you were from Del Rio?" he answered with a question.

She shrugged. "I'm not sure. I'd honestly forgotten you'd moved back here. Life's been kind of crazy the past few months."

"Yeah, no shit. Congrats, by the way."

"Well, congrats to you, too. I think throwing a perfect game in Game Seven of the World Series is a little more impressive than me shooting some targets." She smiled.

Matt smiled back at her. "That was pretty cool. But don't discredit your own championship. I've watched some of your matches on YouTube, and while I'm no stranger to handling firearms, you take it to a whole new level."

She felt her cheeks heat just slightly; even though she'd heard the compliments before, she still wasn't quite used to people talking as though what she did—and that she—was something special. "Still not as awesome as winning the World Series."

"I'm not gonna argue with you—Jenn's taught me better than that."

"Jenn?"

Matt's grin was almost blinding. "My girlfriend."

"Wait. The tall redhead you were with in all the post-game footage?" Caridad vaguely remembered reading something about Matt moving back home in order to be with the love of his life.

His words—not hers.

"That would be Jenn. You'll have to meet her sometime."

Caridad nodded. "Okay. Sure."

"Speaking of meeting people, I have a couple folks you should come say hi to real quick."

Before she could say anything, Matt had tugged on her sleeve and begun steering her away from the restrooms and bar and towards...oh, hell.

⚭

Owen sank the three ball and moved around the table to line up his next shot. He bent over the table, mentally calculating the angles. He moved slightly, positioned his cue stick and pulled back to take the shot.

He couldn't say what it was exactly, but something caused him to look up just as his arm moved forward. He caught the sight of long, straight black hair and curves. The cue caught the edge of the four ball, sending it spinning across the table like a wayward top.

He stood and stepped away from the table. Chase shook his head, grinning, as he grabbed his cue. Owen took a sip of beer and almost choked when Caridad stepped into the pool room with Matt beside her.

Matt basically propelled her into the room, and Owen couldn't help but notice the brief grimace that crossed Caridad's face.

"Look who I found, guys!" Matt said a little too cheerfully.

Owen took another drink of his beer and said nothing, deciding discretion was the better part of valor in this particular scenario.

Matt motioned towards Chase. "Caridad, this is my brother Chase. Chase, this is Caridad Mathews, who also happens to be a sometimes client of Darrin's and is a little bit of a badass."

Chase leaned forward and shook Caridad's hand. "Nice to meet you, Caridad. Don't believe everything my brother says about me."

Caridad smiled and her eyes sparkled. "Nice to meet you, too. And for the record, I've only heard the usual stuff older siblings say about their younger siblings, so it's all good."

"Nice to know."

"And this is Owen Daniels, one of my business partners and my girlfriend's best friend. Well, I guess he's my friend, too. I mean, he's alright."

Owen rolled his eyes and Caridad was beginning to look slightly uncomfortable. They exchanged a brief but charged glance.

"Actually, Matt, Caridad and I kind of already know each other." An image of Caridad in her robe, her breast peeking out from the edge and her lips slightly parted popped into his head. That image was followed by one from just the other day, Caridad standing on her front porch, her eyes glazed and her lips swollen from his kiss. And that one was followed by the memory of her breasts brushing against his chest just moments ago in the hallway outside the bathrooms.

His dick—which he'd finally started to get under control—unfortunately chose that moment to wake back up.

Great.

Matt turned his head and quirked his eyebrow at Owen. "Oh, really? And how do you two know each other?"

If the grin on Matt's face was any indication, his friend was thinking that Caridad was the woman Owen had been preoccupied with. Fantastic.

"Remember Darrin's client I did a guided hunt for opening weekend?"

Matt turned back to Caridad. "That was you? Why didn't you or Darrin say anything?"

Caridad shrugged. "I didn't even decide until the last minute to take him up on his offer. But then I decided it was a good opportunity to get away and clear my head. I honestly forgot you were one of the owners." She tucked a strand of hair behind her ear. "Anyway. I left my brother alone at the bar, so I better get back before he gets himself in trouble. It was great to see you." She glanced at Owen. "Both. And nice to meet you, Chase."

Owen watched as she walked away, his eyes involuntarily drawn to her ass and the sway of her hips. Jesus, the woman could fill out a pair of jeans.

Matt laughed, drawing Owen's attention from Caridad.

"Never in a million years would I have seen that one coming."

Owen casually—he hoped—drank his beer. "Seen what coming?"

"You and Caridad Mathews. You know who she is, right?"

"Yup."

"And that doesn't scare you just a little bit?"

Apparently pretenses were no longer needed, so Owen went with the truth. "Dude, have you ever seen her handle a rifle? It's fucking hot."

Matt threw his head back and laughed. "Oh, this is going to be so much fun to watch."

CHAPTER EIGHT

Caridad needed a gun range. Stat.

Looking back, she still couldn't believe she'd actually made the decision to move back home without researching local gun ranges before hand. She wasn't sure what she'd been thinking, but it apparently hadn't been about her career.

She also needed to find a therapist, but that particular task didn't seem as important to her right now.

While range time was therapeutic in some ways, it didn't do the trick completely. Sure, she could usually push all wayward thoughts out of her head while she was competing, but as soon as the match was over all those thoughts crowded right back in. She hadn't quite figured out how to cope with her anxiety—and what Dr. Tracy had diagnosed as post traumatic stress disorder—off the gun range.

Even after seven years, she still had trouble swallowing the fact that she had PTSD. To her, PTSD was something veterans came home from Iraq and Afghanistan with, or something that first responders and those who'd grown up in abusive homes were afflicted with. She wasn't a veteran, had never been a first responder, and her childhood was pretty good all things considered, so to be told she had PTSD because her ex boyfriend liked to slap her around seemed kind of silly.

Yes, she'd done her research, and she'd come to learn

that people could get PTSD from all sorts of traumatic situations and that the battlefield wasn't always relegated to a desert in the Middle East. Many adult survivors of childhood abuse—mental, physical and sexual—suffered from PTSD, as did men and women who'd been in abusive relationships as adults. Rape survivors often dealt with PTSD—which was understandable, all things considered—as did people who had gone through traumatic, life-threatening illnesses and organ transplants.

In other words, her being traumatized and stressed after being abused and stalked then threatened by her ex was completely normal and almost expected. She just hated that she couldn't always control her reactions, like the other night with Owen when he'd grabbed her arms.

It was funny, because she could pick up a gun with no problem, but as soon as someone touched her arms unexpectedly she was acting on pure instinct. And that pure instinct had almost left Owen with a bloody nose and an inability to ever have children.

Three days later she was still embarrassed by her reaction—to both his unexpected presence and his nearness just moments later. Jesus, could she send out any more mixed signals?

And because her thoughts were spinning around her head, she needed a gun range. Stat.

Unfortunately, the only one she was finding via a Google search was a private range with an out of date website. She'd been able to figure out that the range was still open—ended up there was a Del Rio chapter of A Girl And A Gun women's shooting league, which was a nice little surprise—but she wasn't sure if they would be able to accommodate her on such short notice.

Oh, well. Nothing left to do but call. It was much better than the alternative of slowly going crazy thinking about men.

Three hours and a hundred bucks later, Caridad was unlocking a gate to what was apparently a semi-private gun range. From what she'd been told by the owner, members had a key to the gate and could use the range whenever they wanted to as long as it wasn't already booked. Lucky for her it was a Monday—not to mention the middle of the day—and she had the place all to herself.

Grinning, she swung the gate open before getting back into her truck and pulling through. She got out and closed the gate behind her before following the signs to the main part of the range. She'd noticed there was an International Defensive Pistol Association match on the first Saturday of every month, which meant there was one coming up this Saturday. She figured registration was probably closed for it, but January's was definitely a possibility. She also needed to find some regional three gun matches that she could hit up between now and the first major qualifying competition in February.

She pulled up to one of the bays and got out of the truck. Her actions routine, she unloaded her gear: folding table, range bag, ammo, pistol, target stand, staple gun, and paper targets. Settling in, she set up her first target before walking back to the table and getting ready. As she performed a press check on her pistol and began to load magazines, her brain went on autopilot and focused on nothing more than the magazine and bullets in her hands, the pistol on the table, and the sound of the paper target getting blown by the breeze.

Thank God.

G P

Owen was just closing the tailgate of his pickup when he heard shots ring out.

Guess someone needed some lead therapy.

He checked the door to the range's clubhouse one more time to confirm it was locked, and headed towards his pickup. One little side job down, a million left to go.

Or so it seemed.

It wasn't that he didn't like the little side jobs—they helped pay the bills when he didn't have any larger projects going—it was just that he preferred the bigger jobs. He liked the challenge of making a house come together—from the initial ground work all the way up to driving in the final nail. Sure, the handyman jobs let him get his hands dirty, but the bigger jobs were more satisfying.

Lost in his thoughts, he almost missed the truck parked at the entrance to one of the outdoor bays.

A familiar truck, at that.

Slowing to a stop, Owen scanned the bay until he saw her, about twenty yards from a paper target, rapidly firing the pistol in her hands. Her ponytail had been pulled through the back of a ball cap, and he could just make out her protective ear plugs. She dropped her magazine, letting it fall to the ground, and just as quickly reloaded with a magazine from her tactical belt.

Fascinated, he watched as she walked towards the target, continuing to shoot and hit dead center every single time.

He licked his suddenly dry lips, took a quick drink of water and got out of the truck before he could convince himself not to.

Caridad turned to head back towards the table, only to see Owen of all people walking towards her. Or prowling, really. Whatever.

Wary—of him and her body's immediate response to his presence—she slowly set the gun on the table and began reloading her magazines.

"I see you found the local gun range."

Her stomach dipped and swirled at the sound of his voice. "Yeah. I needed to get in some practice, make sure I stay sharp."

He came to a stop beside her and whistled. "Nice pistol."

It was a Kimber Team Match II, and she loved it almost as

much as she loved her new AR. Almost. "Thanks."

"You're hand loading? Why aren't you using an UpLU-LA?"

She shrugged. "I'm not a big fan of speed loaders. I use them when I have to, but there's something soothing about loading by hand."

She saw him shift out of the corner of her eye. "Fair enough. You pretty much butchered that target."

"That was the point. By the way, what are you doing here?"

"I was finishing up a small remodel of the clubhouse."

She made the mistake of turning to look at him, and was met with nothing but heat coming from those clear blue eyes. She swallowed. "I thought you did residential construction."

"I do usually. This time of year's pretty slow, though, so I take a lot of handyman jobs."

Her stomach fluttered. "So. Um. I think I might owe you an apology."

"For what?"

She licked her lips. "For almost giving you a broken nose the other night."

He shrugged. "No worries. I shouldn't have grabbed you."

His casual acceptance of what had happened floored her. Most people would have either demanded an apology for the slight bruise that bloomed across their forehead, or pried into why she'd reacted the way she had.

She nodded. "At any rate. It seems like we keep getting off on the wrong foot or something."

"I think that might be called lust," he said, his words tinged with laughter.

She snorted and turned back to the table and her magazines. "Something like that."

His arm brushed against hers, causing goosebumps to scatter over her skin.

"Sorry about that."

"No, you're not."

"You're right. I'm not."

She rolled her eyes. "What are you doing, Owen?"

She felt more than saw his shrug. "Trying to get to know you."

"But why?" she set the magazine down on the table and turned back towards him.

Owen angled his body so that they were standing face to face, almost chest to chest. "Because for some Godforsaken reason I like you."

If her hormones hadn't been throwing a dance party she would have laughed at the wry humor in his voice. Instead, she said, "I like you, too."

"If I like you and you like me, when are we going to stop dancing around each other?"

She raised an eyebrow. "I thought you weren't into anonymous sex."

"I wasn't talking about sex."

Oh. "Then what were you talking about?"

"Getting to know each other and seeing where all this liking takes us."

"I'm not following."

He sighed. "A date, Cari. Jesus. Did your ex never even try to woo you?"

"Woo?" she couldn't hold back her laughter. "Look at you, Mister Nineteen Fifties with your wooing self."

"Okay, so maybe woo is a poor word choice, but the point remains—did you and your ex just randomly decide to become a couple?"

She shrugged. "Something like that."

More like they'd gone on a couple of dates, slept together, and decided it was better and easier than staying in the dating scene.

Wow, that was kind of fucked up, now that she thought about it.

"So then go out on a date with me. Friday night."

Feeling dizzy from his nearness and his obvious interest

in her, Caridad closed her eyes and breathed deeply. When she opened them, he was still there, watching her with a hopeful yet weary expression on his face. "Okay. Friday night. You and me and a date."

His smile just about lit up her entire body. "Fantastic. I'll pick you up at seven."

And then his lips were on hers for the briefest of moments—a hard smack that still had the hormonal dance party going at a full ten—before he backed away and headed towards his truck.

Stunned, Caridad ran her tongue over her bottom lip as she watched him drive away.

❧

"So what's been up with you lately? I hear you have a new love interest," his best friend Jenn said an hour later as he sat in the booth across from her.

"Your boyfriend gossips too much."

She stuck her tongue out at him. "Whatever. Considering you haven't said a word to me about a new woman I'm admittedly curious, not to mention a little jealous."

He shrugged. "You've kind of had a lot going on and I haven't wanted to bother you with my silly stuff."

Jenn tucked a red curl behind her ear. "I haven't had so much going on that my best friend can't talk to me."

Their waitress walked up just then, and Owen waited until she'd walked away to respond to Jenn. "There really hasn't been much to say."

She snorted. "That's not what I heard from Matt."

"What exactly did you hear from Matt?"

"That this woman's kind of a bad ass and that she's won a bunch of shooting competitions. I've also heard that she's short—about five three or so—and voluptuous. Long black hair. Dark brown eyes. A bit reserved but a nice person all the same. Oh, and that you were her guide on a hunt at the beginning of this month and that it was just the two of you up at the ranch all by yourselves."

Jenn wiggled her eyebrows, causing Owen to chuckle.

"It's not what you think. At least, not the whole being at the ranch by ourselves part."

Their waitress returned with their drinks and took their orders. Steak fajitas for him, chicken enchiladas for her.

"So what is it, then?" Jenn asked after taking a sip of her water.

He shrugged and ripped a sugar packet open before pouring it into his glass of tea. "I'm not sure what it is. I finally convinced her to go out on a date with me, so maybe I'll have a better idea after this Friday."

"Wait. So you mean to tell me there's a woman out there who was hesitant to go out on a date with you? You? The guy women flock to like bees to honey?"

"Yes, there was. It happens every now and then. And I don't date anywhere near as many women as everyone seems to think I do."

"I never said you dated a lot of women. I simply said women flock to you. I can't imagine why."

Owen balled up the paper wrapper he'd pulled off his straw and threw it at her. "Please. You know it's because of my charm and good looks."

Jenn laughed. Well, guffawed, really. "Your charm and good looks? Whatever. I think they're all just crazy."

He smiled and felt some of his earlier tension drain out of him. There was something about the easy banter between him and Jenn that never failed to relax him.

"Anyway. Enough about me. How are you holding up, especially now that the bed rest has been lifted?"

"Much better now that the bed rest has been lifted. I still have to take it easy and watch how much I'm on my feet. I can't do anything too strenuous for long periods of time, lift anything over a certain weight, stuff like that. There's a chance things could get better as the pregnancy progresses, but considering what happened with Tyler, we're not taking any chances."

Tyler was the name she'd given the baby she'd lost ten years prior. He shook his head. "I still can't believe you managed to hide your previous pregnancy from everyone. I mean, why did you do it?"

Something he'd been dying to know for the past couple of months and hadn't quite gotten around to asking. Why he was asking now was beyond him, other than the fact that Jenn really was like a sister to him and he was still trying to understand everything that had happened back then.

She fiddled with her silverware, her napkin, anything that kept her from looking at him. "It's so hard to explain what all was going through my head back then. I was scared, for one thing. Scared of being pregnant and being a single mom on a beginning teacher's salary. Scared Matt would be livid when he found out. Scared of everything I felt for and about him at that time, since it all was so unexpected considering until that night we'd always been friends at best. I knew I needed to tell him, but I couldn't ever find the words, couldn't ever bring myself to dial his number and tell him 'hey, congratulations on a great season, and not to take your mind off the pennant race or anything but my birth control pill apparently failed and I'm pregnant with your baby.' Yeah, that would have gone over like a lead balloon. I kept telling myself I would tell him once the season was over, that I didn't want to do anything to jinx him that year because he was pitching so well. I knew I needed to tell him, and my parents, hell, his and Chase's parents, Jo, and Chase. I just…couldn't…for some reason. And then I miscarried and it was like, how do you tell the people you're closest to that you'd been pregnant for the past twenty-three weeks and that your cervix was incompetent and couldn't even hold the baby in for a few more months? It was just…it was a really difficult time and I didn't make the best decisions."

Owen reached across the table and grabbed her hand, which had moved on to shredding a paper napkin. "I didn't mean to upset you."

She looked up at him. "I know. It's just still hard to talk about sometimes, even though I know I need to. It doesn't help that I'm scared shitless that this pregnancy won't go full term, either."

"Isn't that what the circle thing and all the bed rest were for?"

Jenn laughed. "'Circle thing?' I think you mean a 'cerclage,' my friend."

"Yeah, that. All I know is that it sounded like the word 'circle' and that whatever it is it's supposed to help keep the baby in the oven until its due date."

She smiled. "Yeah, basically. I'll spare you the details—I really don't want to talk about my cervix with you—but yes, it's supposed to help keep the baby in. My maternal fetal specialist feels like I'm doing well enough, and that we did the procedure early enough, that bed rest for the entire pregnancy isn't required. Granted, that could change at any given point, which sucks royally, but I'll do whatever it takes to keep this baby alive, safe, and healthy."

"You're gonna be a great mom. You know that, right?"

To his horror, tears began to fill Jenn's eyes. She swiped them away quickly and said, "Sorry. Pregnancy hormones. But thank you, Owen. You're gonna be a great honorary uncle."

He grinned. "Damn straight I am."

Their waitress came back and set their plates in front of them.

As Owen was putting his first fajita together, Jenn asked, "So, what's this woman's name?"

He sprinkled some cheese over the still sizzling beef strips. "What woman?"

"The one you're going out on a date with Friday night."

He shook his head, knowing Jenn wouldn't give up until she'd pulled every detail she wanted to out of him. "Caridad. Caridad Mathews."

"Wait a second. Is she from here? As in, did she grow up here?"

"I think so. Why?"

"The name sounds really familiar. How old is she?"

He rolled the tortilla around the meat, cheese and peppers before answering. "Late twenties, I'm guessing. I'm honestly not really sure."

Jenn pulled our her phone and typed something in real quick. He didn't even bother to ask what she was doing since he figured his very nosy best friend was most likely performing a Google search. He'd just swallowed his first bite when Jenn looked up at him and said, "Holy crap. I know why I remember her now."

"Why's that?"

"Her ex-boyfriend's mom used to be one of our eighth grade history teachers. If I remember correctly—and it's been a while, so details are a little fuzzy—Rebecca's son's name was Eric, and he and Caridad were high school sweethearts. She talked about them all the time, and about how she couldn't wait for them to get married and give her grandchildren. She constantly showed everyone pictures of them together. It was kind of sweet and kind of weird at the same time, like it was just too much. And then one day, oh, I don't know, maybe five or six years ago, she just suddenly quit without notice. A few days later the gossip mill really got going, and it ends up Eric had been charged with stalking, assault, and something else that I can't recall. Within a week, though, all the gossip had pretty much died down when the next big thing hit the news."

The food he'd already eaten suddenly felt like a boulder in his stomach. "So her ex was an abusive asshole who'd been stalking her is what you're saying?"

She set her phone down on the table. "If I'm remembering the story correctly, yes. But I also have pregnancy brain, so I could be getting things slightly confused."

He remembered the way she'd reacted when he'd grabbed her arms in the hallway at April's, the distant look in her eyes as she'd simply reacted to him on instinct, and some things began to fall into place. "No, I have a feeling you're probably remembering things just fine."

Jenn's gaze was sympathetic and far too knowing. "Owen, from what I've heard about her in the present day, I don't think she needs saving anymore. It sounds to me like she's done a pretty good job of saving herself."

Her words caused his chest to tighten so that it was now hard to breathe. "I know that."

This time, Jenn was the one who reached out and grabbed his hand. Her words were quiet, but he still felt them like bullets to his soul. "You've got to stop seeking out damsels in distress and trying to be their knight in shining armor, Owen. I know you couldn't save your mom, but that's not on you. It's not your fault the chemo didn't work, or that the cancer had been discovered so late. You've got to stop beating yourself up and trying to save people."

His motions jerky and abrupt, he stood and took some cash out of his wallet and threw it on the table. Unable to meet Jenn's too-knowing gaze, he said, "I've gotta go" and walked out of the restaurant like ghosts were nipping at his heels.

CHAPTER NINE

FOR SOMEONE WHO USUALLY DIDN'T GIVE A RIP ABOUT MAKE-
UP, cute clothes, or having perfect hair, Caridad sure was having a hard time figuring out what to wear for her date tonight.

Date.

Tonight.

With Owen.

The thought sent her brain whirling and her stomach flip
flopping. As did the fact that he would be here in oh—she
glanced at the clock on her nightstand—thirty minutes. And
here she was in nothing but a towel with her hair still dripping
wet from her shower.

Even crazier was the fact that a month ago she'd had a
boyfriend—well, she'd technically had a boyfriend in name
only—and here she was three and a half weeks later getting
ready for a date with someone she'd known for, well, a month.

Her stomach dipped again, and she pressed a hand against
it in an effort to calm herself.

Brian never made you feel this way.

She closed her eyes and inhaled deeply. Exhaled slowly.
Okay, it was time to get this show on the road.

Caridad walked across the room to the closet, which
she'd finally gotten cleaned out earlier this week so that her
clothes were no longer residing in boxes and suitcases, and

rifled through various and sundry items. Part of the problem was that she didn't even know where they were going, so she didn't know how she was supposed to dress. Casual? Fancy? Somewhere in between?

Crap, she hated this dating business.

Besides, let's face it, you don't exactly have anything "fancy" to begin with.

Right. She chewed on her bottom lip as she contemplated her clothing selections. After five minutes of staring blindly at her closet, she gave up and called the most fashionable person she knew.

"Hola. Why are you calling me instead of getting ready for your date?"

"I don't know what to wear." Yes, she sounded slightly desperate, and ordinarily that would have driven her bonkers but right now she was beyond caring.

"Okay, first, calm down. Take a few deep breaths." Mikey paused for a few seconds. "Okay, now that that's done, I think you should wear that pair of skinny jeans you have and that sheer purple top with a cami underneath it."

"But that top gets too hot."

Mikey sighed. "It's like fifty degrees outside. And it's sheer. You're not going to get too hot."

Caridad grumbled but grabbed the jeans and shirt from her closet. "Okay, what else?"

"Since I know you don't own a pair of heels, we're going to stick with ballet flats for tonight. Those nude ones or your black ones would work."

"I think I could have figured out shoes," she said dryly.

"Sometimes I wonder. Anyway, you'll look hot and Mr. Ginger Lumbersexual won't be able to keep his hands off of you."

She rolled her eyes. "He's so not a lumbersexual. I'm pretty sure Owen doesn't care too much what he looks like or what he's wearing."

"Semantics, mi hermana. Semantics. Now go dry your

hair and put on a little bit of makeup—hopefully you can fig-ure that part out on your own, and if not I'm sitting you down and making you watch YouTube tutorials—and don't forget to wear sexy underwear. Preferably not cotton, because cotton panties will not get you laid."

"Who says I'm trying to get laid?"

"Oh, please. I've seen that man, remember? And if you're not trying to get laid I'm going to haul you in to a shrink's office to get your head examined."

"Whatever. I've gotta go. He's gonna be here in like fif-teen minutes and my hair's still soaking wet."

"Later, chica. And remember—ride that unicorn's horn."

"You're such a perv. Later." She hung up before her broth-er could say anything else because seriously, she was nervous enough as it was without thinking about riding Owen's…horn.

With the clock ticking down to seven, she hurried through getting dressed, defiantly pulling on a pair of cotton hipsters because despite what her brother said she was not looking to get laid tonight.

Or maybe she didn't want to get her hopes up.

She made a concession, though, and put on a matching bra before pulling on the jeans and zipping them up. She grabbed a white cami from her dresser, figuring it would go well enough under the light purple top Mikey had suggested.

Fully dressed and with only nine minutes to go, she blow dried her hair as much as possible and swiped on a quick coat of mascara and lip gloss. She looked in the mirror, and over-all things were good, but her hair looked like a limp dishrag. Knowing it would take probably at least another thirty min-utes for it to dry without the aid of a blow dryer, she pulled it up into a quick bun. She'd just stuck in the final bobby pin when her doorbell rang, causing her to jump.

Caridad glanced at the clock. Seven on the dot. Of course he was punctual.

She turned out the bathroom light and grabbed her cell phone off the nightstand before making her way to the living room. She looked through the peephole, saw it was indeed Owen at her door and unlocked it before opening the door to let him in.

"Hey there," she said, her voice slightly breathy. Why the hell was she out of breath?

Maybe because you just sprinted through first date preparations in record time?

"Hey yourself." His smile had butterflies dancing in her stomach, and when he held out his hand and she noticed the bouquet of flowers in his hand those butterflies turned into a full-blown roller coaster. "These are for you."

"Owen, you didn't have to."

"I know. But I told you I was going to woo you, and flowers are part of wooing."

She fought her grin as she took the flowers from him. "Fair enough. Let me try to find something to put these in. I think I found a vase the other day while going through all of Abuela's junk."

If not, one of those empty tequila bottles would probably suffice.

She moved towards the kitchen and belatedly remembered her manners. "Oh, yeah. Come on in. Sorry. It's been a while since I've done this and I'm a little rusty."

Owen stepped inside and shut the door behind him. "No worries."

The space suddenly seemed much smaller with him in it, and Caridad swept her gaze around the living room and kitchen, wondering how it looked through his eyes. Considering the fact that there were boxes everywhere and the place was in a general state of disarray, probably not very good.

Feeling slightly embarrassed, she turned her back and rummaged through the kitchen cabinet she thought she remembered seeing a vase in. "Sorry about the mess. My grandmother apparently became a bit of a hoarder later on in life, and I've been slowly going through things, trying to figure out what to keep, what to donate, and what to trash."

"There's no need to be embarrassed. I used to come over here and help out with yard work every now and then, and she usually invited me inside for a drink and cookies. It wasn't bad until about a year ago. I wanted to offer to help her clean up, go through some things and haul some stuff away, but I didn't want her to think I was insulting her, y'know."

Caridad finally found the vase and pulled it from the cabinet as Owen's words rattled around in her brain. Somehow, she wasn't surprised that he'd come over to help Abuela out. He just seemed like that kind of guy. Still, though, the fact that he'd cared enough to help an old lady out in her later years made her throat thicken with emotion.

Needing a moment to pull herself together, she kept her back to him and slid over to the sink, where she rinsed the dust off the clear crystal vase before filling it with water. She placed the flowers in the vase, admiring the fact that he hadn't gone for roses but had instead brought her lilies, and said, "Thank you for that. I talked to her every week, but she never mentioned you, or that things were getting out of control."

"I kind of got the impression that she was a proud woman."

She smiled and turned back towards him. "Yeah, she was."

"I'm sorry for your loss, though."

She shrugged and walked towards him. "I am, too, but I guess it was just her time to go. Anyway. Let me grab my purse and my keys and we can get out of here and get to wherever it is we're going."

As she moved to walk past him, Owen lightly touched her shoulder. The frisson of awareness that raced up and down her arm made her stop in her tracks.

"You look beautiful, by the way. Not that you don't always look beautiful, you just look extra beautiful tonight. And I am totally messing this up."

She smiled up at him. "And here I thought you were the wooing expert."

"Hardly. Obviously."

"I'm going to show you just how completely inept I am at this whole dating thing by telling you that I had to call my brother to help me pick out my clothes. I pretty much live in jeans, t-shirts, yoga pants and tank tops when I'm not competing, and then I'm in tactical pants or shorts and a polo shirt or t-shirt, which are all highly functional but not exactly feminine."

"Call me crazy, but I thought those pants you had on the other day at the range were kind of hot."

She felt her face warm but couldn't hold back her laugh. "Oh, I am so calling you crazy for that one. There is nothing remotely attractive about those pants."

"I beg to differ. They hugged your ass in all the right ways."

She scrunched up her nose. "That's because my ass is too big."

Owen looked behind her and then back at her face. "Nope. Not too big. I think it's perfect."

The compliment warmed her, even though she knew it probably shouldn't. She knew she shouldn't need a man's approval of her body in order to feel good about it, and most days she didn't. Most days she liked her body and its curves, the fact that she was strong and that it could successfully get her through a super tough three gun course and still feel good at the end of the day. But she was also aware that she didn't fit the societal norm of what was considered beautiful in that she was short, large breasted, had an ass that rivaled J. Lo's, and hips that had been described by more than one person as "child-bearing." More often than not she had to shop in the plus-size section, but every now and then she got lucky and found something in the regular section that actually fit.

So sue her for being happy that Owen thought her ass was perfect. It was nice to know someone found you attractive and desirable, even when you were fairly self-confident.

"Well, thanks." She looked behind him and winked up at him. "And for what it's worth, I think your ass is pretty perfect, too."

"Been staring at my ass, have you?"

"Maybe a time or two." Or twenty. Whatever.

"Uh huh. And as much as I love standing here talking about our various assets, I'm also starving."

She chuckled. "Fair enough."

She grabbed her purse and keys off the kitchen table that had also become her office space while she cleaned out the other bedrooms, and headed back to Owen and the front door. They walked outside and she locked up before turning back towards him. "Where are we going, by the way?"

As they walked towards a Mustang she hadn't seen before—every time she'd seen him he'd been in a pickup—he asked, "You like steak, right?"

"Of course. The bloodier the better."

"Then you're gonna love this place."

꩜

"Since when does Del Rio have such an amazing steakhouse?"

Owen smiled at Caridad across the table. "What? You don't like Manuel's?"

"I haven't been to Manuel's in years, so I don't really know. This place, however, was pretty darned good."

"Glad you liked it." He'd brought her to Cripple Creek, which was a steakhouse on the northern edge of town and had some of the best prime rib in the city. Except for his own, but he hadn't had time to smoke a prime rib in ages.

"Liked it? I loved it. In case you didn't notice, I pretty much cleaned off my plate and would have licked it if I hadn't been in public."

Owen threw back his head and laughed. "Nice to know you have at least a little bit of self-restraint."

"Oh, I have more than a little."

And suddenly he wasn't laughing anymore. "Why is that?"

"Because I often run around on courses with a loaded

weapon in my hands?"

"Fair enough."

Their waiter dropped off the check, and Owen glanced at it before taking out his wallet and laying some bills on the table. "You ready for phase two?"

"Phase two, huh?"

"Yup."

They left the restaurant and climbed back into his Mustang. Once he started it up he pulled out of the parking lot and turned right, heading north on Highway 90.

"Correct me if I'm wrong, but this isn't how you get back to town."

He hated the vague nerves that laced her words. "I'm not going to take you somewhere and dump your body over a cliff or anything. Try to trust me, okay?"

He heard her inhale, and wished he could take his eyes off the road to glance at her, but at this time of year deer had a habit of constantly running on to the road.

"Trust doesn't come easy to me, Owen."

"Somehow I'd already figured that out."

She snorted. "Fair enough. I'll try to trust you. Just keep in mind that if you try anything fishy I *am armed.*"

"Sweetheart, there was never a doubt in my mind that you were carrying."

She actually laughed at that. "Glad to know I'm so predictable."

"I wouldn't say predictable. More like it's just expected."

"Fair enough. So where *are we heading?*"

"You'll see in a few minutes," he said as he turned into Chase's neighborhood.

"Okay, now I'm really curious. You're taking me out to the fancy houses."

He had to laugh at that. "Funny you should say that. I pretty much told Chase the same thing when he had his house built here."

"You're taking me to your friend's house?"

"Uh, no. Because that would be weird."

"Then where the hell are we going?"

"Patience grassahoppa."

"Patience is not one of my strongest virtues."

"Yeah, somehow that one doesn't surprise me either."

He slowly wound through the streets of the small subdivision, heading towards Lake Amistad and one of the many picnic areas along the lake. This time of year they were fairly deserted, especially at night, which was perfect for privacy and getting-to-know-you conversations.

As he rolled to a stop Caridad asked, "You brought me to the lake? It's the beginning of December."

"And it's not that cold out, but if you do get cold I have a blanket in the trunk."

"I don't suppose you have duct tape and rope back there too, do you?"

He turned off the ignition. "Nope. I left that in my truck."

She shook her head, but he was glad when she got out of the car and didn't seem to hesitate about doing so. He grabbed the blanket he'd mentioned, along with a small cooler, out of the trunk before meeting her at the front. Silently, they made their way to the picnic gazebo that overlooked the lake. Owen placed the cooler on the concrete table before sitting down on the hard surface. He patted the space next to him. "Join me?"

She did, sitting close enough that he could feel the warmth of her body but not close enough that they were touching.

"I have to admit that I've never had someone take me out to a deserted picnic gazebo in December. This is definitely a first."

He shrugged and looked out, barely able to see the dark shadow of water below them. "I have to admit that this is a first for me, too. I usually do the dinner and a movie thing, or April's, or something else depending on the season. But it seems like every time we're out somewhere public with lots of people around we don't really get to talk, which means I don't get to know you better."

She turned to look at him, and he could just make out her face in the moonlight. "Why are you so hell-bent on getting to know me better?"

A strand of hair had fallen out of her bun, and he reached up to tucked it behind her ear. "Because I think you're fascinating."

She scoffed and looked away. "I'm not really all that interesting, Owen. I just have the whole chick with a gun thing going for me."

"While I have to admit that watching you handle a rifle is pretty freaking hot, it's not just the chick with a gun thing."

"Then what is it?"

He sighed and looked out towards the lake again. "I honestly don't know. But I can't stop thinking about you, haven't been able to stop since that first weekend. Something tells me the gun thing is only one of your many layers, and I really, really want to peel those layers off until I get to the heart of who Caridad Mathews really is."

She picked at her thumbnail for long moments before saying, "I really don't know that I'm all that interesting, Owen. I'm just a girl who likes to shoot guns competitively."

Deciding to change tactics, Owen opened up the cooler and asked, "You want something to drink? I have a couple of bottles of water and some cokes in here."

"I'll take some water."

He handed her one of the bottles, and grabbed another for himself. He waited until she'd capped hers before asking, "So do you compete for a living, or do you have a day job, too?"

"Well that's a slight change of subject."

"Not that big of one."

She rolled the bottle in her hands and looked out towards the lake. "Competing is actually only a small chunk of what I do. I do speaking engagements, trade shows, that sort of thing. But I mostly do freelance writing for several industry magazines and blogs, and not always under my actual name."

"Why a pen name?"

"It's several pen names, honestly, and it's mostly because of competition, I guess, between different publications. Some places have no problem with me openly writing for other publications, but others want their readers to feel like they have someone exclusively writing for them. For those places, I use a pen name that sounds more like a chat room screen name than an actual name."

"Like what?"

"Oh, God, I think for one place I used the very generic 'Gun Girl.' For others I've used names like 'Three-Gun Chick,' 'Tac-girl,' etcetera. It can get kind of ridiculous."

"I'm guessing that the male readership eats it up, though."

"Surprisingly, no. I mean, do I have male readers and fans? Absolutely. Like I've mentioned before, I get inappropriate comments on my Facebook wall, YouTube, and Twitter accounts on a daily basis. Over the past year or so, though, my readership has become increasingly female, to where women now make up over half of my readers and social media followers."

"That's pretty awesome."

"Yeah, and it's a lot of pressure; I never meant to be the person leading the charge for women in the firearms industry."

"I can see how that could create a bit of pressure."

"To say the least. I mean, I know I'm not the first, and I'm not even the most popular. But for whatever reason people seem to respond to me, so the magazines and blogs keep asking me for more content, which is ultimately good for my checking account."

"How'd you get involved in the gun industry in the first place?"

She shrugged. "About seven years ago I was in a really crappy situation that I was lucky to get out of, and decided I was never going to be helpless again. It started as self-defense, but the more I learned and practiced, the more I loved it. Shooting became a form of therapy for me, a way for me to clear my mind and focus on one thing and one thing only.

When I left town and moved up to Dallas, I found a good range and a gun club up there, started competing in some IDPA matches. Then I started hearing about three-gun matches, and they sounded fun and challenging, so I bought a shotgun and a rifle—really cheap ones at first, I might add—and started practicing and then competing locally. In the meantime I finished up my bachelor's degree in journalism—after figuring out I didn't really want to be a journalist, I might add—and started blogging while looking for full time work. The freelancing thing honestly just fell into my lap. I was at a match and got to talking to another one of the competitors, who mentioned a job opening with one of the big industry magazines. I applied, they liked what they saw, and that was that. So what about you, Mr. Ranch Owner and Construction Guy?"

Owen chuckled and took a drink of water before answering. "Well, I kind of fell into the construction thing. I joined the Army right out of high school, and for some reason I started working on engineering and construction projects for them. I found out I enjoyed it, so when I got out I joined the National Guard and got a job with a local firm and learned from the ground up while saving every penny I possibly could. I worked my way up, took some night courses here and there and got a bunch of certifications, and got lucky when my old boss decided to retire and give me the opportunity to buy the company from him. I'd made some smart investments, and was able to land some pretty decent contracts that helped the company and my portfolio to grow. A few years back Chase found the ranch up for auction, and somehow convinced Matt, Darrin and me to go in on it with him if he could get it. Well, he won the bid—and it was a steal, I might add—and I suddenly found myself a partial ranch owner. The place had been used as a managed game ranch by the previous owners and was in good shape, they just hadn't had great business minds and weren't charging enough to meet overhead and make a profit. We decided to keep it a managed game ranch and did a ton of research on the industry, pricing, marketing, amenities, etcetera and came up with a fee structure that we thought would sustain the place and turn a profit but that would also lend an air of exclusivity for those willing to pay the price. So far it's worked out for us."

"So what you're saying is we're both entrepreneurial spirits?"

He bumped her shoulder with his. "Something like that."

They sat in companionable silence for long moments, until he noticed Caridad was beginning to shiver beside him. He unfolded the blanket and wrapped it around their shoulders, scooting closer to her until their bodies touched from shoulder to hip.

"Thanks."

"No problem. I figured it was smoother than the good ol' yawn and stretch before putting my arm around your shoulders."

Her smile lit up her face. "Much smoother."

"Is it okay if I kiss you?"

She raised an eyebrow. "You haven't ever asked me that before."

"I haven't taken you out on a date before."

"You're a strange man, Owen Daniels."

"Layered, Caridad Mathews, layered."

The corner of her mouth quirked up in a grin. "If you say so."

"I do."

She reached up and rubbed her palm over his cheek before lifting her head up and whispering, "Yes, you can kiss me."

If their first kiss had been raging wildfire, this one was a slow burn, steadily building to something bigger, more powerful. Consuming. Whereas before their mouths had attacked and ravaged, parried and thrust in an effort to overtake the other one, this time it was a meeting of mouths, a gentler getting to know you.

Her full lips were soft beneath his, her tongue like velvet. She tasted like water and the red wine she'd had with dinner, seductive and necessary. As he kissed her, he caressed her cheek, her shoulder, trailed his hand down her arm until he found her hip and wrapped his fingers around it, drawing her closer.

The blanket fell away, but it didn't matter. They were generating enough heat to turn the whole place to ashes.

Caridad made a sound in her throat and moved closer still. Owen angled his head, deepening the kiss while digging his fingers into her hip and holding on for dear life. She moaned, then changed her position so that she was no longer sitting beside him on the table, but was straddling him instead.

Her mouth latched back on to his and he felt her fingers tunnel into his hair before digging in to his scalp, stinging slightly. His dick swelled at the mix of pleasure and slight pain, and his hands reflexively cupped her ass and pulled her closer. The slow burn grew, becoming a bonfire to something quickly raging out of control. He had the thought that now was the time to pull back, to stop, to put the fire out before it became too much, but then she ground herself against his erection and did something with her tongue that had him seeing stars and all rational thoughts fled his brain.

Her hands drifted down, over his shoulders and down his back, around to his sides where they pulled his shirt up slightly and met flesh. He hissed in a breath, and Caridad nipped his bottom lip before kissing him again, making him see stars again. As if from a distance, he heard the *snap snap snap* of the pearl buttons of his shirt being pulled apart, and a small warning bell began to clang in his head. Instead of pulling away, though, he ran his hands up the curve of her backside and under her shirt and the tank top underneath until he met warm, bare flesh.

She arched into him, never breaking their kiss, as their hands explored and teased one another. She scraped her fingernails over his nipples, making him jump slightly. She chuckled and ran the pads of her thumbs over them, sending pleasure spiking through him.

Suddenly impatient, he broke the kiss and drew the shirt and tank top over her head before letting them fall to his side. She leaned back slightly, the moonlight highlighting her kiss-swollen lips and the color flushing her cheeks. He drew a slightly shaking hand up to her breasts.

"You're beautiful, Cari." The words were a whisper, a prayer on the slight breeze, filled with a reverence and a truth he couldn't hide.

"You're not too bad yourself, Owen," she whispered back as he rubbed his thumb over her nipple. The feeling of lace and warm woman shot sparks from his hand to his groin, and all warning bells and thoughts of what he should and shouldn't do flew out the window.

With an ease he didn't realize he currently possessed, he wrapped his hand around her and unclasped her bra. It fell and got caught on the tips of her full breasts, playing a game of peekaboo that he was determined to win. Luckily for him, Caridad shrugged out of it and dropped it beside them, on top of her previously discarded clothing and he was able to look his fill.

Her breasts were magnificent.

Large and full with dusky pink nipples that were currently begging for attention. There was no way he could deny them what they craved, so he leaned forward and latched on to one of those pebbled nipples, laving it with his tongue and teeth while he reached up and rolled the other one between his fingers.

Caridad swayed into him and braced her hands on his shoulders, her breaths coming out on panty little moans that did nothing to calm the situation in his jeans. He switched nipples, bringing his mouth to the other one and she arched against him, the motion so good his vision went a little fuzzy.

It had been a long time since he'd come in his pants, but he was feeling dangerously close to doing so right now.

As he continued to shower attention on her breasts— how could he not when they were that beautiful—her hands moved down and pushed his shirt off his shoulders and down his arms. He helped her out, first shaking it off one arm and then the other, until he, too, was naked from the waist up. She ground against him again, and Owen released her nipple with a *pop before burying his face in her neck.*

"This is going way further than the kiss I'd asked you for."

"Is that a problem?" she asked, her voice husky with arousal.

He kissed the side of her neck. Then her chin. Underneath her ear lobe. "Yes and no."

She tilted her head and arched her neck closer to his mouth. "What do you mean, 'yes and no?'"

"I mean no, it's not a problem because I obviously want you and I'm pretty damned sure you want me to. Yes because I don't usually move this fast." He kissed her neck again, causing her to moan.

"Owen, please."

It was the please that both undid him and brought him crashing back down to earth. With his arms wrapped around her and his face buried in the curve of her neck, he had the thought that Caridad Mathews was going to break his heart.

He wasn't entirely sure he cared, either.

CHAPTER TEN

CARIDAD FELT MORE THAN HEARD OWEN'S SHAKY INHALATION and knew the moment had been lost.

Dammit.

He tightened his arms slightly around her, and she closed her eyes and held on, willing her heart to stop racing. Slowly, reality began to intrude. The cold air at her back, the concrete surface of the table under her knees.

Holy fuckbeans Batman, she'd almost had sex on a concrete picnic table.

She'd officially lost her damned mind.

"Okay, so I suppose a concrete picnic table in December probably isn't the best place to get naked," she mumbled against the top of his head.

He snorted against her neck, the action causing his beard to tickle the sensitive skin there. She bit the inside of her cheek to keep herself from arching into him again.

Slowly, their breaths became calmer. She could feel the steady *thump thump thump* of his heart against her chest, and knew he wasn't unaffected by what had—and hadn't—just happened. Although, to be fair, the erection currently pressing against her kind of let her know that, too.

Aware that this could get real awkward real quick, she finally extricated herself from his lap before reaching across him to pick up her discarded clothing.

They re-dressed in silence.

The sound was deafening.

As she settled her shirt around her waist, thoughts and feelings she was unfamiliar with whirled through her brain. The problem was that usually if a guy had stopped in the middle of a hot and heavy fooling around session like that, she would be pissed. Not that she really had that much experience in the grand scheme of things—she could count on three fingers the number of men she'd been with—but she'd never had any problem asserting herself sexually with those guys. Including the crazy psycho stalker ex, especially since towards the end the only time she felt like she had any power or control in the relationship was when they had sex.

Even if the sex hadn't been that good.

Then again, she was also going off of three men, one of which was a one-night stand after moving to Dallas that had completely failed to ring her bell. Sex with Brian had been good, she supposed, when they had it. He was generous and attentive, had always made sure she enjoyed it as much as he did, and it had been nice.

But this thing she felt any time she so much as thought about Owen?

She had no frame of reference for it, no way of knowing just what this reaction to him was.

Lust, for sure. There was absolutely no doubt about that. It was like any time he so much as looked at her she felt like she was a sparkler on the Fourth of July.

The problem was that it was crazy, out of control lust, and she didn't do crazy and out of control anything.

Apparently you do, since you almost banged a guy on a concrete picnic table.

She grabbed her discarded bottle of water and took a big gulp. Out of the corner of her eye she saw Owen's mouth open to say something, and she swallowed quickly and said, "Don't even apologize for what just did—and didn't—happen."

"I wasn't going to apologize."

She raised an eyebrow.

"Okay, I was going to apologize."

She screwed the cap back on to the bottle. "You don't have to apologize, though. There's nothing to be sorry about, except for the distinct lack of orgasms. You can totally apologize for that."

The corner of his mouth tilted up in a slight grin, and something kind of popped and fizzed inside of her.

"Seriously, Owen, don't apologize. I believe you when you say you don't do anonymous or casual sex, and I generally don't, either." She uncapped the bottle and took another swallow and almost wished it was liquor instead. That would make this next part much easier. "To be honest, I've been with three people. One of them was the guy I just broke up with, who I'd been dating for, God, three years?"

"You're not even sure how long you'd been dating him?"

His tone was questioning rather than censuring, so she shrugged before continuing. "We honestly just kind of fell in to it, so I'm not entirely sure when it began. But it was never one of those all-consuming relationships you hear about all the time. We were more friends than anything, and we just happened to live together and sometimes sleep together. He travels a lot of work. I travel a lot for work. I think we both just got comfortable and didn't want to bother with moving or finding someone new.

"The second guy was a one-night stand right after I'd moved to Dallas." She swallowed and looked ahead, nerves jangling in her gut at telling him the next part of the story, but feeling as though she needed to. "I was lonely and looking for a lot of the wrong things in a lot of the wrong places, and in my oh-so-wise youth I thought that doing the casual hookup thing would be the way to fully reclaim myself. See, the guy before that—my first in so many ways—was my high school sweetheart. We'd started dating in the ninth grade, well, as much as two ninth graders could date, y'know. We went to homecoming dances together. Prom together. We graduated high school together and decided to go to the same community college out of high school so that we wouldn't have to be apart, despite the fact that I'd actually received several academic scholarships to various and sundry universities. His grades weren't as good as mine—he was dyslexic and had a hard time paying attention during classes—but he was intelligent, if that makes any sense. I didn't tell him about the scholarships because I knew it would hurt him. Ends up I should have taken one of them and gotten the hell out of Dodge sooner than I did.

"I got my associates within a year and a half, and transferred in to Rio Grande College even though they didn't offer a journalism major. I figured an English major was close enough, or that I could even just get a General Studies major and choose my own path. He and I moved in together, and it wasn't until then that things started to go downhill. He didn't like how much time I spent on homework or in class. He didn't like how much time I spent actually working since we needed to pay rent and utilities and y'know, eat. Looking back, I now realize how badly he manipulated me at first, chipping away at my self-esteem and my sense of self, even. So the first time he shoved me, I excused it, just chalked it up to him being angry because he'd just been laid off. The problem, though, is that once you let one time slide, it's easier to let the second time slide, and the third, and the fourth, and so on until you don't know who you are anymore. Then one day he grabbed my arms and threw me up against the wall. My head hit so hard it knocked me unconscious. Our neighbor on the other side of the wall heard the sound and called 911. By the time the cops got there I was just coming to. They arrested him for assault and battery and an ambulance took me to the hospital. Luckily I didn't have any broken bones, just a concussion and a broken heart, not to mention severely wounded pride."

She took another drink of her water before continuing, thankful for Owen's silent, steady presence beside her. "He got out on bail—thanks to his mom—and immediately tried to find me. After I left the hospital I went back to my parents' house since there was no way in hell I was going back to that apartment. He found me and made some threats that at the time I thought were bullshit and a guy with a wounded ego spouting off at the mouth. But then the stalking began. I had a feeling it was him, I mean, it made sense all things considered. I reported it to the cops, and they put a detective on the case. He suggested I start taking some self-defense courses and learn how to take care of myself, because they couldn't be around twenty-four seven. I started with your typical self-defense class, one that was actually taught at RGC at the time by someone at Laughlin. I figured if someone in the Air Force couldn't teach me to defend myself, then nobody could. I learned a lot, but he always impressed upon us that kicking a guy in the balls wasn't always going to be enough. So one day I approached him and asked him what else he would recommend and explained my situation to him, and he suggested I learn how to shoot. He actually taught me a lot, and I have to admit that I felt so much safer after buying that first handgun and learning how to use it. I got my CHL not long after that, because the psycho ex's threats were escalating and the cops still couldn't pin the threats and stalking on him. Then one day he made his move and tried to grab me in the freaking Wal-Mart parking lot of all places. Luckily for him, there were plenty of witnesses around because he apparently hadn't cared about anyone seeing him in broad daylight. I applied some of my self-defense moves and had managed to get away so I could draw my gun when another man ran up with a bundle of zip ties in his hand and honest to God zip tied his hands and ankles together. The cops showed up right after that and arrested the psycho stalker ex. I left town the day after he'd been sentenced."

"Holy shit, Cari."

"Yeah. So if I'm a little prickly and a little wary sometimes that's why. It really isn't you, it's all me."

He shook his head. "Where's this guy now?"

She shrugged. "Last I heard he'd moved to New Mexico and was living in a run down trailer and cooking meth."

"Wow Sounds like a real winner."

"Yeah. The only part of that scenario that could have made it even more appropriate would be if he'd moved to Oklahoma instead," she joked.

Owen chuckled. "I can't believe you just went there."

"Oh, I so just went there."

"Obviously." He grabbed her free hand and wrapped his fingers around hers. "Thank you for trusting me with your story."

She squirmed, slightly uncomfortable with his gentleness. "You don't have to treat me like I'm fragile, Owen, because I'm not."

He turned towards her, and even in the moonlight those clear blue eyes were penetrating and filled with something she was wholly unprepared to face much less name. "I know you're not fragile, sweetheart. Something tells me you have a backbone made of steel. But that doesn't mean I don't understand the importance of your story and how it shaped you and made you the woman you are today, which is an amazing woman who I really, really like."

"Awww. You like me," she teased.

Still serious, he nodded his head. "I do. And I respect you."

She sighed. "Which I'm guessing is your way of saying 'no sex for you.'"

He reached up with his free hand and rubbed her cheek with his thumb. "It's my way of saying I want to really get to know you, inside and out. I want to know what makes you tick, how your brain works, the things that make you laugh and the food you cannot stand. I want to know what your favorite song is and if you're a horrible singer or have the voice of an angel. And yes, I want to know what you look like naked, what you taste like and what it feels like to be inside of you, but that desire is a small part of all the things I want where you're concerned."

Caridad's heart stumbled and faltered a little bit at his words, and her stomach was doing this crazy free fall unlike anything she'd ever experienced before.

It scared the shit out of her.

"I don't want to hurt you, Owen, but I'm not sure I'm ready for all that. Hell, I'm not even sure I'm capable of all that."

"Don't sell yourself short, okay?"

She nodded once and tried to swallow down the anxiety that was clawing at her throat. She wasn't sure if it was because things were moving so fast, if it was because she felt like her emotions were completely out of her control or what, but she recognized the tightness in her throat and chest for what it was. Unfortunately, all she could do was close her eyes against it and hope it went away.

Owen watched as panic crossed Caridad's face seconds before her eyes closed. She swallowed once, twice, three times and inhaled deeply, and he felt like the worst kind of asshole for giving her what was obviously an anxiety attack.

Shit, he really had come on too strong.

No time for kicking your own ass right now; you can get to that later.

Right.

He pushed his errant thoughts aside and spoke to Caridad in a low, soothing voice. "Put your head between your knees and breathe."

She bent at the waist and turned her head towards him. Her brown eyes shimmered in the moonlight. "This isn't exactly comfortable, y'know."

He bit back a smile. "I know. But it's already getting your mind off of whatever set you off, so keep doing it."

He could have sworn she rolled her eyes at him, but she kept her head between her legs for a few more breaths before sitting back up and sipping at her water.

"Sorry about that."

"For what?"

"Dumping all that on you and then having an anxiety attack when you said what you did."

If there was one thing he knew he liked about Caridad, it was her honesty and complete lack of guile.

"Don't ever apologize to me for having an anxiety attack, okay? They happen to the best of us."

"They unfortunately happen to me far too often."

"Are you seeing someone about them?"

"Look at you, all psycho analyzing me over there. Yes, I see someone about them. Or, I was seeing someone about them. I've honestly been so busy with sorting through my grandmother's house and trying to keep up with my freelance work that I just haven't had the time to find a therapist here."

"I honestly don't know how many there are in Del Rio. A few, I think, but not many."

"That's kind of my fear. I'm honestly thinking about asking my therapist in Dallas if we can just do Skype sessions or something. I honestly hate the idea of starting over brand new with another psychologist."

"Generally speaking, I think the idea of starting over brand new with most things can be a bit paralyzing."

She shivered, but then asked him, "So what have you had to start over with brand new?"

"How about we get into the warmth of the car and then get you home and we save that for another day?"

"Oh, come on. I showed you mine now it's your turn to show me yours."

Owen sighed and slid off the table. "Fine. But we're getting you home first."

"Fair enough. But don't think for a second I'm dropping this."

"I wouldn't dare."

☙

The ride back to her place was silent, the air thick with all the things they had and hadn't done to each other, not to mention all the things she'd shared with him under the cover of moonlight.

She wasn't sure what had possessed her to tell him about Eric. She rarely talked about that time in her life, tried to push it to the back of her mind so that it didn't consume her every waking hour. Once upon a time he *had* consumed her every waking hour.

And then she'd said, "no more" and walked away from him, from the good and the bad, the pain of his betrayal and the frustration with her mother. She'd also walked away from her brother and her dad, not to mention the grandmother she'd loved more than anyone in the world.

No, Eric had taken enough from her and she was done giving him any of her time, thoughts, or fear.

But she also realized that she'd told Owen because deep down she wanted him to understand. She wanted him to understand her and who she was on a fundamental level. She wanted him to be sure he knew all the fifty shades of crazy he was getting himself involved with every time he touched her, every time he kissed her, every time he insisted he wanted more from her than a casual hookup.

The fact that he hadn't run away screaming was a positive sign.

The fact that he seemed loathe to share any of his own crazy was not a positive sign.

Too soon, he pulled into her driveway and cut the engine.

"You don't really have to come in and share your secrets if you don't want to. I shouldn't have put you on the spot like that."

He pulled the keys from the ignition. "I didn't take you for a scaredy cat."

"I didn't take you for one, either," she shot back.

"Fair enough. If you don't want me to go inside I won't. But if you do want me to, I will."

Her swallow was audible in the still silence of the car. "I want you to. Come inside."

He exhaled a swift breath before opening his door and stepping out of the car. Caridad hadn't even had a chance to get her seatbelt off and collect her purse before he was at her door, holding it open for her. She slid out and stood before kissing him on the cheek. "You really are a gentleman."

"If I wasn't my mom and my grandmother would both kick my ass," he said as they stepped on to the front porch.

She dug her keys out of her purse and unlocked the door. "Raised by women, were you?"

"Two of the strongest, most stubborn women I've ever known. Which is saying a lot considering how stubborn Jenn can be, and how stubborn you are."

She set her purse down on the kitchen table before walking into the kitchen to rummage for something to drink. "Me? Stubborn? I think you're talking about the wrong woman."

He laughed. "You know good and well how stubborn you can be."

"Fair enough. If you want something to drink your options are pretty much water, beer, Dr. Pepper and wine."

"I'll take a beer."

"Shiner or Lone Star?"

"You seriously just had to ask?"

She turned to look at him, a bottle of each in her hand. "Don't hate on the national beer of Texas."

"It tastes like cow spit."

"How the hell do you know what cow spit tastes like?"

"Okay, it tastes like I imagine cow spit would taste."

She shook her head and handed him the Shiner, then opened up the Lone Star just to rile him up. "I never would have pegged you for a beer snob."

"I'm not. Lone Star's fine in the middle of the day in August when you're working outside and need something cold to drink. Or while you're hunting. Or if you're a twenty-year-old frat boy doing keg stands," he said before taking a long pull of his Shiner.

"Point taken. And it's really not my favorite, either. Mikey brought it over the other day and left it here."

"Who's Mikey?"

She smiled and leaned against the kitchen counter. "Jealous, are we?"

"Do I have a reason to be?"

She shook her head. "Nope. Mikey's my brother."

He eyed the Lone Star she'd set in front of her. "How old is your brother?"

"Twenty-two."

"That would explain the Lone Star, then."

"You are a beer snob!"

"Nope. Just stating a fact. The older you get, the worse it tastes."

"Fair enough. So, anyway. Time to spill, lumberjack."

He raised a ginger eyebrow. "Lumberjack?"

She waved a hand in front of her. "Yeah, lumberjack. You've got that whole outdoorsy, I-have-a-beard-and-work-with-my-hands thing going on. Not to mention your penchant for flannel and plaid."

He looked down at his shirt and back up to her. "I didn't hear you complaining about my shirt earlier."

"Oh, I wasn't complaining. The flannel and the plaid suit you. Because, lumberjack."

"Well, at least you're not calling me a lumbersexual," he grumbled.

Caridad burst out laughing. "I'm not, but my brother did."

"Oh, Jesus. I am not well-groomed or metro enough to be considered a lumbersexual, nor do I have enough hair to put it up in one of those man bun things."

"I'm surprised you even know some of those terms."

"One of my best friends is a woman. If you saw the crap she shared on Facebook you would understand."

"Lots of Buzzfeed articles with titles like, 'This guy will make you thirsty AF?'"

"Exactly. And I hate to admit this, but while I've figured out some of the other terms I have no clue what 'AF' means."

"You really need to get acquainted with Urban Dictionary, my friend. It means 'as fuck.'"

"Why wouldn't you just say 'as fuck' then, rather than 'AF?'"

She shrugged. "My guess is it probably started with teens texting it and posting it, trying to keep their parents from figuring out what they were really saying and talking about. Buzzfeed and other places like it probably use it in order to avoid censors. Plus, it looks cool."

He shook his head. "It still doesn't make much sense to me. But whatever. I don't think I'm exactly their target demographic, either."

"I think in that regard you are most definitely correct. Anyway. Enough talk about man buns and weird acronyms you're too old to understand. Time to pay up, lumberjack. I showed you my crazy, now show me yours."

CHAPTER ELEVEN

OWEN TOOK A NERVOUS SWALLOW OF BEER WHILE HE TRIED to figure out just how to answer Caridad's question. Well, demand, really. Whatever. Turnabout truly was fair play.

"I'm not sure my crazy's really all that, well, crazy, to be honest," he said as he picked at the label of his beer bottle. "Like I mentioned earlier, I was raised by my mom and my grandmother."

He hesitated slightly, not because he didn't want to share as much as she had, but more because he didn't want her to think he was looking for pity.

In for a penny, in for a pound.

"I never knew my father. I actually don't even know the man's name, and as far as I'm concerned he's a sperm donor and nothing more since I don't think the term 'father' can even really apply." He shook his head. "As a kid when I would ask my mom where my dad was, she would tell me something vague, like he had to go away for a while. That response worked for a few years, but as I got older I began to ask more questions. When I was a teen she finally told me more, that it was a one-time thing and she'd accidentally gotten pregnant and she didn't know how to find him. It wasn't until a few years ago, after she'd been diagnosed with ovarian cancer and was going through chemo and quickly slipping away that she told me the full story. Ends up he'd definitely had to go away for a while—to prison after being convicted of rape."

A low sound emanated from Caridad, causing him to look up and meet her gaze. Her eyes were glittering, and he could see the questions written all over her face. But she didn't ask. Instead, she shakily took another drink of her beer and gestured for him to go on.

Owen inhaled deeply. "My mom was seventeen when it happened, eighteen when she had me. I still don't know the full details—at the time I was too fucked up to even think to ask her for more—but from what she did tell me it was someone she'd known for years, a friend of the family. Someone she—and her parents—trusted. Luckily—or as lucky as you can be in a situation like that—they were able to collect enough evidence to convict the guy of aggravated sexual assault. I've only been able to do a little bit of research on what constitutes aggravated sexual assault, because honestly every time I've tried it's made me sick, but from the little I've learned and considering he's still in prison, it had to have been a pretty bad situation.

"At any rate, I was around two when my grandfather passed away, so we moved out of our apartment and in with my grandmother because she didn't want to be alone. Somehow, it worked. At the beginning of my senior year of high school all three of us moved to Del Rio. Like I mentioned earlier, after I graduated from high school I joined the Army then the National Guard. After I got out of the Army I moved to Houston for a while. I came back almost ten years ago, and you know some of the story from there, at least professionally. Grandma passed away about a year later. Then, three years ago my mom was diagnosed with ovarian cancer." He ran a hand over his face, the feeling of his beard against his hand grounding him in the here and now rather than those months of sitting beside his mom while she endured chemo treatment after chemo treatment. And all for nothing. "Before Mom, I knew nothing about ovarian cancer, and I don't think she knew much about it, either. Ends up in most women it's hard to identify in early stages and the symptoms are easily misdiagnosed as something else like IBS or just digestive problems. She didn't think it was any big deal, until she started having almost constant abdominal pain. I finally convinced her to go to the doctor, but by then it was pretty advanced. They tried to save her, and she kept her chin up the entire time, but her body just couldn't take the cancer or the chemo. In less than six months she was gone."

"I am so sorry."

Owen glanced up in time to see Caridad wipe away a couple of errant tears. He felt like shit for making her cry. "Hey now. There's no crying in baseball."

She chuckled and wiped away another tear. "I know, I know. And I'm usually not a crier, but holy shit, Owen. That's some heavy stuff you've got going on."

You have no idea.

He shrugged, hoping the movement was casual rather than desperate. "I don't know that my baggage is any heavier than yours, it's just different."

She swiped at her cheeks one more time before grabbing her beer and taking a long swallow. "It's heart breaking is what it is. At least I had a choice in my crap. I chose to be with Eric and to stay with him even after I began to wonder if he had a few screws loose. But you? God, Owen. You didn't have a choice in any of that. It's like you were given a shit sandwich from birth and told to eat it or else."

"That's the thing, though. I did have a choice. I could have chosen to feel sorry for myself, to act out, to do stupid things and blame it on parents or bad genes or whatever. But I didn't. Most of that's completely on my mom and my grandma—neither of them were afraid to whoop my ass if I got out of line, but they also made sure I knew I was loved and wanted. When Mom was diagnosed, I could have chosen to curl up in a ball, to block out reality. But I didn't. And when she died, I was admittedly angry. Really angry, especially with God. She was such a good person; an amazing mom, hard-working. She could have given up when she was raped, and no one would have blamed her for that, but she didn't. I'm not saying things were easy, because they weren't. Money was tight more often than not. I didn't always have the newest toys or the best clothes, but I had a roof over my head, food in my belly, clothes on my back and two women who did everything they could to make sure I grew up as normal, healthy and happy as possible. So yes, I was pissed at God. Why'd He let her suffer so much? Why did she have to go through so much absolute and utter shit in her way too short lifetime when so many people out there—bad people—just breezed through life without a single repercussion or even knowing what the word consequence means? She was so young, just months away from turning fifty, when she passed, that it just didn't seem fair. Most days it still doesn't seem fair, but at least I'm not angry about it anymore."

He took a quick swallow of beer to help alleviate the tightness in his throat.

"I saw how hard being a single parent was on my mom. She tried not to show it, tried to shelter me from the harsher parts of reality, but once I was in my teens it became obvious that life wasn't a walk in the park." He scratched his beard. "She also never dated. When I was a kid I thought it was because she worked all the time. As a teen—before I knew the entire story—I thought it was because I was the product of a one-night stand and she was just averse to dating and sex. I'm honestly not sure what even made me make the leap in my mind, and a psychologist would probably have a field day with it, but I remember being fourteen and hearing my mom crying in the middle of the night. I knew she'd been worried about money, and I'd been mowing lawns to help out. But I heard her crying that night and felt like it was my fault she was crying and so stressed out all the time, and I kind of vowed to never put someone else in that position."

Caridad spun her beer bottle a quarter turn. "And that explains the no casual sex thing."

"I told you a shrink would have a field day with me."

She snorted. "No more than with me, I assure you. I mean, is it kind of surprising to find a man in his mid-thirties who's completely against casual sex? Well, yeah. But is it surprising that someone who's been through experiences like that would be against casual sex? Not as much. At least now it makes a certain sort of sense."

Owen shrugged, heat stinging his cheeks in rarely-felt embarrassment. "Maybe it makes sense, maybe it doesn't. The fucked up thing is that after Mom told me the whole story it just reinforced that vow in my mind, rather than making me feel freer or better or something."

Caridad stared at him for long, silent moments, the only sound his rapidly beating pulse in his ears.

"I'm beginning to have a lot of questions about you, lumberjack, none of which I'm sure either of us are ready for."

The sound of his pulse grew stronger in his ears. "To be perfectly honest, you're probably right."

She turned towards the fridge and opened it. "You want another beer?"

"I should probably head home." He didn't move.

She pulled two bottles from the fridge and handed him one. "Or you could stay here for a while, we can watch a movie on Netflix, and if you're lucky I'll make out with you again."

He took the bottle of Shiner from her and felt the invisible bands that had wrapped themselves around his chest begin to loosen. "Fine. I mean, if you insist."

She popped the cap off her bottle and winked at him. "Oh, I do."

✧

Owen ended up leaving some time after two in the morning. Caridad didn't know the exact time, because she'd honestly been paying too much attention to him and her thoughts to care. Sure, they'd put on a movie and had begun to watch it with the intent of actually watching it, but she'd stopped paying attention while Maverick and Goose were playing sand volleyball.

Which was saying a lot, considering four hot men had been half naked on her TV playing sand volleyball. Usually nothing could pull her attention away from that.

But Owen had.

More specifically, Owen and the questions she had flying through her brain about Owen had pulled her away from one of her all-time favorite movies.

And, yeah, she'd been a little thrilled to find out that *Top Gun* was also one of his favorite movies, and that he didn't think her taste in movies was weird for a woman. Brian had always thought she was a little nutty for preferring "guy movies" over chick flicks. Granted, he also hadn't appreciated her penchant for yelling things like, "get your finger off your trigger if you're not pointing it at something you intend to shoot!" and "you did not just call a magazine a clip" during said guy movies. Yeah, he hadn't appreciated that too much.

She had a feeling Owen would probably just egg her on.

The thing, though, was that while on one hand her brain told her Owen was a fairly straight-forward, what you see is what you get sort of guy, her gut told her there were all kinds of unexpected layers under that sexy outdoorsy exterior. Their sad story exchange had been a revelation in so many ways; she didn't usually open up to people and give them the sordid details, and she'd seen a side of Owen that she never would have expected.

She had a feeling what she'd seen was only the tip of the iceberg.

The thing that was niggling at her the most, though, was the whole no casual sex thing. He was right—a shrink probably would have a field day with him over that one—but in a weird sort of way she got it and even admired it. But there was something there, something she felt like he wasn't saying, that had her spidey senses tingling. If she were patient and let this thing between them play out, odds were that *something* would eventually come to light.

Like she'd told him earlier, though, patience had never been one of her best virtues.

CHAPTER TWELVE

Owen: You doing anything this evening?
Caridad: Trying to convince myself burning the place down isn't a good idea. Why?
Owen: Step away from the matches.
Caridad: I guess I should set this kerosene down, too?
Owen: Probably. Arson's pretty frowned upon these days.
Caridad: Damn. It would solve so many of my problems.
Owen: You don't want the insurance hassle. Trust me. You should get out of there and come over here for a while.
Caridad: I should, should I? What's in it for me?
Owen: Smoked venison roast wrapped in bacon. Potato salad. Peppered corn. Chocolate cake.
Caridad: You had me at bacon. Be there in 30.

"WHAT'S THAT SMILE FOR?"

Owen pocketed his phone and turned back to the chocolate cake he needed to put the finishing touches on. "What smile?"

"The one that's spread all over your face, goofball," Jenn responded.

"Is it a crime to be in a good mood?"

"No. But usually when you smile like that there's a woman involved."

He shrugged as Matt walked in to the kitchen from the living room.

"Did I hear something about Owen and a woman?" the former MLB pitcher asked before leaning over and kissing the top of Jenn's head.

Owen continued to frost the cake.

"Yup. I think he was texting Caridad." Jenn's tone sounded like what he imagined a little sister's tone of voice to sound like at just such a moment—bratty and teasing.

"Oh, yeah. How'd your date go last night?" Matt asked.

Owen looked up at Jenn. "Seriously? Do you tell him everything?"

"Absolutely. I learned my lessons about secrets the hard way. I'm so not going down that path again."

"I think me going out on a date is a little different, Jenn."

"Nope. No more secrets." She smiled up at Matt with absolute love and devotion in her eyes. The swift kick of jealousy was there and gone before he even had a time to react. "You'll understand that one day."

He hoped so. Because what Jenn and Matt and Jo and Chase had? Yeah, he wanted that. Bad.

Owen mentally shook himself and went back to frosting the cake. "I'm sure I will. And to answer your question, Matt, it was interesting."

"Interesting?" Matt asked.

He should have known better and kept his mouth shut. "Yes. Interesting. In a good way. And yes, Jenn, I was texting Cari and she'll be here in…" he glanced at the clock on the stove, "…twenty-seven minutes. So please be on your best behavior."

Jenn batted her eyelashes. "Me? When am I not on my best behavior?"

"Well, I seem to remember a YouTube video from this past summer, not to mention you getting uncharacteristically drunk and then for some still unknown to me reason falling in love with this jerk," he teased.

"I'm an arrogant asshole. Get it right."

"Forgive me. I'll make sure to never make that mistake again."

"Damned straight."

Owen smiled and finished frosting the cake he'd made. Six months ago when Matt had unexpectedly suffered a brain injury from a screaming comebacker, Owen never would have guessed that he and Jenn of all people would fall in love and be expecting a baby at this point. Jenn had hated Matt—or so everyone had thought. Ended up, she'd just been really, really pissed at him for walking out on her after a one-night stand ten years prior, but had been holding on to some strong feelings the entire time. And he never would have thought that he and Matt would become such good friends. Sure, they'd known each other for years and had been business partners for a few of those years, but Matt had stayed in Dallas up until his injury. Prior to that, Owen's impression had been that Matt was a cocky, incredibly talented and athletically gifted guy who was about nothing more than playing baseball and getting laid.

Boy, had he been wrong.

Just goes to show you, never judge a book by its cover.

"By the way, where are Chase and Jo?" Owen asked, pulling himself from his thoughts.

Jenn's shrug was casual, but the expression on Matt's face told a different story. "He hasn't been feeling well the past few days, been complaining of some nausea and loss of appetite, fatigue."

Owen placed the glass cover over the cake stand. "Why hasn't he said anything?"

Anger briefly pinched the corners of Matt's mouth. "Because he's stubborn. I wouldn't have known that if Jo hadn't said something to Jenn earlier today."

"Aren't those all signs the kidney disease is getting

worse?"

"Yup. Apparently Jo's so freaked out she decided to stay in town an extra day and go with him to see the nephrologist on Monday. I'm kind of glad she's doing that, because otherwise I probably would have gone with him myself."

"You can't save him from this," Jenn said quietly.

"I know. But that doesn't mean I won't try."

Jenn reached back and squeezed Matt's hand. Owen felt like a hand was squeezing around his lungs. His heart. His stomach. Ended up fear and jealousy were a real ugly combination.

"Anyway. Jo texted me earlier and said they were still planning on making it, but they might be a little later than usual."

Owen was just about to pull his phone out of his back pocket and text Chase himself when the doorbell rang. Jenn began to slide off the barstool she'd been sitting on, and Owen held up a hand to make her stop. "I am not letting you answer the door right now. Stay."

"I'm not a dog."

"I know, but be a good girl and sit anyway," he teased as he headed into the living room and towards the front door.

When he'd renovated the old barn and turned it into a house, he'd done so with open spaces in mind, so the kitchen, dining and living areas all flowed together and were separated more by furniture than walls. The main living area ran in a long rectangle along the front of the house, with the kitchen being on one end and the front door being on the other. The master bedroom and his home office, along with the pantry, utility room, and guest bath all shot off of the main living area. He'd put in a loft area above the living room, which he used mainly for storing his mom's things he hadn't been able to part with.

He loved his house and the work he'd put into it, but for the first time in years he found himself actually caring what someone else thought about it.

The realization was enough to cause him to almost stumble.

Knowing Jenn and Matt were most likely watching his every move, though, he continued on to the front door and swung it open, a smile on his face.

"I wasn't sure if I should bring anything, but my mom always told me to bring a gift when someone invited me into their home, so here." She held out a six pack of Lone Star long necks and winked at him.

Owen laughed as he took the beer from her. "I'm sure these can be put to good use. As target practice."

Caridad reached for them. "Oh, I don't think so, mister. That is not how you thank someone for bringing you a gift."

"How about this, then?" he asked before leaning in and covering her mouth with his. Even though he kept his hands to himself he still felt her body soften as her lips moved against his in a kiss that quickly went from "hello" to *hello*.

Jenn's wolf whistle from the kitchen startled him enough that he almost dropped the beers, not to mention almost biting through Cari's tongue. He broke the kiss far quicker than he would have liked and grinned sheepishly at Caridad before saying, "I swear to God, Jenn, as soon as you have that baby I'm going to smack you."

"No you won't. You don't believe in hitting girls."

She really was the bratty little sister he'd never had but had always kind of wanted. "That's beside the point."

Caridad lifted an eyebrow and whispered, "You could have warned me I would be meeting your friends."

Owen lowered his voice. "Sorry. You seemed so excited at the mention of bacon I didn't want to give you a reason not to come over."

"Fair enough. And for the record, I probably still would have come over. I mean, you said there's bacon."

"And chocolate cake."

"Hopefully not together."

"Have you never tried chocolate-covered bacon? It's

amazing."

"Are you sure you're not the pregnant one?"

"Absolutely positive. Anyway. Come meet Jenn." Owen raised his voice so that he could be heard by his other guests. "She's that bratty woman in the kitchen who thinks she can get away with murder just because she has a bun in the oven."

"Whatever. I think I can get away with murder because you adore me and Matt's head over heels in love with me. Plus, baby. There is that."

Owen smiled and humor glinted in Caridad's eyes. He grabbed her hand and wound his fingers through hers as he led her through the living room into the kitchen.

"As you can see, this is all one big open space. Pretty self-explanatory. Bedroom, office and bathroom are all on that side," he tilted his head to the right, "if you want to see them later or need to use the facilities. Pantry and utility room are back here off the kitchen and between the garage and main living area."

"It's beautiful. This place puts the barndominiums I've seen on Pinterest to shame."

"I know, right? I keep telling him he needs to start selling plans or building these things for a living, because they're all the rage." Jenn smiled as they neared the eat-in kitchen island and held out her hand. "Hi, I'm Jenn, otherwise known as Owen's best friend and Matt's better half. You must be Caridad."

Caridad took Jenn's hand in her own for a brief shake and smiled. "That I am. Do I want to know how you know who I am?"

Jenn's green eyes twinkled with mischief, which, really, was fairly common. "Matt mentioned running in to you last weekend at April's and told me there was a definite 'vibe' between you and Owen. Then Owen here confirmed on Monday afternoon—after much poking and prodding, I might add—that y'all were going on a date last night. So how'd it go? Did our resident Casanova knock your socks off?"

Caridad looked from Jenn to him, a slight look of confusion on her face. "Casanova?"

"I'm gonna put these beers in the fridge out in the garage. Be right back," Owen said.

Before he could even take one step, though, he felt a tug on his waistband, stopping him in his tracks. He looked down at Caridad and saw that the confusion remained, but that she was also apparently enjoying his discomfort. Fantastic. Now he apparently had two women in his life who liked to give him hell.

"Seriously, lumberjack? Casanova? Do you have a reputation I haven't heard about yet?"

"Lumberjack?" Matt asked.

Owen's face suddenly felt as if it were on fire. Sometimes it sucked being a ginger.

Caridad looked as if she was barely holding back laughter when she answered. "Yeah, it's my nickname for him. My brother thinks he has that whole lumbersexual thing going on, but I think he's just got a lumberjack thing going on."

Jenn cocked her head to the side. "Y'know, now that you mention it, I can kind of see that. We should totally take some photos and send them to Buzzfeed. They'd be all over him in a heartbeat."

"Dear God, no. I take back every mean or teasing thing I've ever said to or about you," he said to Jenn.

His best friend just laughed. The wench. "Oh, come on. It could help your construction business. Think of all the female clients you could suddenly get. Not to mention the ranch. Dude, y'all should totally do a Devils Ranch calendar or something. You, Matt, Chase and Darrin? That would sell like hotcakes."

"What the hell is that baby doing to your brain?" Owen asked.

Jenn rubbed a hand over her belly, which had just started to swell over the past couple of weeks. "Sometimes I wonder. It's probably a good thing I had to take the year off from teaching. God only knows what I would have ended up saying to my seventh graders."

"You probably would have had them reading Kathleen E. Woodiwiss or something," Matt said.

Jenn sniffed. "I'm pretty sure that would be frowned upon by the administration. That being said, it's not like I wasn't reading Johanna Lindsey and Virginia Henley novels in the seventh grade anyway, so I'm pretty sure some of my students are well beyond *A Wrinkle In Time* and *Where the Red Fern Grows.*"

"I loved *A Wrinkle In Time*," Caridad said.

"Me, too! It's actually one of my favorite books to teach."

"So I have to ask, who are the other authors you mentioned? I've never heard of them."

Jenn looked from Owen to Caridad, an expression of disbelief on her face. "You've never heard of Johanna Lindsey or Kathleen E. Woodiwiss? *The Flower and the Flame*?"

Cari shook her head. "Nope. I'm a suspense sort of girl, or Christopher Moore if I want something funny."

"Who's your favorite suspense author?" Owen asked.

"Oh, Brad Thor, hands down. Vince Flynn runs a close second."

"I almost cried when I found out Flynn had passed away. Mitch Rapp is such a great character."

"No kidding. I swear, if there was ever a Scott Harvath/ Mitch Rapp mashup I would be all over that."

"Oh really?"

"Not like that, you perv. Well, maybe. They both sound pretty hot."

"Sorry to cut into y'all's verbal foreplay here, but I'm starving," Matt said.

"Oh, leave them alone. It's cute."

Owen rolled his eyes at Jenn. "Cute is for kittens and puppies, not men. And yeah, we probably should eat before it gets cold. The roast's probably rested enough by now anyway."

He walked over to the oven to take the venison out, and

realized he still had a six pack of beer in his hand. Holy crap. What was it about being around Caridad that made him lose track of time and his surroundings? It was like some of his brain cells just shrunk up any time she was near.

He put the beer in the fridge in the garage, which was generally where he kept drinks, and went back into the kitchen. He'd just pulled the venison out of the oven when he heard the front door open and Chase's voice say, "Sorry we're late. I've been feeling like crap, took a nap and accidentally overslept."

Owen did not miss the worried look that passed over Jo's face.

"No worries. I'm just now getting around to carving the roast anyway," he said as he set the pan on the island before pulling the foil off of it. "Caridad, I'm sure you remember Chase, who's definitely the better Roberts brother in my opinion. And the lovely woman with him is his fiancee, Jo, who currently lives in Austin but will be moving here as soon as the semester's over."

Jo and Cari shook hands, and Cari asked, "Oh? Are you a teacher like Jenn?"

"High school guidance counselor."

"That sounds about as fun as rolling in a fire ant bed while covered in honey," Caridad deadpanned.

Owen snorted out a laugh while Jo went into what could only be described as convulsions she was laughing so hard. Once she'd caught her breath, she said, "That's probably the best description for my job ever. And sadly accurate. Yet for some reason I love it."

Caridad shrugged. "I shoot targets for living. What are you gonna do?"

"Cari's the current women's three gun champion," Owen said, feeling a weird sense of pride at sharing that information.

"Cool! I competed in a couple of IDPA matches a couple of years ago and enjoyed it, but never really had the time to do more than that," Jo said.

"You did?" Chase asked.

"Yeah. Through my women's shooting league. You should try it some time, you'd probably enjoy it."

A look of uncertainty crossed Chase's face, and now that he was standing closer and under the bright kitchen lights, Owen could see that his other best friend looked a little pale and a lot worried. The man who usually couldn't sit still pulled out a bar stool and sat down.

"You need some water, cowboy?" Jo asked.

"Please?"

She kissed him on the cheek before asking, "Anyone else need anything from the fridge while I'm out there?"

"I'll take a bottle of water, too," Caridad said.

"Sure." Jo walked out of the kitchen and Owen returned his attention to Chase.

"You okay man?"

Chase toyed with the salt shaker. "I hope so, but my gut's telling me no. Hell, my brain's telling me no, not to mention my body."

Owen exchanged a worried glance with Matt before going back to carving the roast. "Well, you know when the time comes I'll be the first person signing up to donate a kidney."

"You'll have to beat me to it," Matt said.

Caridad pulled out the barstool next to Jenn and sat down before asking, "Someone care to explain to me what's going on?"

☙

Caridad looked from Owen to Matt to Chase to Jenn, saw the tension in their faces, the set of their shoulders, and remembered the worried look in Jo's eyes when she'd asked Chase if he needed some water. Even though she'd just met Jenn and Jo, their anxiety was palpable, and even though she'd only met Chase once it didn't take a rocket scientist to figure out the man wasn't feeling well.

And Matt and Owen? She'd watched Matt throw a perfect

game in Game Seven of the World freaking Series and not show an iota of the nerves he was showing right now. While she was still trying to figure out the puzzle that was Owen, there was no doubt in her mind that he was worried about his friend. Big time.

"Oh, hell, Cari. I'm sorry. We're all so used to talking about this by now that it honestly slipped my mind to explain it to you," Owen said.

"I get that. I'm the new person in the mix and y'all are obviously all very close."

"Why is there cow spit in your fridge, Owen?" Jo asked as she walked back into the kitchen and set a bottle of water in front of Chase before handing her one, too. Caridad's gaze flew from Jo to Owen, who was doubled over with laughter. Caridad's lips twitched, and she tried to fight the smile that wanted to bloom across her face.

"Cow spit? Eww. What the hell, Owen?" Jenn asked, making Owen, Jo, and Caridad all laugh.

"Lone Star, Jenn," Jo said. "There's Lone Star—aka cow spit—in Owen's fridge."

"Ohhhh." Jenn looked at all three of them and shook her head. "You are all crazy."

As their laughter wound down, Owen shook his head and then said, "Anyway. Back to the subject at hand. Chase, you mind if I give Cari the Cliffs Notes?"

Chase opened the bottle of water and sipped from it. "Not at all."

Owen spoke as he continued to slice the roast he'd just pulled out of the oven. "Chase had this thing with his kidneys as a kid that went undiagnosed for far too long. By the time they figured out what was wrong and fixed it, some scarring had already occurred. He stayed pretty healthy through high school and college, mostly thanks to how active he was."

"You pitched for UT, right?" Caridad asked Chase.

He smiled, his brown eyes lighting up. "Yup. Won a College World Series with them."

"I remember that. You got drafted pretty high, didn't you? I seem to remember people talking about how you were crazy for not turning pro."

He chuckled. "Those people weren't aware of my kidney function at the time."

"Ah."

"Yeah. At any rate, I didn't go pro because my body couldn't take the stress at that level, and that decision was probably one of the things that helped me stay healthy as long as I have. But over the past year or so I've been getting sicker, and this past summer found out I was in stage four chronic kidney disease, which basically means I'm one stage away from dialysis or a kidney transplant. For some reason it seems like I've been rapidly getting worse over the past few months, and I'm worried I'm going into renal failure."

"Wow. That's some heavy stuff."

Chase ran a hand through his hair. "No shit."

She pointed at Owen and then at Matt. "And I'm guessing you two are duking it out to see who's first on the possible donor list?"

"Absolutely," Owen said.

"Although, as Chase's brother, I'm obviously going to be the best match."

"Only if all the markers match up."

"They will."

"This isn't baseball, honey," Jenn said. "You can't will everything to be a match the way you can put a ball exactly where you want it in the strike zone."

Matt grinned. "Sure I can."

Jenn sighed and shook her head.

"So, yeah, that's the basic run-down," Chase said. "Re-thinking about dating Owen now that you know he's crazy enough to give up a kidney?"

She smiled and glanced at Owen. "Nah. I've probably done crazier things."

Owen looked up from the roast he'd just finished cutting

and smiled, causing her heart and stomach to spin and free fall. She'd probably done crazier things? Yeah, like falling in like with a guy who she suspected was still hiding something from her.

That felt pretty darned crazy.

CHAPTER THIRTEEN

"Holy crap that was good. Excellent cook and fantastic kisser? I might just have to keep you around," Caridad's tone—and the smile on her face—indicated she was teasing.

Owen settled onto the couch beside her and smiled back at her. "Glad you enjoyed it, and that you're not too mad at me for forgetting to warn you about everyone else being here."

"I'll admit, at first I felt a little bit like one of those dreams you have where you're standing naked in front of everyone in high school, but lucky for you your friends are pretty awesome. It also helps that I've known Matt for a while and that I'd already met Chase."

He took a sip of his beer. "Still, though, I totally forgot my manners and should have warned you."

She nudged his side with her elbow. "Don't sweat it, lumberjack. Or should I call you Casanova?"

Her eyes sparkled with teasing laughter, but Owen still felt like a two-ton boulder had been placed upon his shoulders. "I think the Casanova thing is definitely blown out of proportion by Jenn."

"Still, though, there's a reason why she calls you that."

He rubbed his palm over his beard. "Fair enough. I guess I have a bit of a reputation among my friends for being a ladies' man."

"Wait. How does Mister No Casual Sex have a reputation as a ladies' man?"

"See, that's where it gets a little complicated. I like women. I respect women. I enjoy their company. Going out on a couple of dates with someone isn't the same as sleeping with them, or even being serious about them. There's nothing wrong with taking a woman out on a date, having a good time, and remaining acquaintances if not friends when the night's over. No hard feelings, y'know."

Cari looked down and picked at her thumbnail before looking back up at him, the teasing laughter now replaced by a serious, thoughtful expression. "So is that what you're doing with me?"

"God no. I don't know how else to say this except, well, I actually really like you. Not that I haven't liked the women I've dated in the past, because I have. But they were more a way to kill the loneliness and just spend an evening or two with someone other than myself or my usual group of friends. As much as I love Chase and Jenn—and Matt and Jo by extension—sometimes I just need to be around other people and have different conversations. It's also admittedly nice to spend time with people who don't know almost everything about me. This thing with you and me, though? It feels real, if that makes any sense."

She nodded her head and let out a breath Owen hadn't realized she'd been holding. "Here's the thing, I like you, too. Obviously. But sometimes this feels like everything's moving way too fast and it's all spinning out of my control."

He felt a little like he'd just been punched in the gut, even though he should have known Caridad would balk at some point. To say she was gun-shy when it came to men and more specifically relationships seemed like an understatement. He took a deep breath to center himself and said words he didn't really want to say but knew he needed to. "If you want me to slow down and back off, I will."

A look of surprise mixed with slight disappointment

crossed her face, there and gone in less than a few seconds. But he'd seen it, and that gave him hope.

"But I'm not giving up, and I don't think you want me to, either."

She stared at him a brief moment before saying, "You've got this weird mix of alpha male and sensitive guy going on, and it's totally throwing me off."

He shrugged. "Like I said before, I was raised by women and my best friend's a woman, so I get the sensitivity thing to an extent. But I'm still a guy."

"No." She shook her head. "You're a really good guy. One of those guys who's simply decent down to his very core. I was beginning to think guys like you didn't exist anymore."

"I like to think I'm a limited edition."

"Something like that." She looked away and then back at him. "So if you go out on all these casual dates and remain friends afterwards, that either means you're so amazing in bed they forgive you immediately or you don't so much as kiss these women good night. Quite frankly, I'm not sure which one of those to believe."

Was it suddenly hot in here?

Trying to project a calm, cool guy aura and not one of a man who was kind of messed up inside, Owen gave what he hoped was a flippant grin and said, "Somewhere in between."

Caridad raised her eyebrows. "Explain, lumberjack."

Owen swallowed and try to will his heart rate to slow. "I don't kiss all of them goodnight, no. But I don't sleep with any of them."

"Which makes sense, considering your whole no casual sex thing, which I have to admit is both frustrating and admirable from where I'm sitting. But what about girlfriends? Have you managed to stay friends with any of your exes?"

His mouth and throat were suddenly as dry as the Sahara, although he shouldn't have been surprised at her line of questioning. "I have all of two ex girlfriends. And no, we're not still friends."

She chewed on her bottom lip, and if Owen hadn't felt so uncomfortable he probably would have found the sight erotic. As it was, he felt a slight stirring in his jeans that was completely inappropriate given the topic at hand.

"So you're not still friends with your two exes, but you are still friends with most of the women you've gone on a couple of dates with. I feel like maybe this is silly of me to keep harping on this, but I have a feeling that you're not being completely up front with me about something. And that has me confused and worried, because on the surface you're the most honest, up-front person I've come across in a long time."

Agitated now, Owen got up and walked into the kitchen where he poured what was left of his beer down the sink before getting himself a glass of water. He paced to the island, and back to the sink. Island. Sink. Island. Sink.

"Okay, so I'm getting the feeling there definitely is something you're not telling me."

"You think?"

Caridad got up from the couch and joined him in the kitchen, where she grabbed his hand and brought his pacing to an abrupt halt. "I showed you my crazy last night. Remember? Psycho stalker ex boyfriend and all. I didn't mention that when all of that went down, my mom just kind of shut down. She'd thought of Eric like a son, and couldn't believe he would ever do something like that. For a long time she lived in complete denial about what had happened, and even insinuated a few times that it was somehow my fault. Things are better now, but there's still a rift there and I'm not sure it'll ever be fixed. And my brother? Oh, God. Mom's favorite place to reside is in a land called Denial, I swear. You hear all these horror stories about parents disowning their kids for being gay, and all the great ones about how accepting they are. Mom? It's like she stuck her fingers in her ears and never heard Mikey when he finally came out. She doesn't deal well with things she doesn't understand. She never has. So whatever it is you've been holding in, locked up tight? I'm pretty sure it couldn't begin to match my levels of crazy."

He turned away from her and set the glass on the island. The feeling of her hand still in his, though, anchored him somehow, even though he still felt nauseated at the idea of showing her his particular brand of crazy.

She squeezed his hand and he squeezed back, closed his eyes and said the words he'd never uttered to another living soul.

ଙ୨

"I've actually never had sex before."

Caridad blinked a few times. "Excuse me?"

That was so probably not the correct response.

"Yeah."

Owen still wasn't looking at her, but she squeezed his hand tighter as she tried to process what he'd just told her.

"But, how? I mean. You're…you're what? Thirty-four? Thirty-five? And you're so…my God, Owen, do you know how good of a kisser you are? And you're…I don't know, sensual, I guess. I hate that word because it seems really corny and kind of gross in a way, but that's the only way I can think of to describe you and—"

Her babbling was cut off by his mouth on hers. She could feel his desperation, his hesitation, and yes, his sensuality in the movement of his lips against hers. He turned and then backed her up against the island, bracing his hands on either side of her hips and she pressed her body in to his. She didn't know how it was possible that someone his age—and this good at kissing—was a virgin, and she still wasn't entirely sure how she felt about that, but his lips and tongue against hers were doing a really good job of scattering all of her brain cells.

Before her brain could completely short circuit, though, she broke the kiss and said, "Owen. Stop."

He backed away from her faster than she'd known a man could move. It made her smile, even though inside she was a bit of a confused mess.

"Not that I don't enjoy kissing you, because I do. You're a pretty amazing kisser, like I said. But I don't know that making out right now is going to help matters."

He rubbed a slightly shaking hand over his beard and closed his eyes. "Sorry. I don't know what came over me or why I did that just then."

She grinned in an effort to lighten the mood. "Because you can't resist me?"

"I think that's definitely a part of it."

He didn't look happy about that.

"Okay, so. Let's back up a few steps here and get back to the question I was having a really hard time expressing. How the hell are you still a virgin?"

His shrug was casual, but the blush that crept up his cheeks gave him away. He shoved his hands in the pockets of his jeans and leaned against the counter opposite her. "I just…I told you about what happened to my mom and that I'd decided as a teen to never put someone in the position of being a young single parent. It just…I don't really know how it happened, exactly. I didn't necessarily plan on being the thirty-four year-old virgin, it just happened. I've gotten close to sex—I'm not a saint by any stretch of the imagination—but I guess it never felt right. I'm not exactly a super religious guy, so it's not even about saving myself for The One or anything like that, but the longer I kept not having sex, the easier it's gotten to wait until it feels right."

She blew out a breath and hesitated to ask the question that was on the tip of her tongue. In the end, though, curiosity won out. "So when you say you've been close to having sex, exactly how close are we talking here?"

"Trying to see how far you can push me?" He grinned.

"Partially. I'm honestly kind of curious, too."

"I've done pretty much everything except insert tab A into slot B."

A laugh burst from her lips. "Seriously? Tab A and slot

B?"

"What? Do you want me get technical about it?"

She shook her head. "There's no need to go into technical territory."

"Good. Because this conversation's embarrassing enough as it is."

She rubbed the outside of his calf with the toe of her Converse. "Aww. Don't be embarrassed. Also, you didn't completely answer my question."

"I am not giving you down and dirty details."

"I didn't ask for those. Honestly, that would be a little weird. I'm just trying to figure out what everything but actual sex involves. Oral sex? I mean, I've heard of some of those true love waits kids going so far as to have anal sex and saying it doesn't count since the penis didn't enter the vagina, but that seems a little disingenuous."

"I can't believe you just went there."

"Oh, I so just went there."

"Obviously." He crossed his legs at the ankles and looked away from her. "For the record, anal sex is going even further than good, old fashioned sex. I honestly don't understand the appeal of it, but I've never been a position to appreciate regular sex. So I guess to answer your question, oral sex has not been off the table, but even then it's not something I've done with a lot of people. It's just so intimate."

She chewed on her bottom lip. "So what you're saying is you've made it to third base but never slid across home plate?"

"You really just went with the baseball analogy?"

She fought a smile. "What? How else do you want me to say it? Hmm, let's see...so you've made it into the red zone but never to the end zone?"

Owen looked like he was struggling not to grin. "I don't even know what to say to that right now."

"I'm just giving you a hard time, mostly because I'm not entirely sure what else I'm supposed to say right now."

"I don't really know what to say, either." He shook his head. "I can't believe I just told you that."

She rubbed his calf with her shoe again. "You've seriously never told anyone? Not even Jenn? Because the two of you seem pretty close."

"We are. But she's like a sister to me and I'm like a brother to her, so our sex lives are generally off the table. Believe me when I say it was pretty awkward giving both her and Matt advice this past summer."

"I'm sure that must have been interesting at the very least, but Matt and Jenn aren't the topic at hand. You are."

"Yeah, and I don't want to be."

"Too bad, mister, because I have all kinds of questions swirling through my head right now."

"Do I want to know?"

"Probably not. Or, rather, you probably do but you're trying to convince yourself you don't."

"I feel like I should be on a couch and calling you Doctor Mathews right now."

"Well, if anyone's qualified to give backseat therapy, it's probably me."

Owen waggled his eyebrows. "First Doctor Mathews and then backseat therapy? That sounds dirty."

"Anyway. Perv." She drew in a breath and tried to gather her thoughts, which were kind of all over the place. "So... okay, crap, I don't even remotely know how to ask this considering we're just getting to know each other and all and there's definitely been no talk of next month much less forever, and shit I'm rambling."

Owen chuckled. "It's okay. And I think I know where you're going with this."

"And where is that?"

"Yes, I've been waiting for the right person. Yes, I really like you. Yes, I want to see where this goes. But if the whole no sex thing is a total no-go for you, I get that. Hell, I respect that."

She gathered her hair at the base of her neck and held it up, cooling her heated skin. "Here's the thing, though—I respect you, and I respect your decision. I may not completely understand it, because on the surface it seems a little extreme, but I still respect it. I'm not exactly the type to go jumping into bed with random guys anyway, so I'm not sure it's that big of a deal. At least not right now. I'm just…kind of torn, I guess, in that I don't typically move fast and yet all I want to do with you is go far too fast. I don't want to push you into doing something you don't want to do, which is kind of a weird gender role flip sort of thing to say. I want to get to know you, but I also want to rip your clothes off. It's a very strange dichotomy going on in my head right now."

Where the hell were these words coming from? She never spoke like this to men. Never. And yet here she was being completely honest and baring herself emotionally for Owen.

Kind of like he just did with you, dummy.

Yeah, there was that.

"If it makes you feel any better, I have that same war going on inside my own head." He crossed his arms and looked down at his feet. "Dating for me is usually pretty casual. Like I said, I like having the company of women and having good conversation."

He shook his head before looking back up at her with those clear blue eyes. "The thing is, Cari, this really doesn't feel casual."

She swallowed the anxiety that suddenly clogged her throat. Just like that, it was too much. His words. His confessions. His hot looks and embarrassed smiles.

Panic slid through her veins, cold as ice, before settling in her stomach and her chest. The rational part of her brain knew she was perfectly safe, but that part was being silenced by the panic and fear that suddenly threatened to consume her. Hastily, without thinking about what she was doing because she was honestly incapable of that at the moment, she turned away from him and almost sprinted to the front door.

Owen was right behind her, and she could hear the worry in his voice when he asked, "Cari, are you okay?"

But his voice sounded far away. Miles away. She nodded or shook her head—she honestly wasn't sure which—and fumbled with the door knob for long seconds that only helped to escalate the panic inside of her. Finally, she got it open and she stepped out on to the porch and took a deep breath of the cold early December air. It did nothing to calm her pounding heart or the jittery feeling inside, so she raced down the front porch steps, her fingers failing to grasp the keys she'd tucked into her pocket.

Behind her she vaguely heard the sound of Owen's footsteps, but the panic had become a train in her head, drowning out all sound other than the too-rapid beating of her pulse.

She finally grabbed the keys and managed to pull herself into the truck. One try, then two, before she slid the key into the ignition and cranked the engine. She put the truck in Reverse and backed out of Owen's driveway.

On the short drive home, and even after she'd locked herself up in her grandmother's house, the only thing she could see was the worry and confusion that had clearly been etched across his face.

Owen debated going after her, but ultimately his pride won out.

For the time being.

As he watched Caridad's taillights traverse the distance between his house and hers, he replayed the conversation in his mind, trying to figure out what he'd said to cause what had obviously been a panic attack.

This really doesn't feel casual.

One minute, she'd been fine, but as soon as he'd uttered that simple phrase it was as if she'd completely clammed up.

Down the road, the lights of her truck turned off, and a few moments later the glow from the living room light shone through the front windows. Okay, Good. At least she'd made it home safely.

Because she had so far to go, you big idiot.

Confused, worried and yes, embarrassed, Owen walked back to his front porch and sat in one of the giant wood rocking chairs he'd made years ago after he'd built the deck that wrapped around three quarters of the building. A sigh escaped as he propped his elbows on his knees, staring out into the inky darkness.

The night air was cool, and idly he thought that maybe he should go in or get a jacket. In the end, though, he stayed where he was and instead sought out the star he thought of as his mom's, the one that twinkled right beside the moon.

He drew in a ragged breath and scratched his beard. "Well, Mom, I think I might have screwed the pooch on that one."

The star twinkled in response.

"Yeah, I know. I just need to give her some time. Some space."

In his mind, he could still see his mom's smile. Sometimes he could even remember the way it felt when she would hug him close and tell him everything was going to be all right.

He would give anything for one of those hugs right now.

CHAPTER FOURTEEN

IT WAS TIMES LIKE THESE CARIDAD WISHED SHE HAD GIRL-
FRIENDS to talk to. In the absence of that, though, she did the
next best thing and called Dr. Tracy first thing Monday morning.

The receptionist—Brenda—picked up on the second ring,
"Dr. Tracy's office. How may I help you?"

"Hi, Brenda, it's Caridad."

"Hi Caridad! How are you doing down there in Del Rio?"

She couldn't hold back her smile at the older woman's
warm greeting. "I'm doing okay, I guess. That's actually why
I called. I'm having trouble finding a therapist here that I feel
comfortable with, and was wondering if Dr. Tracy would be
willing to do some Skype sessions or something."

"Hmmm. I don't know. Let me buzz her real quick. I'm
going to put you on hold for just a second."

"Thanks, Brenda," Caridad said before the line clicked
over to the adult contemporary music that let patients know
they were on hold. Kelly Clarkson's "Stronger (What Doesn't
Kill You)" piped through her phone's speakers, causing her
to smile.

Leave it to a therapist to have upbeat hold music.

She was quietly singing along when the music abruptly
ended and Brenda popped back on the line, "Caridad, you still

there?"

"Yes, ma'am."

"Well, I just spoke with Dr. Tracy and lucky for you her ten o'clock canceled. She's more than willing to do a Skype session with you. What's your screen name?"

Caridad glanced at the clock on her laptop screen. It was 9:30. Score. "It's, um, the number three gun Caridad. All together."

"Perfect. I'll shoot this over to Dr. Tracy and get you on her calendar. It's been lovely talking to you, dear."

"It's been nice to talk to you, too, Brenda. Take care."

She hung up the phone and stared at her laptop screen, wondering what she was going to do with herself for the next thirty minutes.

Might as well get some work done.

Not wanting to get started on a writing piece only to be interrupted, she opened up her various social media accounts and spent the time sharing, re-tweeting and pinning various and sundry blogs and videos. She was in the process of watching the latest episode of Love At First Shot when Skype rang with an incoming call.

She closed out the video and answered. "This is Caridad."

"Hi, Caridad. It's Dr. Tracy. How are you?"

Dr. Tracy's smiling face popped up on her laptop screen, instantly making Caridad feel more at ease.

"I'm okay. I'm not sure if Brenda told you, but I'm having trouble finding a therapist here in Del Rio."

Dr. Tracy nodded. "Yes, she did, and I'm sorry to hear that."

"Would you be open to having some therapy sessions like this in the future?" Caridad asked. "I've been okay for the most part, but every now and then I need someone to talk to so I can sort out all the crazy in my head."

"Caridad, you are not crazy."

"Logically I know that, but that doesn't keep me from sometimes feeling like I am crazy."

"What's happened to make you feel that way?"

She sighed. "It's kind of a long story, so I'll try to give you the condensed version."

"Fair enough."

"Well, first, my grandmother was apparently a hoarder later on in life. This place is a mess. And there are a lot more memories and feelings popping up than I'd bargained for, especially the couple of times I've seen Mom."

"That's to be expected, though, considering your past with your mother and everything that happened to cause you to leave town."

"Oh, I know that, and I feel like I'm dealing with those things better than I'd expected to. It's Owen that I'm really having trouble with."

Dr. Tracy barely raised an eyebrow. "And who is Owen?"

Caridad fought the urge to fidget. "You remember that hunting trip I came down here for right before I broke up with Brian?"

"Yes."

"Well, Owen was my guide. He's one of the owners of the ranch, so he's friends with Darrin. Kind of. They're business partners. Whatever. There was an attraction even then, but since I was with Brian I didn't do anything about it. I'm not the type to cheat, but you know that. Anyway. Ends up Owen's also my neighbor and we've, ah, been spending some time together."

Dr. Tracy was silent while Caridad tried to find the best way to express her thoughts. Finally, she just blurted out, "He's a thirty-four year-old virgin."

To give Dr. Tracy credit, her facial expression barely changed. "While that's certainly unusual in this day and age, it's not completely unheard of. Does this bother you?"

Cari shrugged. "Yes and no. I mean, on one hand it's kind of weird. On the other, his reasons make a really messed up sort of sense. And I don't know that I want to be the one that changes the state of his, uh, virginity."

"Okay, let's back up a little bit here and do a little exercise."

In a weird sort of way, Cari loved Dr. Tracy's "little exercises." They were sometimes painful and hard to deal with, but when it came down to it those exercises simply *worked.*

"Okay."

"First I want you to tell me how you felt with Brian. Don't think about it, just give me the first few words that pop in to your mind."

Caridad closed her eyes. "Safe. Comfortable. Calm."

"Good. Now how did you feel when you broke up with him?"

"Relieved. Free. Excited. Scared."

"Those are all good. How did you feel when you first met Owen?"

"Excited. Scared. Horny." She blushed at the last one, causing Dr. Tracy to chuckle slightly.

"What did you feel when you he told you he was a virgin?"

"Confused. Curious. Horny."

Caridad opened her eyes and barely caught Dr. Tracy fighting back a smile.

"None of those emotions are bad, and none of them are remotely crazy."

"Logically, I know that, but it just feels crazy to want someone so badly in such a short period of time. I mean, am I ready for that?"

"Ready for what?"

Cari huffed out a breath. "To feel so much for someone. I think about him all the time and love spending time with him. Hell, I even met his friends the other day and really liked them, too—including Jo and Jenn, and I don't exactly have a lot of females I consider acquaintances much less friends. He said the other day that whatever's going on between us doesn't feel casual to him—right after he told me about the virgin thing—and I had a panic attack. It's the second one I'd had in two days, and the first one had been when we'd been out on a date. He says these things that are at once incredibly sweet, super intense, and holy crap arousing, and it's like my brain and my insides get twisted up into pretzels and all of a sudden I can't breathe and I have the urge to either run as fast as I can or throw him down on the nearest flat surface and have my way with him."

"So tell me about Owen."

Dr. Tracy's request threw her off just a tad, considering everything she'd just spilled, and Cari blinked rapidly a few times before taking a deep breath and saying, "He's incredibly hot. He's got this beard that drives me crazy—in a good way—and this red hair that's just…gah. I've never had a thing for gingers, but he's just…holy smokes…and these eyes… they're this crazy clear blue color, like, that really light blue that kind of freaks you out because they look kind of cool and icy at first but then you realize they're not cold at all and there's all this heat there. He has this great laugh and smiles a lot, which is kind of amazing considering some of the shit he's been dealt in life, and he's smart and driven. He owns a construction company, and he renovated a barn—by himself—into a house, and it's really nice. Warm and inviting, all these open spaces. And on the surface he seems like this super laid-back, easy-going guy who just likes to make people laugh, but he's really this intense man who has all these layers. Still waters running deep and all that jazz. He says stuff that throws me off, and for someone who's never had sex he's probably the most sexual—no, sensual, even though I don't like that word—person I've ever met. And he's a fantastic kisser. Like, really, really good."

"Caridad, I want you to take a look at yourself right now."

She drew her brows together. "Why?"

Dr. Tracy tsked. "Don't ask 'why,' just do it."

Caridad looked down at the little box in the corner of her laptop screen, the one that had her face in it. She clicked to make the image bigger.

Her eyes sparkled. A flush stained her cheeks. And she was smiling.

"Oh."

"Yeah, 'oh.' What do you see?"

"Am I falling for him? I can't be falling for him already. I barely know him. I mean, well, I feel like I know him, but we haven't known each other that long and I just got out of a relationship and holy fuck I am so not ready for this."

She felt her chest tighten as black tinged the edge of her vision.

"Caridad. Breathe. Like I taught you when you first start-ed seeing me."

She did her breathing exercises, counting backwards from ten until she got to one.

"Better now?"

She nodded. "A little. Sorry about that."

"You know you don't have to apologize to me for having a panic attack. I know it's been a while, but I'm going to give you a homework assignment."

"Okay."

"First, I want you to keep an open mind about Owen. Sec-ond, I want you to try some free writing like we did when you first started seeing me. When you start feeling anxious, I want you to free write. You know the drill—don't censor yourself or worry about grammar, spelling or punctuation."

Caridad nodded. "Okay. Got it."

"I really do think you've got this, Caridad. You're strong. You've done great with identifying triggers and learning how to utilize healthy, effective coping mechanisms. You just need to learn to trust yourself and your feelings."

She swallowed as she felt anxiety start to take over again. Trust herself?

Somehow that seemed like the hardest thing she could possibly do.

CHAPTER FIFTEEN

CARIDAD STEPPED BACK FROM THE GUEST ROOM CLOSET AND wiped her hands on the back of her yoga pants.

God, this place was a mess.

At least she'd managed to formulate a bit of a game plan, though, which she was calling Operation Get Rid of Abuela's Crap. Short and to the point. She liked it.

The first step in Operation Get Rid of Abuela's Crap was to go through her grandmother's clothes and take them to… somewhere…and donate them. Del Rio didn't have a Goodwill or Salvation Army, but she was sure she could find someone who wanted or needed all this junk.

After ending the call with Dr. Tracy Caridad had felt like she needed to do something to get her house in order, so she'd come in here and stuffed almost all of her grandmother's clothes in garbage bags. She'd kept a few sentimental items like her grandmother's wedding dress and a christening gown she'd found in a box on the top shelf, but everything else had to go.

She looked at the bags of clothes—six of them—sitting on the floor and back up onto the top shelf of the closet. Next to the box holding the christening gown was another box. She'd lifted the top off of it briefly, seen what looked to be a mixture of photos, newspaper clippings and handwritten notes, and shoved it back onto the shelf before moving on to the next thing. Now that she was done with the clothes, however, curiosity was getting the better of her.

Bottom lip held between her teeth, she stood on her tip toes, reached up and grabbed the box. It was heavier than she'd thought it would be, piquing her curiosity even more.

She carried it into the living room, where she sat it on the coffee table. Staring at it almost as if she expected something to pop out of it, she plunked down on the couch. She hadn't gotten a good look at the contents earlier, but the very brief glance she'd had had been of her dad's face.

This was either going to be a very good or very bad trip down memory lane.

Stalling, Caridad got up and grabbed a bottle of water from the fridge before returning to the living room. She sat back down, eyeing the box nervously, before slowly reaching forward and opening it. She set the lid down beside it and pulled it closer, nerves dancing in her belly.

Why she was so nervous about a bunch of old photos she had no idea. But the fact that this box had been hidden away—like the photo album Mikey had found—made alarm bells ring in her head.

She reached in and smoothed a hand over the top photo— one of her father smiling into the camera—before grabbing a handful of photos and pulling them out of the box. She sifted through them, noting that they were mostly of her father in his teens and that there was nothing written on the back of them. Her father's high school years flashed before her eyes. In some of the photos he was with her mom. In others by himself. And in others he was with friends, or in football pads with a serious expression on his face, or smiling as he looked up from a desk or lunch table.

She set the first bunch of photos aside and reached into the box for another handful. This time she grabbed photos and what looked to be newspaper clippings, the paper yellowed and slightly faded.

Her father's byline was under the headline.

Curious, she scanned through the first article, which was about schedule changes for the upcoming school year. The next was a story about a fundraiser the senior class was holding. There were more, stories about homecoming games and valedictorians and awards various organizations and students had won. Typical high school journalism stuff.

Something she'd never known about her dad—that he was a writer, too.

She set the articles aside and grabbed another stack of items. More photos, including some with her very pregnant mom and others by himself. As she watched her dad mature with every photo, she also saw him get sadder and sadder. By the time Caridad began appearing in photos, the bright smile her dad had flashed in high school was gone, replaced by a dull light in his eyes and a permanent frown.

Which was weird, because the very few memories she had of him, he'd been smiling and laughing.

She set aside the third stack and removed more items from the box. Additional photos, featuring Caridad as a baby and toddler. Her scowling parents. Neither of them looked very happy.

One photo in particular caught her eye. Her dad was holding her, a wistful smile on his face as she threw her head back and laughed. Caridad smiled at the photo—she looked like such a happy, carefree child—and flipped it over like she'd done with every photo so far. Unlike those others, though, this one actually had writing on the back of it.

You bring lightness to my dark.

Okay, that was a little weird.

She looked at the next photo—one of her dad and her mom—and flipped it over.

I don't make you smile anymore.

Next was a snapshot of her mom, a candid photo that caught her with worry etched across her face as she looked out their kitchen window.

Your beauty is too good for my ugliness.

Next came a photo of Caridad smiling a toddler's smile, her hair in pigtails as her dad pushed her on a swing at a playground.

I hope you never lose your laughter. It's the most beautiful sound in the world.

Caridad playing with their dog, Zeus, on the kitchen floor.

The only good thing I've ever done.

Gloria looking over her shoulder as she arranged flowers in a vase.

I will always love you.

Caridad unwrapping a Christmas gift, the Christmas tree bright and shiny behind her.

The best gift I'll ever have.

Her dad, his expression hollow. Grim. Almost lifeless.

I tried. I promise, I tried.

Caridad's hands shook as she set the stack of photos aside and reached for the final item in the box—a thick manila envelope.

Not sure if she really wanted to look inside or not, she took a deep breath and removed the envelope. Slowly—so slowly—she turned it over and undid the clasp. Flipped up the seal. Opened it and slid her hand inside. She withdrew a thick sheaf of documents as anxiety roiled in her stomach.

The top sheet was a death certificate.

Fernando Garcia.

Her dad.

She was staring at her dad's death certificate.

With a sort of morbid curiosity—and a really bad feeling considering what had been written on the backs of those photos—she read through it, noting his birth date, his spouse and location of death, which was the hospital. That made sense, considering she'd always been told he'd died from injuries sustained in a car accident.

She kept reading until she came to the cause of death.

The certificate fluttered out of her hands.

The little suicide box had been checked.

Next to it, in the Cause of Death box was, "Gunshot wound to the head."

Caridad got up and barely made it to the kitchen trashcan before puking.

When she was done, she rinsed her mouth out at the sink then sat at the kitchen table, her hands shaking and thoughts careening through her head like wayward bumper cars.

She glanced at the pile of memories on the living room floor and felt a chill go up her spine, followed by anger.

Why hadn't they told her the truth?

She understood not telling her when she was a child, but why not as an adult? Why had they kept that from her?

If anything, though, this at least explained why her mom had been so upset when Caridad had purchased her Glock after the incident with the crazy psycho stalker ex boyfriend. Well, kind of. Had her mom feared Caridad would follow in her father's footsteps?

Not likely.

Considering the things that had been written on the backs of some of those photos, it was obvious her father had been depressed. Really depressed—at the very least. Which brought up all kinds of questions: what had caused him to go from that happy teenager in the photos to a man who could no longer bear to live? Had he sought help at all? Had anyone even noticed his downward spiral and that he'd been crying out for help?

She could always ask her mom, but Gloria was awful about confrontation and Caridad had a feeling she would get nothing but stony silence rather than answers to any of her questions.

Not sure what to do with herself, she got up and grabbed her phone off of the coffee table before going back to where she'd been sitting at the kitchen table. The one thing she did know, though, was that she didn't want to be in this house alone right now with knowledge she didn't know how to process.

Caridad: I need to get out of here. You up for a late lunch or early dinner or something?

Mikey: Sorry. Can't. Hot date.

Caridad: Seriously?

Mikey: Seriously. But what's up?

Caridad: Oh, nothing, really. Going through Abuela's crap and just found out my father killed himself.

Mikey: You didn't know that?

Caridad: No. I was told it was a car accident.

Mikey: That's shitty. Why would Mom keep that from you? I've known it was suicide for years.

Caridad almost dropped her phone.

Caridad: What? How did you know but I didn't?

Mikey: I overheard Mom and Dad talking about it one day. Never asked about it, though.

She barely resisted throwing her phone across the room in frustration. Seriously? How had her half brother known about her father's suicide years before she'd found out about it? And why the hell had she found out about it by going through a freaking box in a closet?

Her fingers tightened around the phone. This was so fucked up.

Mikey: You ok? I can cancel my date if you need me to.

She grinned at that.

Caridad: Don't cancel your date. Go have fun. I'll figure out something to do.

Mikey: Owen maybe? *waggles eyebrows*

Caridad: I don't think so. Love you.

Mikey: Love you too. Call me if you need me.

Caridad: Will do. :)

She sighed and set her phone down, her gaze once again drawn to the pile of photos and papers on the living room floor, torn between wanting to cry and just burn the whole place down.

After several long moments, she decided to grab her keys

and go for a drive instead.

Owen drove over to Chase's with a feeling of dread in the pit of his stomach. Chase's text message had been short and hadn't said much, just asking their little group to meet him at his house around three. A part of him had been tempted to come up with an excuse to not be there—he'd had enough bad news over the past few years, thank you very much—but in the end there was no way he couldn't not be there for his best friend.

So now he was turning into Chase's neighborhood, his gut telling him Chase's doctor's appointment hadn't gone well today.

Within minutes he was parking in front of Chase's house. Jo's car was in the driveway, and Matt's JEEP was already out front, as was Matt and Chase's parents' sedan. Looked like he was the last to arrive.

He took a deep breath before cutting the ignition of his truck and getting out. He didn't bother knocking since he was expected, and closed the door to find a tensely quiet house. Six pairs of eyes turned towards him as he walked into the living room.

"Relax, guys, that embarrassing infection's cleaned itself up."

Matt snorted. Jenn rolled her eyes. Jo smirked. Chase shook his head and Bo and Sarah—Chase's parents—looked at each other before looking quizzically back at Owen.

He walked into the living room and sat on the couch on the other side of Jenn. "And now that I've broken the ice with that really inappropriate not to mention awful joke, what's up? I don't see a preacher anywhere, so I'm guessing this isn't surprise nuptials or something like that?"

He winced when Jenn elbowed him in the ribs.

Chase cleared his throat and ran a hand through his hair.

"Just spill it, bro. I don't think any of us are expecting

good news considering the way you've been feeling," Matt said from Jenn's other side.

Chase exhaled. Owen didn't miss how Jo squeezed Chase's hand in support. "It's not good news." His Adam's apple bobbed up and down before continuing. "My clearance has dropped significantly and my creatinine has shot up. I'm also apparently anemic, which is something I hadn't had to worry about before but is pretty common with kidney disease."

"So what's next?" Matt asked.

"Unfortunately I've gotten bad enough that I can now apply to be on the transplant waiting list and start looking for living donors. My nephrologist thinks I have a little bit of time before we need to start dialysis, but he's going to monitor me closely so that I can start as soon as necessary if it comes to that."

"When can we apply to be donors?" Owen asked.

"I'm not sure yet. I have the paperwork and am going to fill it out tonight and get it back to the transplant coordinator tonight or tomorrow morning. After that, it's my understanding that I have to go through a physical and psychological workup; they'll do more labs, chest X-Rays, make me talk to a shrink." He grinned at Jo. "Sorry, babe, psychologist or social worker."

Jo rolled her eyes, but the high school counselor's smile was filled with nothing but love for Chase.

"After that, they'll present me to the transplant committee at the hospital, but that's pretty much all I know at this point."

"Which hospital are you going to go through?" Bo asked.

Chase shrugged. "Part of that depends on what health insurance will or won't approve. I'm guessing it'll be somewhere in San Antonio, though, considering that's where my nephrologist is based and it's the closest city with a top tier transplant hospital."

They all grew silent, each person lost in his or her own thoughts. Sarah sniffled. She'd obviously tried to silence it, but everyone heard anyway. Chase drew her in for a hug, and mother clung to son, silent sobs wracking her body.

Owen looked away and blinked rapidly. It seemed like just yesterday he and his mom had been doing the same thing, except she'd been the sick one and he the one trying to figure out how to hold it all together.

He couldn't imagine what it must be like for Bo and Sarah, knowing their son had a disease that had no cure and that could kill him without a transplant or dialysis. Although, from what he understood, dialysis wasn't a viable long-term solution.

Beside him, Jenn leaned in to Matt, her head on his shoulder as tears welled in her eyes and threatened to spill over. Sarah pulled away from Chase and went to her husband, who wrapped her in his arms. Jo, openly crying, reached out and grabbed Chase's hand.

And God, what must Jo be going through right now? Knowing the man she planned on marrying had an incurable disease? Again, he couldn't imagine what he would do if the person he loved was in a position similar to Chase's.

Suck it up, just like you did with Mom.

With the three couples murmuring to one another, Owen suddenly felt like the odd man out. Wrapped up in each other, none of them noticed when Owen got up and quietly slipped out of the house.

CHAPTER SIXTEEN

CARIDAD GLANCED UP AT THE SOUND OF A CAR DOOR CLOSING, and felt a little jolt when she looked over her shoulder and saw Owen walking towards the picnic table she was sitting on. A little tingle of pleasure zipped through her veins, followed by the realization that Owen was not okay. His mouth was set in a grim line and his shoulders slumped as if he'd just been told Santa and the Easter Bunny were both make believe.

She caught his gaze with her own and held it until he reached the table, where he sat down beside her on the cool concrete surface.

"Sorry if I'm interrupting some personal time or something," he muttered.

She shook her head, even though he was staring straight ahead and probably couldn't see the motion. "You're not. Well, you kind of are, but it's okay. I just needed to get out of the house so I could think clearly."

He sighed and pinched the bridge of his nose, but didn't respond, and even though a vast majority of her was scared as hell of the way she felt when she was around him, she couldn't not try to offer him an ear when he obviously needed one. "What's wrong?"

He shrugged. "Why'd you need to think clearly?"

Ouch. If his body language and inability to look her in the

eye hadn't let her know he was upset with her, his flat tone definitely got the point across.

"Just needed to." Her unwillingness to open up even now was probably a bit childish and immature, but dammit, it wasn't as if he was giving her any indication he even wanted her to.

She slid off the table and began to walk towards her truck.

"So that's it? You're just gonna walk away again without telling me why?" And there was the emotion that had been sorely lacking just moments before.

Caridad stopped and took a deep breath before saying, "Owen, you know why I left the other night like I did."

At least, she hoped he knew.

"Actually, I don't. I know a lot of things were said Saturday night. I told you things I've never told another soul, and those things apparently made you hightail it out of my house as if your ass was on fire."

She whirled around and stalked towards him, poked him the chest before saying, "You threw a lot at me the other night, Owen. A lot. And yes, I freaked out. I panicked. But it wasn't because of the virginity thing, if that's what you're thinking."

He lightly grabbed her finger and held on. Her gaze snapped up to his, and where his eyes had been cold and lifeless just minutes before, they were now a hot, burning blue like the heart of a flame. "Then what was it, Cari? Did I get too real for you? Too close to you? Did I move too fast? Open up too much? Because, fuck, I feel like I'm on a constant roller coaster with you. One minute it's up, up, up and the next we're flying back down to earth so fast we're about to go off the damned rails."

And because she'd had a shit day and was still feeling raw and vulnerable after not only talking to Dr. Tracy but finding that goddamned box and all its secrets, her brain disconnected from her mouth and out tumbled words she'd never intended to say. "I ran away because it was too much, Owen! You make me feel too much. You make me feel so much it scares me shitless. I wasn't looking for this. I wasn't looking for you, dammit! And there you are, looking all hot and sexy with your beard and those stupid, scuffed up boots and kissing me so that my brain falls out of my freaking ears and I just…I can't, Owen. I can't do this. I can't allow myself to fall for you because the last time I let myself fall in love I ended up in the hospital and having to get a fucking restraining order."

He let go of her finger, and she took a step back, her chest rising and falling far too rapidly for someone who'd just been standing in place. But her heart was racing and adrenaline was flooding her veins like it did after a particularly difficult competition course, and oh shit. It was worse than she'd thought.

She wasn't about to fall, she was already falling.

And that was completely unacceptable.

Because…because…bad past experiences.

That sounded weak even to her.

"I'm not him, Cari," he said softly.

She snorted. "Logically I know that, but in my head? God, it's so messed up. Beyond messed up. It's this tangled mess of crap that I feel like I've been trying to straighten out for years, but every time I think I'm getting somewhere a new knot forms."

He reached out and tentatively grabbed her hand, questions in his eyes. She wrapped her fingers around his in response.

"I can be patient. You probably need to know that about me, that I can be incredibly patient and stubborn when necessary."

She fought a smile. "You? Stubborn? I never would have guessed."

"Well, it takes one to know one."

"Fair enough."

He tugged her closer, and she sat back on the table beside him.

"I'll help you untangle those knots if you let me."

She rested her head on his shoulder. "I know. And I'm

glad you're willing to, but I think it's something I need to figure out myself if I ever want to have a healthy relationship, if
that makes any sense."

He squeezed her hand. "It does. But I'm here if you need
me."

"Thanks for that."

She felt him kiss the top of her head, the sweet gesture
bringing tears to her eyes for the umpteenth time that day.

"So what brought you out here seeking clarity?" he asked.

Caridad blinked rapidly. "My father killed himself."

"Okay. I thought he'd been gone for a while?"

"He has been, since I was a toddler, actually. I'd been told
he died in a car accident, but it ends up that was a big, fat lie."
Her chuckle was humorless. "I found a box with his death
certificate in it today. Ends up he thought a bullet through the
brain was better than being here for his wife and daughter."

Owen wrapped his arms around her and pulled her close,
so that her head was resting on his chest. She wound her arms
around his waist and sniffled, fighting back the tears that
threatened to fall.

"I'm sorry, Cari. So, so sorry."

She swallowed the lump in her throat before asking, "So
what about you? By the expression on your face when you
first got here I'm guessing you didn't come out here for the
spectacular view."

"My best friend's dying."

She drew in a sharp breath.

"Wow, that was a little melodramatic," Owen chuckled,
but it sounded hollow. "Maybe 'dying' isn't the right word,
but he could die. Chase found out today he's officially in kidney failure and can qualify for a transplant. He doesn't need
dialysis just yet, thank God, but he's gone downhill so quickly
I'm worried he won't find a kidney soon enough."

"Holy shit, Owen. I am so, so sorry."

His chest rose and fell underneath her head and his fingers
combed through her hair. "Me, too."

They sat together in silence until the sun dipped below the horizon, casting the lake and the world around them in a rosy glow.

"Sometimes I get so mad at God." Owen barked out a harsh laugh. "Actually, there have been more than a few times when I've questioned Him over the past few years, even questioned His existence at times. I mean, how could a God that's supposed to be so loving cause so much pain? Why do so many bad things happen to so many good people? But then I have moments like this, when the sun sets and everything's bathed in gold and pink and orange, and I want to kick myself or being a stupid, selfish asshole for even doubting."

She wrapped her arms tighter around his waist. "I know exactly what you mean. It's so easy to be angry all the time, to doubt and question. It's a lot harder to give up even a small bit of control and just have faith and believe."

"And this is what happens when two control freaks collide," he quipped.

She chuckled. "You know what's funny about that? When I first met you I wouldn't have pegged you as a control freak at all. You come across as this easy-going, laid-back guy, but you're not."

"Thanks for that."

She looked up at him, unable to tell if he was serious or being sarcastic. "Thanks?"

He nodded. "Yup, thanks." He shrugged. "The thing is, I know I come across as easy-going and laid-back, and in a lot of ways I am. It's easier sometimes to be that guy, rather than the one I really am."

"I read a quote once from Greta Garbo that's stayed with me for years: 'Anyone who has a continuous smile on his face conceals a toughness that is almost frightening.' I think you might be the first person I've ever met that made that make sense to me."

He snorted. "That may be, but how many quotes are there out there about wearing a mask for so long that you begin to lose yourself?"

"Do you feel like you're losing yourself?"

"Sometimes. Other times—most of the time—I know who I am and think I've maybe just gotten a little off track." His quietly murmured words hit home, like an arrow aimed true at its target.

"Yeah, I know what you mean," she muttered.

"Think maybe we can help each other get back on track?" he asked quietly.

"Maybe."

But what if in getting back on track, they realized they were going in completely different directions? Or worse—on a collision course that would leave them both shattered and burned.

Owen followed Caridad back to her house, his mind racing, trying to process everything that had happened in the past forty-eight hours. Not to mention the fact that he wasn't entirely sure what he was doing following her back to her place. They'd had a moment, sure, but that's all it had been—a moment.

At least that's what he kept telling himself.

When she walked inside, he followed, silent, as if being pulled by some invisible chain that had tethered him to her.

He swallowed and cleared his throat before speaking. "Cari, I—"

She turned and placed a hand on his chest. "I know I keep throwing mixed signals at you, and I wouldn't blame you at all for walking away right now and never looking back, but I really don't want to be alone right now."

He took a deep breath and nodded. "Okay."

"Okay?"

"Okay. Truth is, I don't really want to be alone right now, either."

She nodded once before slowly moving away, but then

surprised him by taking his hand in her own and leading him to the couch. They sat, and she grabbed a remote off the coffee table before turning on the TV then pulling up Netflix.

"You up for watching a movie?"

"Sure."

"Anything in particular?"

He shrugged. "Not really. Just nothing about people dying, because I really don't want to think about people dying right now."

"Fair enough."

She clicked in to New Releases and thumbed through them, paused. "How about *Magic Mike XXL?*"

Her eyes sparkled and she was barely holding back a grin. Owen bit back his own. "Uh, how about no?"

"Awww, come on."

"Let's not and say we did."

"Fine," she pouted. It wasn't a very effective pout, though, considering her shoulders shook with silent laughter.

She backed out of new releases and went into suggested Christmas movies. "I figure it's December, so why not?"

He hadn't been able to watch Christmas movies since his mom passed away. Instead of telling her that, though, he just said, "Whatever you want."

She scrolled through and finally clicked on *Elf.* "I think goofy humor and smiling is needed tonight."

"I like smiling. It's my favorite," he quipped.

She snorted and started the movie.

It took them both a while to relax, but eventually Caridad's head ended up on his shoulder. Before the movie was even halfway through, he looked down and realized she'd fallen asleep.

She was beautiful while awake, full of life and a fire that refused to be extinguished. Asleep, though, she was amazing with her features relaxed and her guard down. He kissed the top of her head, and she snuggled closer to him, a sleepy, contented sigh barely escaping her lips. He pulled her closer, realizing now that he'd been a cotton-headed ninny muggins for thinking he could stay away from her for any amount of time.

CHAPTER SEVENTEEN

CARIDAD WOKE UP SLOWLY, BECOMING MORE AWARE OF HER surroundings in foggy stages. Sleepily, she stretched, and then jerked when her ass came in to contact with a very hard something behind her.

The fog lifted, and all at once she became aware of the arm wrapped around her waist. The hand resting under her t-shirt on her stomach. The beard tickling the back of her neck.

Kind of confused and kind of horny, she squeezed her eyes shut and tried to remember what had happened last night after she and Owen had come back to her place. She could recall looking for movies and starting *Elf*. She remembered laughing a couple of times, and leaning in to him at one point. After that, though, everything was blank.

I must've fallen asleep.

She really hoped she hadn't drooled on him.

Owen grunted and pulled her closer, strong even in his sleep.

Well, to be fair, she didn't exactly resist, either.

There was something comforting, something *right*, about being held by him like this that made her stomach do somersaults and her heart beat faster.

But why did it feel so right?

Why was his presence comforting?

She was a strong, independent woman who was fully capable of taking care of herself. She didn't need a man, especially a complicated virginal man.

And oh, God, what if she had morning breath?

Caridad, stop it.

She opened her eyes and focused on the black screen of the TV across from them, slowly drew in a breath and exhaled.

She was so tired of worrying all the time. Tired of the anxiety that crept into her mind at random moments, throwing her entire world into a tailspin. She'd felt off-kilter from the moment she'd met Owen, and as hard as it was to embrace that feeling, she also knew she didn't want to keep going on like she had been.

Scared.

Scared of the things he made her feel. Scared of the way he looked at her. Scared of the things he said. Scared of the attraction that burned bright between them.

Scared of completely giving her heart to someone again.

And that was the crux of it, really. Waking up beside him like this, snuggled in to each other and his arm holding her close, she couldn't hide from the truth anymore.

She'd started falling for him that very first weekend and hadn't ever stopped.

She was still falling.

Maybe had already fallen.

She drew in a deep, shaky breath and blew it back out.

"You're thinking so hard you woke me up." Owen's voice was low and gravelly with sleep, the sound of it causing yet another somersault in her belly.

"Sorry. I didn't mean to."

His nose nuzzled in to her neck, and then she felt the light brush of his lips there, just below her hairline. Goosebumps popped up on her arms and legs, and she arched against him involuntarily, like her body suddenly had a mind of its own.

He kissed the back of her neck again and murmured, "What were you thinking so hard about?"

His pinky finger sneaking under the waistband of her yoga pants must have short-circuited her brain, because she said, "I'm tired of being scared, of fighting this."

His hand stilled, but he kissed the back of her neck again, causing more shivers to race across her skin. "What is 'this,' exactly?"

She rolled her eyes, even though he couldn't see her reaction. "You know what I'm talking about, Owen."

"I know, but I need to hear you say it."

His lips pressed into the curve where shoulder met neck, and she tilted her head to give him better access. "This attraction. My feelings for you. I'm scared shitless, but I'm so tired of fighting it."

Owen's hand moved again, lower, under the waistband of her panties until he cupped and teased her.

"You're so wet already." The raw hunger in his voice did crazy things to her body.

She arched against his hand, pushing her backside against the very hard erection straining against his jeans. "Yeah, well, you feel like you're pretty good to go yourself."

He chuckled, the sound low and incredibly sexy, and she turned her head before lifting her mouth up to his.

If their last kiss had been sudden and explosive, a frantic, desperate search for *something,* this kiss was the exact opposite. It was slow and sensual, a meeting of lips and tongues, a sweet mingling of breaths that caused her thoughts to float away like dandelion fluff in the breeze. Instead of a desperate search for something, Owen's mouth against hers felt a lot like coming home.

♋

Owen felt like he was in an alternate reality. One where he and Caridad were done with their will they/won't they dance and where he had his hand down her pants and her mouth on his.

Oh, wait. That was reality.

And because that was reality, he couldn't ignore the feeling of satisfied anticipation that bloomed through his chest. Or the hard-on in his jeans.

He also couldn't ignore the wet heat against his fingers, or the way her hips arched against his hand when he did something she liked.

He broke the kiss and trailed his lips across her cheeks. Her jaw. Her forehead before drawing away so he could watch her every movement and expression.

He continued to slowly circle her clit with the pad of his index finger, dragging his finger across it every so often, teasing her and torturing himself. A frustrated groan escaped from Cari's lips, and he fought a smile.

"Tell me what you want," he whispered into her ear.

She whimpered, but didn't respond. His hand stilled.

"I hate you right now," she finally said.

"No, you don't."

"Cocky bastard," she huffed.

"What do you want, Cari?"

Almost as if the words were being dragged out of her, she finally, slowly said, "I want you."

He rubbed a finger across her clit. "Do you want this?" he asked before pressing his erection into her backside, "or do you want this?"

"Can't I have both?" She sounded almost breathless.

He chuckled. "Are you sure you want both?"

"You are such a tease."

He moved his hand lower and slid a finger inside of her. God, she was so wet. Hot. Tight.

She shifted, pushing into his hand. Constrained by clothes, his movements were shallow and jerky, but he was able to press the heel of his palm against her clit, and he was rewarded by her sharp intake of breath.

"Jesus, Owen." Her voice was shaky.

"What do you need?"

She pushed against his hand again. "Just keep," she drew

in an unsteady breath, "doing," a tiny moan escaped her lips, "what," another unsteady breath, "you're doing."

Her hips picked up their rhythm, moving faster and faster against his fingers. He watched her face, the expressions playing across it, the way she bit her lip and her eyebrows drew together as he continued to thrust his finger inside of her. She was obviously getting frustrated, so he pressed his mouth against her ear and went with his gut, figuring she simply needed to get out of her head and focus on what she was feeling.

"Do you have any idea how hot you are, fucking my hand like that?"

Her eyebrows relaxed a little.

"You're so wet, Cari. Your hot little pussy likes my finger, doesn't it?"

She bit her lip harder, but her eyebrows relaxed even more. Score one for intuition.

"I wonder how you taste? Will your pussy be sweet against my tongue?" She pressed hard against his hand. "You like that, huh? God, I want to taste you so bad, Cari, bury my face against you and fuck you with my tongue until I make you scream."

She panted out the words. "I'm. Not. A. Scream—oh fuck me."

The only thing better than watching Caridad's face as she came was feeling her clench around his finger, the way her body tensed before completely coming undone.

It was so fucking beautiful.

She was so fucking beautiful.

Her body began to relax in slow increments, and she opened her eyes then turned her head so she could look at him. Her voice was barely a whisper when she said, "I want you."

And he knew the questions in her eyes weren't because of her, but because of him.

But he wanted her, too.

He kissed the tip of her nose and slowly removed his hand from her pants. Disappointment crossed her face, until he brought his finger to his lips and sucked it into his mouth, tasting her on his skin.

"Sweet. So fucking sweet."

Silently, she got up from the couch, held her hand out to him. He took it and allowed her to pull him towards the back of the house. They stepped into her bedroom, and still silent she turned to him and slid her hands under the hem of his t-shirt, pushing it up until she tugged on it. He lifted his arms, and she pulled it off his body and over his head, tossed it somewhere on the floor. She ran her hands over his stomach, his chest, traced the outline of the tattoo that covered his left pec.

She glanced up at him. "What does it mean?"

He cleared his throat. "It's a Celtic cross, symbolizing the bridge between heaven and earth."

She traced the teal ribbon that wound around the black ink of the cross. "For your mom?"

"Yeah."

She kissed the center of it, her lips barely there and then gone, before taking a step back and pulling her shirt over her head and tossing it the way of his.

He swallowed thickly, entranced as she reached around and unclasped her bra. She relaxed her arms, and the straps and cups dangled, clinging until she shimmied them away.

Jesus Christ she had amazing breasts. Full and heavy with dusky pink nipples that were already hard. He watched as she reached for the waistband of her yoga pants and peeled them off, kicking them to the side.

"You are so fucking beautiful."

She blushed.

"I mean it, Cari." He reached out and lightly ran a fingertip along the curve of her breast, down along her rib cage, following the flare of her hips. She was voluptuous in all the best ways, soft. Her belly slightly curved out rather than being flat and taut, and he loved it. Just like he loved her wide hips, the fullness of her thighs, and her generous ass. He hadn't realized he could get any harder, but seeing her like this, like a Renaissance era painting come to life, had him nearly coming right then and there.

Not going to happen. Not so soon.

She smiled, and he loved the confidence in her eyes as she reached for the button of his jeans. He let her unbutton and unzip them, let her drag the denim and his boxers down his legs. He stepped out of them, kicked them to the side.

Her gaze dropped down to his dick, and a strangled chuckle escaped from his lips.

She looked back up at him and raised her eyebrows. "You've been keeping that hidden from the women of Del Rio? How?"

"What exactly are you saying?" he teased.

"You know exactly what I'm saying."

"Come on, I need it spelled out for me. I'm not exactly experienced in these types of things."

She stepped forward until her hard nipples brushed against his chest. "You know exactly what I'm saying, Owen. And I'm not going to stroke your ego by telling you you have a, uh, really wide dick."

"I have a big dick, huh?"

She slapped his shoulder. "You're incorrigible. Now, a little less talk and a lot more action."

"As you wish," he said before capturing her mouth with his and walking her backwards towards the bed, where he laid her down before kissing his way down her neck, her chest, until he reached those magnificent breasts.

He drew a nipple into his mouth, rolled the taut peak around his tongue before sucking. Her hips bucked underneath him, and her fingers threaded through his hair. He plucked at her other nipple with his fingers, making her body roll against his. He switched breasts and lashed the other with his tongue and teeth, eliciting a barely there groan from Caridad.

He let go of her nipple with a *pop* before kissing his way further down her body, paying special attention to the underside of her breasts. Her ribs. Her stomach. He nipped and sucked his way across her hips, down her thighs and back up, then he slid his tongue against her clit. Her fingers dug into his scalp and pulled him closer.

He loved her with his mouth and fingers, bringing her to the edge and slowing down when she got too close. He thrust his tongue inside of her like he'd told her he wanted to, the taste of her sweet on his tongue.

A low moan escaped from her as she thrust harder against his face, her hands insistent on the back of his head. With one last long, slow lick, he kissed his way back up her torso before claiming her mouth with his own.

Her hands swept down his back, grabbed his ass briefly before snaking their away around front. Her fingers closed around him, and he broke the kiss, a hiss of satisfaction whistling through his teeth.

"A part of me wants to tease you the way you've been teasing me," she said.

His hips flexed in her hand. "Oh, yeah?"

His voice sounded slightly breathless, even to him.

"Yeah." Her hand slid up his shaft and back down, squeezing gently as the base and making him turn to jelly temporarily.

"But?"

She licked her lips. "But I want you inside of me more." Uncertainly clouded her eyes. "Unless you don't want that. I'm not going to push you."

He kissed her hard and fast. "Give me a second."

He got up off the bed and went over to his jeans, grabbed his wallet out of his back pocket and then the condom he'd put in there a week ago. When he turned back to her, her eyebrows were raised. "First, that is a kick ass tattoo on your back. Second, I guess that means we're doing this."

He laid back down on the bed beside her and handed her

the condom. "Only if you're certain it's what you want. I'm not going to push you."

Her hands shook as she ripped open the foil packet then slid the latex over his length.

He found it funny that she was more nervous than he was. You would think she was the virgin, not him.

"Um, so, how do you want this?"

Yup, she was definitely nervous.

He bit back a grin and instead of responding, leaned in and kissed her. She began to relax against him as he took over, her body rolling against his as their tongues caressed one another. He wedged a thigh between her legs, continuing to kiss her. She wrapped a leg around his waist, and then moved her other one so that she could wrap it around him, too.

He thrust his tongue against hers as he slid into her body, the movement natural, guided by pure instinct. He slid in slowly, wanting to savor the moment as much as he wanted to give her body time to adjust to his girth. Her legs tightened around him, pulling him closer. She broke their kiss, and her chest rose and fell rapidly as she looked up at him.

"Holy shit. I'm taking your virginity."

"You complaining?" he asked as he slowly withdrew.

"Not at all." She gasped when he slid back home. "Fuck you feel good."

Her nails dug into his back and he buried his face in her neck. "Back at ya," he mumbled into her hair.

She chuckled and moved with him, their movements slow and luxurious, like a boat gently bobbing in the water on a calm summer's day. Her hands explored his skin, and her occasional gasps echoed in his head. Gradually, their rhythm picked up, her hips bucking against his and her legs pulling him closer, harder.

He wanted this to never end, to go on and on forever so he could die a happy man buried deep inside of her. Unfortunately, the pressure building at the base of his spine let him know that wasn't going to be the case today, so he slowed the pace slightly and asked, "What do you need?"

"Lift up just a little." Her voice was low and husky, and she was as completely lost in the moment as he was.

He lifted up on his arms, putting a little bit of space between their bodies, and he almost came when she reached down and touched herself.

"You're killing me, Cari."

She arched her back. "No dying yet."

Fair enough. "Do you need it harder? Faster? Slower?"

"This is good." The finger working against her clit picked up speed. "This is perfect."

He looked down between their bodies, watching her hand as it moved. He'd never seen anything sexier. His balls tightened, and he gritted his teeth, forcing himself to maintain the same pace despite the fact that his body was screaming at him to pound into her hard and fast.

Caridad's hips undulated underneath him, picking up speed. "Harder."

Oh, thank God.

He slammed into her, causing her breasts to bounce wildly and his brain to short circuit. Oh fuck.

The very short tether he'd had on his self control snapped, and he gave in to his body's urge to pound into her harder and faster. He fused his mouth to hers, kissing her with very little finesse but a whole lot of passion.

He couldn't hold on any longer. Couldn't hold back the orgasm that ripped through him, or the shout that tumbled from his lips.

As he came back down, still moving inside of Cari like he never wanted to stop, she stiffened beneath him before relaxing, her muscles spasming around him, milking him and prolonging his own climax.

For long moments, the only sound in the room was that of their harsh breaths. He opened his eyes and stared at the woman beneath him. Her forehead glistened with sweat and her black hair was a tangled fan across the bedspread. Roses bloomed across her cheeks, and he could feel her heart racing against his own.

"I'm sorry," he murmured.

Her eyes flew open. "For what?"

Slightly embarrassed, he said, "I didn't last long enough."

She had the audacity to smirk. "Did you not feel what just happened?"

"Yeah, but I came before you did."

"Seriously, Owen?"

"Yes. Seriously."

She chewed on her bottom lip and looked away briefly before saying, "I can't believe I'm about to say this because I don't know that your ego needs any stroking, but that was the best sex I've ever had."

And suddenly he felt ten feet tall and like he could leap over buildings with a single bound. "Really?"

"Really."

"Huh. How 'bout that."

"Don't get all cocky on me now that you've given up your V card and been told you give good sex."

"Me? Cocky?"

"Yes, you."

She smiled up at him and laughed. Since he was still inside her, he felt that laugh *everywhere*. *"Oh. Wow."*

She stopped laughing. "What?"

"When you laughed. I could feel it."

"Really? What did it feel like?"

"Honestly, it kind of hurt."

"I'm sorry."

"No need to apologize." He kissed her lightly. "I should probably go take care of the condom."

"Yeah, probably." She sounded wistful.

He withdrew slowly, immediately missing her warmth wrapped around him, and made his way to the bathroom where he disposed of the condom and cleaned himself up a bit. He opened up the linen closet and grabbed a wash cloth, wet it down with warm water, and took it with him back to the bedroom.

"What's that for?"

Suddenly unsure, but working on some weird instinct, he didn't respond. Instead he sat down beside her and silently ran the cloth over her sensitive flesh. Feeling her gaze upon him, he looked up. Tears swam in her eyes, but her mouth crooked up in a half smile.

"You're a good man, Owen Daniels," she whispered.

He tossed the cloth into an empty laundry basket and crawled in to bed beside her. He wrapped his arms around her and pulled the covers up over their bodies before responding. "You're a good woman, Caridad Mathews."

She grasped his hand and lifted it, kissed the back of it before twining her fingers with his and snuggling back against him.

He breathed in the scent of her hair and sex, and could have sworn he felt his heart tumble to the ground.

CHAPTER EIGHTEEN

Two days later, Caridad was still trying to process everything that had happened Monday afternoon and Tuesday morning. Amazing, how her life had gone topsy turvy so quickly.

She stared at her computer screen, the blank page staring back at her.

Every time she'd tried to start the article that was due next week, her brain had lost focus and gone back to images of Owen naked and inside of her.

She really liked him that way.

They'd left her house late Tuesday afternoon, when Owen discovered the abysmal state of her kitchen. He took her back to his place, where he made them this amazing chicken, pasta, and basil pesto dish. They managed to make it five minutes after cleaning off their plates before tearing into each other and barely making it to his bedroom.

She'd ridden him hard and fast, until they'd both screamed each other's names.

Her nipples tightened and her clit throbbed at the memory.

Crap. There was no way she was getting any work done while she was this horny.

With a sigh, she pulled up Facebook, hoping for a distraction.

Had she really taken a thirty-four year-old man's virginity?

Oh my God, she totally had.

It was like being in some weird alternate universe, especially considering he hadn't, well, acted like a virgin. If anything, she'd been the awkward one, not him.

It was disconcerting, to say the least.

She noticed she had a friend request, so she clicked on the icon to see who it was. She tended to get a few requests a week from people who didn't know her and who apparently didn't understand that her public page existed for a reason. Jenn's face popped up, and Caridad hovered over the request for a few seconds before deciding to accept it.

That taken care of, she cleaned out her notifications, responded to a couple of comments on her fan page, and then scrolled through her news feed absentmindedly.

She was just about to click through on a Buzzfeed article about dogs who forgot how to dog when the message window opened up.

Jenn: Hey there. I know this is probably weird, but have you talked to Owen since Monday?

Sensing a bit of a land mine, she responded with: What makes you think I would have talked to Owen?

Jenn: A) Because you live next door to each other. B) He's absolutely crazy about you. C) When I stopped by his house Tuesday morning I noticed his truck in your driveway.

Caridad: If you knew all that, why'd you ask if I'd talked to him?

Jenn: I didn't want to be presumptuous. ;-)

Caridad snorted.

Caridad: Whatever. Yes, I've obviously seen him. And yes, he's okay. At least, I think he's as okay as he can be right now.

Jenn: He left Chase's the other night without saying a word to any of us. We all kept trying to call and text him and he didn't answer, which is completely unlike Owen. I was worried.

Caridad: He must have turned his phone off or left it in his truck, because I never heard it.

Granted, she'd also passed out pretty quickly Monday night, and Tuesday they'd been busy doing, well, other things.

Jenn: And now he won't answer my texts or calls, and I have pregnancy hormones so I'm freaking out and vacillating between crying and wanting to eat everything in sight.

Caridad: I'm sorry.

Jenn: Eh. It's just a part of being pregnant. As long as this baby survives it'll be worth it. Anyway. Now that you think I'm a weird preggo stalker best friend who's far too clingy, I wanted to tell you again how awesome it was to meet you the other night.

Usually someone like Jenn would have weirded her out; she didn't do perky and she certainly didn't do girl talk. But there was something completely guileless about the other woman—not to mention her obvious affection for Owen— that made it impossible for Caridad to not like her.

Caridad: :) It was nice meeting you, too.

Jenn: Owen totally sprang us on you, didn't he?

She laughed.

Caridad: What gave you your first clue?

Jenn: Oh, it might have been the deer in the headlights look.

Caridad: I can only imagine. I wanted to be mad at him, but y'all were all so nice it was impossible.

Jenn: We should do something some time. Not being able to teach this semester has me going a bit stir crazy, and while I love Matt he's a guy. Which is how I got in this mess to begin with. Because, penis.

Caridad snort giggled.

Caridad: Penis has been known to get we womenfolk into trouble from time to time.

Jenn: No shit. BTW, did you see that lumbersexual article Buzzfeed posted this morning? I'm not usually into the whole man bun thing, but those guys really were hot.

Caridad: But were they hot AF? ;-)

Jenn: Totally. They'll give you major thirst. Or something like that. I think I used it right. I'm getting too old for all this slang crap.

Caridad: LOL It gets kind of ridiculous sometimes.

Jenn: Anyway. I'll stop harassing you now. Glad Owen's in good hands. ;-)

Caridad shook her head, but didn't bother fighting the smile that crossed her face as she clicked over to Buzzfeed's Facebook page and looked for the lumbersexual post Jenn had mentioned.

Oh, those guys were definitely hot AF, but none of them held a candle to Owen with his natural, raw masculinity and alpha male pheromones.

Hell, she had it bad.

୧ৡ

Owen's phone vibrated in his back pocket for what seemed like the hundredth time that day and he barely resisted the urge to throw it across the room without even looking at the caller ID.

Jenn. Again.

He sighed, knowing he couldn't keep ignoring her.

"What's up?"

"Holy shit, you're alive!"

Her teasing tone managed to coax a small grin out of him. "Did you think I wasn't?"

"I was beginning to wonder, after your disappearing act on Monday."

She sounded curious more so than accusatory, which he took as a good sign. Still, though, he rubbed a hand over his beard and closed his eyes. "Yeah, sorry about that. I just needed some air."

"You're worried about him."

"Of course I'm worried about him. He's like a brother to

me, and he has an incurable disease."

"Chase isn't your mom, Owen," she said. The words were uttered softly, but he still felt them like individual punches to the gut.

"I know that. Logically, I know that. But I've also done research and talked to Chase about it, and I know that he can get to a point where he won't be able to survive without dialysis, and that without a transplant his life expectancy will be cut down dramatically. It sucks."

"It does, but he already has you and Matt who are willing to donate a kidney to him, and I'm sure there are others who would be willing."

He leaned back in his chair and propped his booted feet up on the edge of his desk. Eyes closed, he said, "I know, Jenn. I'm just worried. And the other day I was the odd duck out. I just needed some space, is all."

"I get that. Hell, I was in your shoes not that long ago."

"Please don't give me the whole 'you'll find somebody' spiel. Those suck."

She laughed. "I'm kind of insulted that you think I would even go there."

"Well, you do have that whole lovey-dovey, new relationship glow thing going on."

"Be that as it may, you know I'm not going to insult your intelligence or feelings like that."

"I'm a guy. I don't have feelings."

She coughed out a, "Bullshit," making him laugh.

"I love how you men are always all like, 'I'm a guy. I don't do emotions. I'm a big strong man. Rawr.' When in fact y'all can be more emotional than us women."

"Shh! Don't give away our secret."

"I don't think it's much of a secret at this point, babe."

"Fair enough."

"So speaking of *feelings,* what's going on with you and Caridad? I really liked her, FYI."

He couldn't hold back the smile that spread across his

face. "I'm honestly not a hundred percent sure what's going on with Caridad and me."

"But there's something."

"You are such a girl."

"Hello, Captain Obvious."

"We're just enjoying each other's company."

"Is that what you kids are calling it these days?"

"Jenn, I'm older than you."

"Not by much. Besides, I'm pregnant, so humor me."

"I'm not letting you play the pregnant card on me."

"Yes, you are. You totally are."

He rolled his eyes to keep from laughing. "Whatever. Anyway. I've gotta go. I'm in the middle of bookkeeping and I want to get this done some time before next Christmas."

"Bookkeeping. Eww. Have fun with that."

"Oh, yeah."

"Love you."

"Love you too."

He ended the call and set his phone on his desk before turning his attention back to his computer screen. He hadn't been lying when he'd told Jenn he was taking care of bookkeeping, and he definitely was not enjoying it right now. Usually he would just whiz through the day to day stuff, leaving the heavy lifting to his accountant, but today he was having a hard time focusing on numbers, invoices, and purchase orders. Instead, all he could see was Caridad as she'd been just this morning, naked in his bed.

For the past couple of days all he'd been able to think about was sex. Specifically, sex with Caridad.

No wonder teenage boys act like raging idiots.

Shaking his head to clear his thoughts, he once again tried to focus on Quickbooks.

Fifteen minutes later he was about to give up all hope of being able to concentrate when his phone rang, saving him from accounting hell.

Chase.

Apparently today was not his day to continue avoiding the elephant in the room.

Giving in to the inevitable, Owen answered.

"What's up?"

"Where the hell did you go on Monday?"

He rubbed a hand over his beard before responding. "I just needed some space. Sorry about that."

"I'm not mad, you just worried me, especially when you wouldn't answer your phone."

Well, hell. "Sorry."

"So, you okay?"

"Shouldn't I be asking you that?"

Chase laughed. "Probably, but I've had time to adjust to all of this, considering I've known it was probably going to happen since I was a teen. You, on the other hand, haven't. Plus, you just lost your mom and…"

"It's been three years."

"And it still seems like it was yesterday. All I'm trying to say is that I hate that I'm putting everyone through this."

"Uh, Chase, I'm not sure if you've noticed or not, but you're the one who's sick."

"Not that sick."

"Yet."

"We're catching it as it's happening rather than after my kidneys have completely failed. I'll be fine."

How could he sound so positive? "Well, now that we've gotten the pep talk out of the way."

"Right. Anyway. Jo and I are doing an impromptu Christmas party Saturday night, figured it would be nice to get everyone together under happier circumstances. Bring Caridad."

"A—what if I already had plans and B—why do you assume I would bring Caridad?"

"A—if you have plans that's fine, but we would really like you to be there and B—because we all saw your truck at her house Tuesday morning."

"What the fuck? Why's everyone spying on me?"

"Because we were worried." Chase's tone held absolutely no remorse.

"And who's 'we all,' by the way?"

"Oh, all four of us—Matt, Jenn, Jo and me. We took a field trip." He sounded far too entertained by that.

"Well, I hope you all remembered your juice boxes and animal crackers."

"If by juice boxes you mean wine for Jo and by animal crackers you mean fully loaded nachos for Jenn, then yes, we did."

Owen rubbed his forehead. "Jo was drinking wine and Jenn was eating nachos while y'all did a drive by on my house on Tuesday *morning?"*

Chase snorted. "It was just as weird as it sounds, believe me."

"Desperate times call for desperate measures?"

"Something like that. Anyway. So I'll see you Saturday night?"

"Of course. What time?"

"We're thinking around five. That work for you?"

"Absolutely." Owen swallowed. "And Chase?"

"What's up?"

"Sorry for being a dick the other night and running out like that."

Chase laughed. "Seriously, man, I'm already over it. Saturday. Be there."

The call ended and Owen stared blankly out of his office window before getting up. Screw it. He'd rather do Christmas shopping than accounting anyway.

CHAPTER NINETEEN

"I'm dressed okay, right?" Caridad asked Owen for what felt like the fiftieth time Saturday afternoon. Which was weird, because she didn't do this girly, worrying about what she looked like thing.

Except for now, apparently.

Because, crazy.

Owen pulled her close and kissed her. "You look beautiful as always."

She slapped his chest, but secretly was kind of turning into a puddle of goo on the inside. "You're just saying that so you can keep getting in my pants."

"No, I'm saying that because it's true."

She looked up at him, saw the seriousness in his expression and smiled. "Well, you're not too bad yourself, lumberjack."

He kissed her again, the casual gesture quickly turning less-than-casual. She broke away, gulping in air. "If you don't stop that, we're going to be late."

He nibbled at her earlobe. "I'm okay with that. I'm sure they'll understand."

"But, you'll mess up my hair," she weakly protested as he walked her backwards towards her bed.

His only response was to kiss her again while his fingers

unbuttoned her pants.

Oh, screw it, that's what buns are for.

GꙨ

In the end, they got to Chase's neighborhood at 5:08, which Owen considered to be perfectly acceptable, especially considering Chase had said, "around five" not "at five" specifically.

Semantics were important.

Cars lined the street, and Owen found a space to park a couple of houses down. Looked like he would be handing out gifts at a later date.

He opened Cari's door for her and held her hand as they walked up the sidewalk towards Chase's house.

"Nice place," she said.

"Yeah. You should see the backyard. It's amazing. He has one of those swimming pools that looks like it was just cut out of the earth, and you can see the Sierra del Burro mountains across the border."

"Hunting must pay really well."

He shrugged. "It certainly doesn't hurt, but he's also in commercial real estate. Honestly, most of the money we make off the ranch we put back into it. The rest of it, we invest."

"That must have sounded incredibly snoopy."

He squeezed her hand as they reached the front door and pulled her close. "I love your curiosity, for the record."

"Good." She lifted up on her tip toes and kissed him lightly. "Because I am really, really curious."

"I've noticed," he mumbled against her mouth.

"Jesus, you two, get a room."

Caridad jumped at Matt's voice, causing her teeth to nip Owen's bottom lip a little too hard. He ran his tongue over it before turning to Matt. "Like you have any room to talk."

The other man smirked before stepping aside. "Fair enough. I just thought it would be fun to give you as much hell as you gave Jenn and me."

"If I recall correctly, I didn't give you two hell so much as advice."

Matt shrugged and closed the door behind them. "You say advice, I say hell. Same thing."

Owen rolled his eyes and led Caridad into the house, which was packed with people, some he knew, others he didn't. "You want something to drink?"

"I would love something to drink."

"I'll see if they have any Lone Star for you," he said, winking at her.

She rolled her eyes. "You're never going to let me live that down, are you?"

"Nope."

They entered the kitchen, which was just as packed, and he finally spotted Jo and Chase leaning against the island. Chase's Great Pyrenees, Winchester, was glued to his side.

"Holy shit. Is that a dog or a miniature pony?" Caridad asked quietly, making him laugh.

"That is Winchester, and he's basically a big ball of dog hair."

"Pretty good name for a dog."

"I agree."

Chase nodded his head at Owen. "Glad you made it. Hi, Caridad. Drinks are in coolers out on the patio if you're thirsty."

Owen led her to the patio doors and outside.

"Holy shit that's a lot of peo—oh, wow. You weren't kidding."

Owen smiled. "I wasn't kidding."

"I'm pretty sure this looks a lot like something I've put on my Dream Home board on Pinterest."

He groaned and opened up the first cooler. "You, too?"

"Me what?"

"Pinterest. I swear. I hear Jenn talk about it constantly."

"Cool. I'll have to find her and follow her."

He shook his head. *Women.* "Anyway. Looks like this

one's water and cokes." He opened up the second cooler. "And this one's Shiner, Shiner Cheer, and Bud Light. Sorry. No Lone Star."

She chuckled. "I'll take a Cheer."

He handed her a bottle and grabbed one for himself before standing up and leading her back inside. They walked back over to Chase and Jo.

"Dude, who the hell are all these people?"

Chase and Jo glanced at each other, a smile playing at Jo's lips, before Chase said, "Friends and family, mostly."

Sure enough, Bo and Sarah were in the living room, talking to an older woman Owen had never seen before. Jenn was curled up in a recliner, Matt standing behind her and rubbing her shoulders. Chase's assistant Kim was in the living room, shooting daggers at him.

Fantastic.

There were at least a dozen other people he didn't recognize, varying in age, but they all seemed to know each other so he figured they must be the family Chase had mentioned.

He was just about to open his mouth to ask Jo how her semester was going when Winchester gave a deep WOOF and sprinted into the living room. Owen raised his eyebrows and said, "I didn't know he actually knew how to run."

Chase laughed. "He does when it suits him, but it's a rare occurrence."

Owen turned to Caridad and explained, "Winchester is notoriously lazy and slow."

"I don't know that I would want all of that running full speed towards me."

"I wouldn't, either," Jo said. "But he's a big teddy bear."

A child's delighted squeal pierced the air, and seconds later a female voice said, "Trevor Jacobson! No running inside the house! If you want to play with Winchester, take him outside."

"Yes, Mama."

A little boy skipped in from the living room, almost being dragged by the big dog, but he stopped and said, "Hi Mr. Roberts. Hi Mr. Daniels. I'm gonna play with Winchester if that's okay."

"That's totally fine, Trevor," Chase said as Trevor's mom, Miranda Jacobson entered the kitchen. Daniel Hernandez, their ranch manager followed close behind her.

Trevor and Winchester disappeared out the back door and Miranda blew blond bangs out of her eyes. "Sorry about that. He's been wound up ever since I told him we were coming here this morning. I really need to get him a dog."

"I can help you with that," Daniel said. Eagerly.

Owen glanced at Chase, and he could see the laughter in his best friend's eyes. Looked like their ranch manager had a bit of a crush on the pretty wildlife biologist.

Miranda eased away from Daniel slightly. "Thanks, Daniel, I'll think about it."

Daniel's face fell briefly, and Owen felt kind of bad for the guy. It was never fun getting kicked in the teeth by a woman.

"Thanks for inviting us," Miranda said as she hugged Chase. She turned to Owen and hugged him, too.

"Of course I invited you. You're part of the Devils Ranch family, therefore part of my family," Chase said. "And speaking of family, I don't think y'all have met yet. Miranda, this is my fiancee, Jo. Jo, this is Miranda, otherwise known as the best wildlife biologist employed by Texas Parks and Wildlife."

Both women smiled and shook hands, exchanging greetings. Miranda turned to Owen, a curious expression on her face. He cleared his throat and glanced at Caridad. "Miranda, this is Caridad, my," he paused, unsure what to call Caridad. His girlfriend? Friend? Date? "Hopefully my girlfriend. Caridad, this is Miranda."

Caridad gave him some serious side eye, but plastered a smile on her face and shook Miranda's hand.

Chase caught Owen's gaze above the two women's heads, and made a face at him that clearly said, "What the hell, man?

You're totally inept."

No shit, Sherlock.

An awkward silence fell over the group, until Miranda turned to Chase and asked, "Have you heard anything else from the Devils River Conservation Association, or anything about West Texas Water Company?"

Chase shook his head. "Nope. Haven't heard from either of them."

"Hopefully that means he's given up on the idea."

"I doubt he has. Even though we got some good rain late in the summer, the entire state's still in a drought and cities are struggling to provide water to people," Chase said.

"What's going on?" Caridad asked.

Chase gestured towards Owen, so he explained, "Back in late July we got a letter from the Devils River Conservation Association about West Texas Water Company, who's oh-so-brilliant owner has proposed pumping water out of the Aquifer under Val Verde County and into San Antonio."

"That sounds incredibly short-sighted."

"Exactly," Chase said. "Not only would it severely impact the groundwater that feeds into the Devils River, but it would also deplete the water supply for everyone in Val Verde County, especially Del Rio and San Felipe Springs, which is where the city's water comes from."

"The environmental impact isn't worth it, though," Miranda said. "If they need water that badly they should just recycle gray water like other cities have started doing. We've gotten lucky that we've gotten just enough rain at just the right times over the past few years, otherwise the wildlife population would be really bad off by now. We need what little water we do have here, here, helping the people, livestock, and wildlife of Val Verde County. You can't rob Peter to pay Paul."

"The water situation in this state is turning into a real cluster, that's for sure," Chase said.

"I just hope the city of San Antonio realizes what a mistake it would be and shoots the guy down."

Owen nodded at Jo's statement. "Same here. If worse comes to worse, though, I'm sure there will be enough people willing to drag it out through the legal system in order to make them think twice about it."

Chase took a drink of his ginger ale. "Let's hope it doesn't come to that. I think we all have enough on our plates without throwing a legal battle into the mix."

Matt ambled into the kitchen. "What about a legal battle?"

"We were catching Miranda and Caridad up on the water thing," Chase said.

"Ugh. Don't get me started on that guy. And yeah, we all have far too much on our plates right now without adding legal crap on top of it."

"Oh, come on, it's just kidney disease, moving in with your fiancee, getting married, retiring from pro baseball, and having a baby. No big deal," Owen said sarcastically.

Matt snorted. "I'm actually trying to figure out which is scarier—Chase getting married or me becoming a dad."

"You becoming a dad," Chase deadpanned, making everyone laugh.

"Love you, too, little brother."

Chase rolled his eyes. "Again with the feelings."

"Whatever. I'm just secure enough in my masculinity to freely express my emotions."

Chase stared at Owen. "Who is he and what has he done with my brother?"

Owen shrugged, fighting a smile. "Could be a pretty good alien abduction."

Before Matt could respond with what was sure to be a smart ass remark, Sarah walked into the kitchen with a tall, gray-haired man Owen did not recognize. "Chase? Pastor Robinson's here."

Sarah's eyes were full of questions, and every eye in the kitchen turned towards Chase and then the Pastor, then back to Chase.

Who just smiled before giving the older man a hug.

"Thanks for coming, Pastor Robinson. I know it was short notice, but we really appreciate it."

"Oh, it's my pleasure."

"Chase? Jo? What's going on?" Sarah asked.

Chase turned to Jo and asked, "You ready to do this?"

Jo's grin was bright enough to light up a moonless night, and she grabbed Chase's hand and said, "Absolutely, cowboy. Let's do this."

"Holy sh—crap," Matt said, glancing at the Pastor and editing himself mid-sentence. "Is this what I think it is?"

Chase raised his voice and said, "Hey, everyone. We have a surprise for y'all out in the backyard. It won't take long, I promise."

People began to murmur, and Owen asked Chase in a low voice, "Congratulations?"

Chase smiled before turning and leading everyone out into the backyard. Jenn was already there, a wide smile across her face. A bower covered with sunflowers and orange roses had apparently magically appeared since he and Caridad had stepped outside earlier, and Winchester sat beside Jenn, a white pillow attached to his neck and beginning to list to one side.

Chase and Jo stepped under the arch, Pastor Robinson joining them.

As everyone crowded into the backyard, their murmurs became louder.

Caridad stood on her tip toes and whispered in Owen's ear, "Did you have any idea about this?"

"Not a freaking clue," he whispered back.

Chase cleared his throat and the crowd instantly quieted. "Obviously, this isn't just a Christmas party, and obviously all of you know about what's going on with me. Jo and I talked about it, and both of us agreed that we both wanted a small, casual wedding with our closest friends and family present. So thanks, y'all, for being here."

The couple turned back to Pastor Robinson, who removed

the Bible he'd had tucked under his arm, and smiled at Chase and Jo before beginning. "Let us pray."

Heads immediately bowed.

"Heavenly Father, as we gather here today to see Chase and Jolene wedded in holy matrimony, we ask that You watch over them and guide them, not only as they begin their lives together, but as they face the challenges that are sure to come. We ask that You wrap them in Your arms and fill them with Your spirit. We ask for healing, for support and comfort for those who love them, Your blessing, and Your guiding hand. In Jesus' name we pray. Amen."

The gathered family and friends quietly echoed the Pastor.

"Let us begin."

Jo and Chase turned towards one another, love shining from their eyes.

"I think we all know Matt's the more emotive Roberts brother," Chase began, eliciting a laugh from the audience, "but you, Jolene Dolly Westwood, bring out the emotion even in me."

Chase swallowed and blinked rapidly before continuing. "As I thought about what to say, the only thing I could come up with is that I'm lucky. We're lucky. You were my child-hood playmate and best friend, the first girl I ever loved and the first girl I ever wanted to kiss. We drifted apart, but fate's funny like that. Well, fate and broken hip bones—thanks for that, by the way, Nelly."

The elderly woman Owen had noticed earlier laughed, and up closer Owen could see the resemblance between her and Jo.

"I can't believe how lucky I am to have you by my side, loving me and fighting for me, supporting me and caring for me. You make me laugh, even when I don't always want to, and you remind me to breathe when sometimes it seems too hard. I am so incredibly happy that I get to spend the rest of my life waking up next to you, seeing your beautiful smile, and calling you mine."

Chase drew in a deep breath and closed his eyes briefly. "I know our time together isn't infinite, but, rather, far more finite than either of us would like. And even though I sometimes think it isn't fair to you, selfishly I am incredibly glad that you're willing to put up with me and the challenges that lie ahead, because I don't think I could do it without you by my side.

"I love you, Jolene Westwood, and will continue to love you for the rest of my life, however long or short that may be."

Several sniffles could be heard, and Owen blinked rapidly at the sudden stinging in his eyes.

Jo's chin quivered before she straightened her spine, obviously gathering herself before speaking.

"You, Chase Ashley Roberts, are my soul mate. My best friend. My partner in life and the person who makes me feel loved in a way I never have. I am so incredibly grateful to have found you again, and that you were willing to open your heart back up to me after such a long absence.

"There is no one I would rather spend the rest of my days with—how many of those there may or may not be. I know our life together won't always be easy, and that's okay. Life isn't easy. It isn't often fair. All we can do is make the most of what we've been given, and love each other enough to get through the rough patches. But there's no one I would rather experience those rough patches with, because even the roughest of patches with you is better than the smooth days without you.

"I love you, Chase Roberts, and will love you for the rest of our lives."

Someone passed around a box of tissues, and most everyone took at least one.

As the guests delicately sniffled and wiped away tears, Pastor Robinson nodded at both Chase and Jo and then launched in to the rest of the wedding vows. Owen looked down at the top of Caridad's head as his friends promised to love and cherish each other in sickness and in health, and frowned.

He was incredibly happy for Jo and Chase, but also re-alized the road ahead was not going to be easy for them. He couldn't imagine entering a marriage knowing one partner had an incurable disease that could dramatically shorten their time together. Conversely, the absolute conviction and resolve that Jo exhibited was inspiring. Talk about a strong woman.

While he certainly had no desire to enter into a marriage with that kind of ax hanging over his head, he did want what Chase and Jo had. Love. Respect. A teammate in this crazy thing called life. Someone to come home to at the end of the day and to hold in the middle of the night.

Did Cari want those same things, or was she content to keep going it alone, stubbornly independent and borderline unwilling to lean on anyone even for a few seconds?

She looked up at him smiled, her eyes glittering with un-shed emotion, and realized something: he wasn't sure logic mattered, because where she was concerned he had a hair trigger heart. All she had to do was look at him and he was a goner.

That's a little inconvenient.

CHAPTER TWENTY

"So that was...interesting," Caridad said as she flopped down on her couch.

Weddings made her tired.

Probably because they made her feel lonely, which made her feel sad.

And wasn't she just Little Miss Sunshine?

Owen sat beside her, picked up her hand and brushed his thumb back and forth across her wrist. Warm little tingles shot out from there, all the way to her toes and stopping in fun places in between.

"Good interesting or bad interesting?"

"Oh, good, definitely. They obviously managed to surprise everyone, though."

"Did they ever. I can't believe they managed to keep that from everyone."

"Well, it'll certainly make for an interesting story years down the road."

He chuckled. "Oh, today's surprise wedding was only the tip of the iceberg. Their story is quite interesting."

"I kind of picked up on that." She relaxed further back in to the cushions. "So what is their story?"

Owen toed off his boots and propped his feet up on the coffee table. "Jo, Chase, and Jenn were childhood best friends from an early age. They're the same age and were in the same grade, lived in the same neighborhood and just clicked. Jo's home life left a lot to be desired from what I've gathered, and her mom was not known for her fidelity. I haven't been told the entire story—just enough to piece things together— but when they were in high school Jo's mom hit on Chase's dad. You met Bo and Sarah tonight—they're fantastic parents and still madly in love with one another. Jo freaked out and stopped talking to Chase, even though by that point they were both head over heels for each other. This past summer Jo came back after her grandmother had hip surgery, she and Chase reconnected, and that's that."

Caridad chewed on the inside of her cheek. "So Jo just stopped talking to Chase because her mom was an adulteress?"

"Pretty much, yeah."

"Well that seems silly."

"No shit. But think about it, they were teenagers. Does anyone make good decisions at fourteen years old?"

She thought back to what she'd been like as a fourteen-year-old, how desperately head over heels she'd fallen for Eric, and conceded his point. "Fair enough. Teenagers aren't exactly known for their superior decision-making skills."

"Exactly. And anyway, the point is that they got a second chance at love, which is a hell of a lot more than most people get."

"Oh, I don't begrudge them their happiness. Not at all. I actually kind of admire Jo; I don't know many people who would willingly go in to that situation, knowing the man you're marrying may not be around to see your kids graduate from high school."

The silence in the room was heavy yet comfortable, like a hand-made quilt.

"What about you?" Owen asked quietly.

"What about me?"

"Would you marry someone, knowing you might not get

to live to be old and gray together?"

She shrugged. Once upon a time her answer would have been an unequivocal yes. Back when she'd believed in happily ever after and true love and all that jazz. Back before her faith and face had been slammed against a wall. "I want to say yes."

"But?"

"But I honestly don't know." She looked down and picked at some gun grease under her thumbnail. "Once, I would have said yes. Now, I just don't know."

A solid weight settled in her chest, shrouded in a gray sadness that made her want to kick and scream and cry at the unfairness of it all—after she curled into a ball in a dark corner somewhere and gathered her emotional reserves. Because head case.

Owen opened his mouth as if to say something, but whatever he was going to say was cut off by a knock on her door.

"You expecting someone?" he asked.

Considering it was almost midnight, no. She shook her head and got up. Owen tugged on her hand. "Let me get it."

She raised an eyebrow. "Seriously? You do realize who's hand you're holding, right?"

"Fair enough."

She rolled her eyes when he got up and followed her to the front door. She looked through the peephole, but the front porch light must've burned out because it was completely dark outside. Not even the moon provided any light.

With one hand on the grip of the Kimber Sapphire she concealed carried, she cautiously unlocked the door and cracked it open, mentally kicking herself for not putting her tactical flashlight in her CanCan Holster earlier.

Rookie mistake.

"Who's there?" she asked, her voice strong and commanding like she'd learned years ago in her self defense classes.

No one answered, and the hairs on the back of her neck stood up.

"¿Quién es?" she repeated in Spanish.

Still no answer, but she sensed someone on the front porch, hidden from her view. Which made her nervous. But she would be less nervous with a closed, locked door in between them and whoever was on the front porch, so she quickly closed and locked the door before backing up.

Owen was right there, his presence warm and comforting, and that kind of pissed her off in an admittedly irrational way. But dammit, she was fully capable of taking care of herself. She didn't need him. She didn't need anyone. She'd learned that the hard way.

She swallowed before silently moving to check the back door and the door to the car port.

Locked. Good.

She walked back in to the living room, and Owen told her, "I'm not letting you stay here alone tonight."

She nodded, torn between wanting to tell him she could handle it on her own and pulling him close and never letting him out of her sight.

She wasn't entirely comfortable with either of those reactions.

They'd just sat back down on the couch when the sound of knocking shot through the small house. Owen and Caridad glanced at one another, and he could see the fear and determination in her gaze. He knew she could take care of herself, but dammit, she didn't have to.

And he sure as hell wasn't letting something happen to her while he was around.

Cari got up and walked to her bedroom before coming back to the living room. In her hand was a small flashlight, making Owen smile.

That's my girl.

He got up and joined her at the door, neither of them saying a word. Cari silently unlocked the door, waited a beat and then threw it open at the same time she turned on the flash-light, which she aimed out the screen door.

Illuminated in the light was a tall, thin man with a shaved head and hollowed cheeks.

The beam from the flashlight trembled slightly in Cari-dad's hands before it steadied, and Owen watched in fascina-tion and admiration as Caridad's spine stiffened and she took control over herself and the situation.

The man on the other side of the door said nothing, but the wild look in his eyes—along with the dilated pupils—did not bode well. An odd, acrid scent emanated from him, as if he'd been around something chemical and the smell had embedded itself into his clothes and skin.

"What are you doing here Eric?"

Eric. Eric? Oh, shit. Something Caridad had said the other day about him floated through his memory. "Last I heard, he was living in a trailer in New Mexico and cooking meth."

That would certainly explain the smell and the wild eyes, not to mention the whole skin and bones look.

But what the hell was he doing on Caridad's front porch at midnight?

"Heard you were back in town. Had to see it for myself."

"I'm not any of your concern anymore."

Eric laughed, the sound hollow. "You've always been my concern, Caridad." His wild-eyed gaze flickered up to Owen and his features drew into a mask that would put a character in a horror movie to shame. "And now you're fucking someone else? Who the fuck do you think you are? You're a whore! That's who. A fucking no-good whore!" he yelled, spit flying from his mouth.

Owen tensed and put his hand on Caridad's shoulder, in-tent on getting her out of the way so he could take care of this piece of trash himself. He'd be damned if he was going to let some no-good, abusive, strung-out dick disrespect his woman like that.

Instead of moving, though, Caridad stood her ground and

had the audacity to glare at him. What the fuck?

"Let me handle this, Owen."

"Cari…"

"I said, let me handle it." Her tone had gone cold, devoid of any of the warmth he'd managed to coax out of her over the past few weeks.

But he wasn't going to let her get hurt, so he moved to step around her and put himself between Eric and Caridad.

"Dammit, Owen, I said let me fucking handle it!" she yelled, making him stop in his tracks.

Eric laughed, or cackled, really. "So you're fucking a pussy-whipped bastard, huh, Caridad? Does he let you order him around and do the things I used to do to you? I bet you get off on hurting him, watching him bleed, don't you?"

Caridad pointed at Eric, anger rolling off of her in waves. "What you did to me was abuse, Eric. You beat me—physically and emotionally."

The screen door flew open and before Owen could react Eric was inside the house, face to face with Caridad as he knocked the flashlight out of her hand and wrapped his hand around her wrist. Caridad winced, but didn't cry out. Owen moved again, determined to take this guy out, but Caridad shook her head and said, "Owen. I said let. Me. Handle. This."

Everything in him screamed to land one good punch on Eric's face, break his nose, show him how it felt to be pushed around and beaten like he'd done to Cari. He had a feeling, though, that if he tried to help again Cari would be just as likely to shoot him as she would Eric.

And he liked living, thank you very much.

Eric's hand around Cari's wrist tightened and he tried to pull her closer.

"I really suggest you let me go, Eric."

"Or what? You're gonna cry and scream and run to your mama? She won't believe you, y'know. She never did."

"You're an asshole, you know that?"

"And you're a slut, fucking around on me like this. Apparently I didn't teach you well enough."

Before Owen could react, Eric's free fist made contact with Caridad's cheek, the sound reverberating through the room and his skull like a gun shot.

"You're going to pay for that," Owen said before advancing on Eric.

"Owen, I'm okay. Let me take care of this."

"I'm not going to let him beat the shit out of you!"

She took her gaze off of Eric for a brief second, long enough to look at Owen and let him see her resolve. "He's not going to."

Eric's fist rose again, but before he could make contact Caridad twisted out of his hold and away, putting distance between her and Eric. Eric drew a knife from his pocket and took a step towards her. Owen took a step towards Eric because there was no way in hell he was laying hands on Caridad again, and Caridad stuck her hand down the front of her jeans and within a fraction of a second was pointing a gun at Eric.

Owen stopped. Eric, however, did not, the blade of his knife flashing in the kitchen light.

"You won't do it, Caridad. You're scared. You've always been scared. So scared. So easy to manipulate."

"You're wrong."

Eric lunged towards her, the knife pointed directly at her torso. As if in slow motion, Owen saw Caridad's thumb flip off the safety, her finger pull back on the trigger, heard the sound of the gun firing. His ears rang as Eric collapsed to the floor, blood quickly soaking the front of his shirt.

"Cari?" Her head snapped up and she looked at him, her eyes focused and clear. Good. "Are you okay?"

She nodded then licked her lips. "You might want to call 911."

"Right."

His phone. Where was his phone? Back pocket. That's where. He slid it out and dialed 911, tried to explain the situation as calmly as he could considering he was barely managing to not lose his shit.

You would think someone who'd been in the military would be able to handle something like this better.

Yeah, but something like this has never involved the woman you love.

He informed the operator that he didn't know if Eric was still breathing and had no intention of getting close enough to him to find out for safety reasons. He then gave the operator Cari's address while Caridad kept her gun trained on Eric, calm as can be.

It was a weirdly scary turn-on.

And completely inappropriate.

After what seemed like hours the sound of sirens could be heard in the distance, drawing nearer with rapidity. A Val Verde County Deputy Sheriff appeared, followed by another officer, and stepped inside the house. Owen hung up his phone, and Caridad flicked the safety on before setting her handgun on the floor.

The deputy introduced himself and then flicked his gaze from Owen to Cari to Eric and asked, "So what happened here?"

As the other officer checked Eric over—for weapons and a pulse, Owen assumed—Caridad recounted the night's events in a tone so cool and collected Owen wondered if maybe she was in shock. He'd seen her operate before and knew she just went to a completely different level when she had a gun in her hands, but this was beyond what he'd seen in the deer stand, at the range, or in any of her YouTube competition videos.

As she was explaining to the deputy what had happened, a couple of paramedics walked in with a stretcher and various and sundry medical equipment. The other officer declared Eric clear of any weapons, allowing the paramedics to check his gunshot wound and vitals. The female paramedic called in something on her radio, but all Owen could make out was the word "coroner."

He swallowed the bile that threatened to rise up in his throat.

The deputy took Caridad's statement and then Owen's as they waited for the coroner to show up.

Some time later, after the coroner had showed up and collected Eric's body, the deputy asked them if they could follow him back to the Sheriff's office. Caridad smiled tightly and said, "I'll be more than happy to, sir, once I've had a chance to call my attorney."

The deputy nodded. "Understandable." He handed Owen and Cari both a business card and asked them to call him in the morning once they were able to make it down to the station. The entire experience with the paramedics, coroner, and Sheriff's department was oddly surreal, almost as if they were in some third dimension.

After the deputy left Owen went into the kitchen, filled a baggie with ice and wrapped a kitchen towel around it before taking it back to Caridad, who still stood in the middle of the living room. She took the ice pack from him and pressed it to her jaw, which was beginning to swell.

She closed her eyes and inhaled. "I think you should go home now, Owen."

"Cari—"

"Don't 'Cari' me, Owen! Just go home, okay?"

"But—"

"I'm serious, Owen, and I'm not in the mood to argue. Just go home."

"I'm not leaving you here by yourself after what just happened."

"I think I can obviously take care of myself. I'm a big girl now. Ha ha."

He ached to touch her, to hold her, to make sure she really was okay even though it was blatantly obvious to him she wasn't. Instead of doing that, though, he simply said, "How about we make a deal? I'll sleep on the couch and give you your space, while I get some peace of mind that you're okay."

She turned away from him, walking into the kitchen where she unwrapped the bag of ice, opened it and dumped the contents in the sink. "I'm okay, Owen. Promise."

"You might be, but I'm not. He *hit* you, Cari, and you wouldn't let me do anything to help! He fucking hit you!"

She turned back to him and yelled, "And I fucking killed him, Owen! I told him years ago that if he ever hit me again I would kill him. He apparently didn't believe me, so now he's paid the price. I don't need you to rescue me! I had it handled!"

Her words pelted his heart like hail on a windshield.

"Stop being so stubborn! You don't have to go through everything alone. Don't you get that?"

"Yes, I do, Owen." She was like a balloon that had suddenly been deflated, and she slouched against the kitchen counter. "Nothing good stays that way for long."

"Cari—"

"If it'll make you feel better to stay the night, fine. I'll get you a blanket and a pillow."

Caridad walked slowly out of the kitchen and down the hall, where he heard her open and close a door shortly before returning to the living room and setting an afghan and a pillow on the coffee table. She didn't even glance at him before going back to her bedroom. He heard her door close and rubbed his hands over his face.

What the hell had just happened?

CHAPTER TWENTY-ONE

CARIDAD TOSSED AND TURNED THE REST OF THE NIGHT, UN-ABLE to close her eyes without seeing Eric's lifeless body.

Somewhere around dawn she curled up into a tight ball in the middle of her bed as silent sobs wracked her body. She shook. She ached. Her chest felt hollow and like she couldn't catch her breath.

She'd killed him.

Logically, she knew that she'd been protecting herself and, yes, Owen. Even if he thought it should be the other way around. Emotionally, though? Oh, God.

I killed him.

The words played on an endless loop in her head, fueling her tears and stealing her breath.

And then there was warmth behind her, dipping the mattress and wrapping his arms around her. She wanted to push him away, be strong, prove that she was fine on her own.

Except she wasn't fine.

She was nowhere near being fine.

Owen's scent enveloped her, the familiarity both soothing and frightening. She hadn't meant to feel this way. Didn't want to feel this way.

She hadn't wanted to shoot Eric.

She wasn't sure how long she bawled like a baby, but as

her sobs finally decreased in both quality and quantity, she was begrudgingly glad for Owen's stubbornness, even if she would have preferred to lose her shit without him seeing it.

Her heart rate finally slowed and sobs turned to sniffles, she cleared her throat and said, "I probably need to call my attorney."

"Probably." Owen's voice was rough, as if he'd been crying, too.

But he was a big strong alpha male, and big strong alpha males didn't cry.

They also don't listen when you tell them you can take care of things yourself.

Anger tried to build back up, but she was too damned exhausted for it to really take hold. So instead of trying to kick him back out, she uncurled her body and stretched out alongside him, her back to his front, and let his warmth and his scent lull her to sleep.

Owen held Cari as she slept, somehow barely managing to not squeeze too tight out of sheer gratitude that she was okay.

Well, okay was definitely a relative term in this situation, all things considered.

The swelling in her jaw had gone down over the past few hours, but a bruise was definitely starting to bloom on her cheek. Looked like it was going to be a nasty one, too.

At the thought of what Eric had done Owen's fists clenched so tight his fingers began to tingle.

Calm down. Breathe in. Breathe out.

He still couldn't believe Cari had ordered him to stay out of it. If she'd just let him step in when he'd first tried to, maybe none of this would have happened. Maybe she wouldn't have been hit and then wouldn't have killed a man in self defense.

Maybe.

Shoulda. Woulda. Coulda.

He never wanted to be that scared again, though. There were so many ways that situation could have gone even more sideways, ending up with Caridad the one in the morgue rather than Eric.

And he'd just stood there like a pansy and let his woman get the shit knocked out of her.

Owen inhaled deeply before slowly exhaling, wishing the action would take his self-disgust right along with it.

GP

Some time later Caridad woke up to an empty bed, the sheets cool beside her where Owen had been just hours before. She stretched and yawned before sitting up and then swinging her legs over the edge of the mattress. Feeling a little like a cast member of *The Walking Dead,* she plodded towards the bathroom.

After splashing some water on her face and brushing her teeth, she tread softly down the hallway into the living room, expecting to find Owen on the couch or in the kitchen.

Except he wasn't there. The boots that had been on the floor in front of the couch were gone, the blanket folded up with the pillow sitting on top of it. The blood on the floor had been cleaned up, too, which she honestly was not complaining about.

She wandered into the kitchen and found a note on the counter top, written in an unmistakably masculine scrawl.

Funny, that was the first time she could recall seeing Owen's handwriting.

Cari,

You looked like you needed sleep, and something came up that I had to take care of. Didn't want to wake you. Call me if you want me to go down to the Sheriff's office with you for moral support.

Yours,

Owen

She crumpled the note up into a ball and threw it across the room.

Then promptly ran across the room and picked it back up, smoothing the paper and tracing the words with her fingertip.

No. None of this.

None of this mooning over a man bullshit. It did absolutely no good, especially when said man was hard-headed and refused to listen when she told him to stand down.

But he held you when you cried.

So.

And he gives amazing sex.

Truth.

But she wasn't backing down from her principles just because he gave her butterflies and mind-blowing orgasms.

Or, y'know, held you while you totally lost your shit.

Ugh.

She stuffed the note in a drawer and went back to her bedroom to grab her phone and call her attorney.

Hours later she'd been allowed to leave the Sheriff's office with the news that charges would not be filed against her. Since she'd previously had a restraining order against Eric along with documented domestic violence—not to mention Eric's criminal record, which had become quite impressive over the past few years—combined with Owen's statement, the Sheriff said he thought it was a pretty cut and dry case of self defense.

Case closed.

If only she could close down her brain that easily, she thought as she pulled up to her parents' house.

She turned her truck off and stared at the front door, wondering why she'd even come by in the first place. She wasn't in the mood to deal with her mom.

Sighing, she got out of the truck, walked up the front walk and opened the front door to the house she'd spent the majority of her childhood in. It had been a good home to grow up in. Warm. Full of laughter and the amazing scent of her mom's cooking. It hadn't been until she'd gotten older—until she'd pressed charges against Eric—that her memories of this house had become tainted.

As she closed the door behind her, Bruce looked up from his recliner and said, "Hey, Cari. We weren't expecting you."

"I know." Her bottom lip quivered. "Sorry. I can g—go."

Bruce swiftly got up from his chair and made his way to her before pulling her in for a tight hug. Caridad hugged him back, the familiar scent of cigar smoke and Old Spice making her feel safe. His hand rubbed her back as tears silently leaked onto his shirt, soaking the front of it.

"What's wrong, baby girl?"

She smiled weakly at his endearment. When was the last time she'd let her dad call her that?

Somewhere around the time Eric had shattered her trust and faith in men.

He screwed me up so much worse than I ever realized.

Caridad pulled away and swiped at the tears running down her face. Bruce gasped and asked, "What the hell happened to your face? That boy you've been seeing didn't do that, did he?"

Her movements stilled. "What boy?"

"That one Mikey was teasing you about a couple of weeks ago, the one who owns the ranch."

He thought Owen had caused the bruise on her cheek?

She burst into laughter, the sound going from jolly to hysterical in less time than it took to tie her shoes.

"I'll kill him," Bruce muttered.

"Too late. He's already dead."

"The ranch owner's dead?"

She shook her head. "No, Daddy, not Owen. Eric. Eric's dead."

Bruce led her to the love seat and pushed down on her shoulders until she sat. "Maybe you should back up and start from the beginning."

"Probably. Are Mom and Mikey home? I'd rather only tell this story once rather than three times."

"Gloria! Mikey! Caridad's here."

Her mom walked into the living room, wiping her hands on a kitchen towel. The smile on her face quickly fell as soon as she laid eyes on Caridad's cheek, and her gaze got that far-away look that drove Cari nuts.

Mikey walked in, his eyes glued to the screen of his phone. "Hola, sis."

Gloria sat down and Mikey leaned against the door frame, never taking his eyes off of whatever he was doing on the device in his hands.

"Mikey, could you put the damned phone down for a few seconds? Something's happened," Bruce said.

Her brother glanced up, irritation marring his features, but the moment his gaze fell on Caridad's face the phone clattered to the floor, forgotten.

"What the hell happened to you? Did Owen hit you?"

She shot up from the couch and tugged at her hair. "For the love of tits, no, Owen did not hit me! Owen would never hit me or any other woman. And what makes you think a guy did this anyway? I could have been in a car accident or fallen and bumped my head for all y'all know."

Did no one think she was capable of defending herself, taking care of herself? Did they all think she was some help-less damsel in distress that needed to be saved?

Screw that.

She was the hero of her own life story. Or however the hell that famous quote went.

"Well then who's dead?" Bruce asked, clearly confused.

"Dead?!" Gloria exclaimed.

"What the actual fuck?" Mikey asked.

Caridad raised her hands and yelled, "Stop! All of you. If you would just shut up and let me talk..."

Her parents and brother remained blessedly silent. "Fine. Now that we've got that out of the way, long story short is that I had an unexpected visitor last night by the name of Eric. He forced his way into my home, grabbed me, hit me—which is where the bruise came from—and threatened me with a knife, so I took care of the situation."

"What do you mean you 'took care of the situation?'" Gloria asked, her voice weak.

"I drew my concealed carry weapon and shot him in the chest. I killed him."

Gloria flinched at Caridad's sharply spoken words, and Mikey's face drained of all color.

"He'll never be able to hurt me or another woman ever again, which he'd apparently made a habit of once he left town and move to New Mexico. He had a rap sheet as long as my arm, including several charges for domestic abuse and drug possession."

Gloria sat down and reached up and grabbed Bruce's hand. "Are you okay?"

Wait. Her mom actually sounded like she *cared.* What kind of alternate universe was this?

The vulnerable look in Gloria's eyes caused Caridad to sigh and say with complete honesty, "I don't know yet. I need to call my therapist, because I know I'll be dealing with the psychological repercussions of this for quite some time. But that can wait until tomorrow. Today, I've just been going through the motions and taking care of what absolutely had to be taken care of."

Mikey slid down the wall and plopped down on the floor. "Holy shit, Cari. I can't believe...I can't even..."

"I know. Me either."

"If you need to stay here a while you're more than welcome to do so," Bruce said.

Caridad smiled. "Thanks, Dad." She swallowed thickly and then asked, "Can I, um, talk to Mom alone?"

"Sure thing, baby girl."

Once Bruce and Mikey had left the room, Caridad sat down on the sofa beside her mom and gathered her thoughts before saying, "Can I ask you about something?"

"Sure." She sounded uncertain.

Caridad took a deep breath and plunged right in. "The other day I was going through one of the closets with a bunch of Abuela's stuff in it, and I found a box that had a bunch of old photographs and news clippings and stuff in it. It also had my father's death certificate in it." She lifted her gaze and looked Gloria straight in the eye. "Why didn't you ever tell me he killed himself?"

Gloria flinched, and then crumpled before Caridad's eyes.

"Mom? You okay?"

Her mom blinked back emotion before speaking. "I didn't want you to think poorly of him, or that you'd done something to cause it."

"Why would I have thought that? I was just a kid."

"You wouldn't have then, but you might have later. When it became obvious to me that the only memories you had of your father were the good ones, I didn't want to taint those in any way."

"Are you saying there were bad memories?"

"Oh, Caridad. There were so many bad memories, and so many good ones."

"What happened, Mom?"

"Well, your father…he was a lot like Eric."

"Meaning?"

Gloria nodded. "He was abusive. He was also sick but too proud to ask for help or take meds when they were prescribed to him. Your grandmother and I had him committed once, and he was diagnosed as schizophrenic and manic depressive. When he was on his meds, he was the sweetest, loving man. Off of them, though, he was mean and abusive with violent mood swings. The first time he hit me, I told myself it was because he'd forgotten to take his meds, that it wasn't actually him. I begged for him to take his meds and get help. He said he would, but he never did. He would take the pills for a few weeks and then stop taking them again. The second time he hit me, I took you and left. A few days later the cops showed up at my parents' doorstep looking for me so they could tell me my husband was dead."

"Jesus, Mom."

"I gave almost all of your father's photos to your grand-mother, and I let her keep the death certificate because honestly I didn't want to be reminded of it." She reached out and took Caridad's hand in her own. "I know I should have told you, and that you shouldn't have found out the way you did, but I was just trying to protect you."

Caridad looked down at their clasped hands and asked, "Then why did you blame me when I came clean about Eric abusing me? You were so disappointed in me, and it seemed like you took his side and thought it was all my fault."

"Oh, cariña. I was never disappointed in you. I was sad for you. I hurt for you, and it made me relive a lot of things I hadn't ever wanted to think about again. I didn't handle that situation as well as I should have, and for that I am sorry."

"I can't believe I killed him, Mama," she whispered brokenly.

Gloria pulled Caridad close and Cari rested her head on her mom's shoulder.

"I can't imagine what you must be going through right now, but you don't have to go through it alone."

"Thanks." She sniffled. "Te amo, Mama."

"Te amo, cariña."

CHAPTER TWENTY-TWO

FOR DAYS AFTER THE INCIDENT WITH ERIC, OWEN WAS AT HIS wit's end.

Stick a fork in me, I'm done.

He'd called and texted Caridad every day since he'd left Sunday morning, and she hadn't responded or answered the phone. He'd seen lights on over at her place the past two nights, along with her truck parked in the driveway, so he knew she was home.

He was done losing his mind over a woman who repeatedly shut him out and pushed him away only to pull him back to her.

No matter how much he loved her.

So now he found himself sitting in April's, bellied up to the bar, and drinking. Alone.

Winning.

He'd worked his fingers to the bone this week, picking up any and every odd job he could and then going home and renovating the loft that didn't really need to be renovated. But it had been something to do with his hands and focus his mind on, when what he'd really wanted to do was pound on Caridad's door and beg her to just let him in.

God, he was pathetic.

It also didn't help that someone else in the bar was apparently in a similar mood as him, considering the past three songs had all been about heartache and breakups, and William Clark Green's "Fool Me Once" was currently playing, which was far too appropriate for his current situation. He raised a silent toast to his unknown broken-hearted brethren.

He'd known she was prickly from the beginning, known she had baggage and obvious issues, and yet he'd been unable to stay away. Like the proverbial moth to the flame—and really, how cliché was that?—he'd been unable to resist her occasional smiles and sharp wit, not to mention her strength and determination.

One day, you'll meet a woman as stubborn as you are.

His mom's words echoed through his head, causing him to smile ruefully. Thanks, Mom.

Owen tipped back his beer and drained the rest of the bottle before signaling to Shae to bring him another. The young woman set a Shiner in front of him.

"Thanks."

"No problem. One of the gang coming to drive you home?"

Shae was the primary bartender at April's and they'd all gotten to know her over the past year or so that she'd been working there.

"I'm fine."

"That's your sixth beer, Owen. You rarely drink that much."

He sighed and pulled out his phone. "Fine. I'll get someone to drive me home if that makes you feel better."

The only problem was that he didn't know who to call or text. Chase and Jo had gone back to Austin for the week, since Jo still had to finish up the fall semester. Jenn was pregnant and didn't need to be in a bar and Matt would probably just give him hell. No way was he calling Caridad.

Matt it is.

Owen: Shae's threatening to confiscate my keys if I don't have someone come up here and take me home.

There. That didn't sound drunk at all.

Not that he was drunk, but the bartender was probably right that he didn't need to be driving after having six beers.

Matt: You're the most literate drunk ever.

Owen: I'm not drunk. Maybe a little buzzed.

Matt: Be there in a few, Buzz Light Year.

Owen rolled his eyes and took another pull from his beer bottle. Ten minutes later Matt plopped down on the barstool beside him and asked, "So what has you getting drunk on a Thursday night?"

"Good evening to you, too," Owen said, feeling slightly surly.

"Oh, I'm sorry. I didn't realize you wanted to exchange formal greetings. In that case, good evening, Owen. What the hell has crawled up your ass?"

Owen snorted. "Nothing. Just needed a drink."

"How's Caridad doing since the break-in?"

Owen's head whipped around so quickly he almost gave himself whiplash. "How'd you know about that?"

"Dude, it was in the newspaper. Plus, Darrin mentioned it to me. So what happened?"

He shrugged. "Her ex boyfriend decided to forcibly enter her home, hit her, and threaten her with a knife. She shot him. He's dead. The end."

"She okay?"

"I guess."

Matt's shrewd gaze looked at him a little too closely, making Owen want to squirm. He guessed he now knew what it felt like to be a rookie batter facing the great Matt Roberts.

"Let's go play a game of pool," Matt said.

"Let's not."

"Yes, let's," Matt said, grabbing Owen's bicep and hauling him off his bar stool. The fact that Matt was able to do that let Owen know that he was maybe feeling the beer a little more than he'd realized—he wasn't exactly a featherweight.

Matt dragged Owen to the pool room, grabbed two cues

off the table and tossed one to Owen. He barely caught it. Matt set up and racked, then told Owen, "Okay, Daniels, get it off your chest."

"What is up with you and all this talk about feelings?" Owen muttered.

Matt just smirked, the asshole. "I'm a more evolved man than most, my friend."

"Chase is right—you really are kind of weird."

Matt sank a ball—Owen didn't even care which one—and said, "We're all kind of weird, some of us are just more comfortable than others letting our freak flags fly."

Fair enough. A heavy feeling in his chest, he said, "I fucked up somehow, but I don't know what I did."

Matt laughed. "I'm pretty sure that's a normal occurrence when you're in a relationship. We men fuck up and we apologize, even when we have no clue what we did wrong in the first place."

"Well that's stupid."

"I agree. But it happens. Just because we don't know what we did wrong doesn't mean we didn't do something wrong." He sank another ball and moved around the table. "A wise man once told me that the key is figuring out what set her off and upset her in the first place."

Owen pinched the bridge of his nose, a memory from this past summer and a similar conversation between him and Matt popping into his brain. "Wait. Didn't I tell you that?"

"You did. So take your own advice and figure out what set Caridad off in the first place."

"That's the problem, though. I have no clue." He leaned against the wall and spun the pool cue between his hands. "We were great Saturday night at Chase and Jo's wedding and went back to her place afterward. Then her ex showed up and everything went down, and after the cops left she was *pissed* at me and told me to leave. I couldn't just leave her alone after what had happened, so I slept on the couch and left the next morning after making sure she was going to be okay."

Matt's head snapped up. "Wait. You were there?"

He nodded.

"Okay, so let's back up here. You say y'all were fine before the ex showed up, but somewhere in between that and the cops leaving everything went sideways?"

"In more ways than one."

Matt gave up all pretense of playing pool. "So what exactly happened?"

It was an easy story to recall, considering it had been playing on a constant loop in his head all damned week. "There were a couple of knocks on the door, a couple of different times. She opened it to see who was out there, and he called her some awful names and said some nasty stuff. I tried to step in because, hey, this guy was clearly intent upon doing harm to her, and she told me to back off and let her handle it. I didn't like that, but I respected it, so I didn't jump in. Things escalated and he forced his way inside. I tried to jump in again, and she told me to back off again. He grabbed her wrist then punched her in the face. I tried to go after him and she told me to back off again. I argued with her because the asshole had just punched her in the fucking face, and she got mad at me. Everything after that happened far too fast. She managed to back away from him and draw her gun. The stupid ex apparently didn't realize who he was dealing with and taunted her while advancing towards her with a knife he was waving around like an air traffic controller, and she shot him. Just as cool as can be."

"Holy shit, man."

Owen rubbed a hand over his face. "Yeah."

The silence in the pool room was heavy, broken only by the music playing through the sound system.

"So it wasn't until you tried to jump in that she got pissed at you."

Owen thought back, once again recalling the events of that night. "That's what it seems like."

"And you kept trying to jump in." It was a statement rather than a question.

"Well, yeah. I wasn't going to just stand there and let him assault her."

Matt's gaze turned thoughtful. "I'm not a woman—" Owen snorted and Matt continued, "but my guess is that she didn't want you protecting her."

"But...that's what I do. I protect the people I love. Why wouldn't I protect her?"

"Have you told her that?"

"Told her what?"

"That you love her."

"No. She hasn't exactly given me a chance to."

Matt shook his head. "You have to make your own chance."

Maybe he was a little too buzzed, because that made no sense to him. "What?"

"She may not give you a chance to tell her you love her."

"Well, obviously."

"And I don't know her entire story, just bits and pieces here and there, but from what I do know she's a strong woman who was in a bad situation and got herself out of it. We all react differently to traumatic events. Hell, look at Jenn and me, and Chase with how he broke up with Jo when he found out his health was getting worse. Caridad's had a double whammy of traumatic events, both involving someone she loved and trusted at some point. It doesn't take a shrink to figure out she's got trust issues."

"That might be an understatement."

"Can you blame her, though?"

"Absolutely not."

"I saw the way she looked at you Saturday night at the wedding. She might be mad at you right now, but she also cares. Somehow she's fallen for your ugly face."

Owen didn't rise to Matt's bait, and instead slouched against the wall. "I just wish I knew how to set things right."

❦

Friday afternoon Caridad was still pissed off. Was she being irrational? Absolutely. But no matter what she did, she couldn't seem to get rid of the jumpy, itchy feeling that had her feeling like a feral dog that snapped at anything that got in her path.

Owen had continued to call and text her, and she'd continued to ignore him.

She felt a little like an asshole for that, but her feelings were so jumbled right now she was afraid speaking to him would do more harm than good.

Or maybe that was just a convenient excuse to help her keep avoiding what was sure to be a difficult conversation.

Denial isn't just a river in Egypt.

She slumped in her chair and stared at the article she'd been working on for the past few days. And by working, she meant she'd stared at her laptop screen and retyped the first sentence at least a couple dozen times.

Productivity was not her strong suit this week, but she hadn't been able to focus on much of anything, other than the moment she'd shot Eric and then later the devastated look in Owen's eyes when she'd told him to leave. She wasn't sure what it said about her that the look in Owen's eyes bothered her far more than Eric dying on her living room floor did.

Not that that didn't bother her, because it did, it was just that, well, she wasn't going to apologize for defending herself. She knew herself well enough to realize that a massive breakdown was probably imminent; she'd been mostly detached since Sunday afternoon and knew that particular state wouldn't continue.

She'd had a Skype session with Dr. Tracy this morning and rehashed all of it. She'd also mentioned her fear that she was too detached, and Dr. Tracy had reassured her that there wasn't something wrong with her and that odds were it was a defense mechanism, her brain's way of protecting herself.

Then again, she'd also said that if the detachment lasted for too long she would be worried.

But how long was "too long?" Caridad didn't know, and Dr. Tracy hadn't specified. Caridad suspected she'd done that on purpose.

Maybe she needed to force herself to deal with it. Just rip the bandage off and be done with it.

Except she really, really didn't want to.

She was kind of pathetic.

She got up from her chair and walked into the kitchen. She got herself a glass of water and stood at the sink as she sipped it, staring out the window and across the way to Owen's house. His face flashed in her head, those blue eyes that seemed to see past all of her defenses and straight into her soul.

Her stomach flipped and her nose burned.

She barely registered the tear that ran down her cheek, or the one that followed. Instead, all she could see were Owen and Eric, their faces flipping back and forth in her mind like a demented game of Whack-A-Mole.

One man had put her through hell.

The other had been more patient than Mother Theresa.

One said mean, ugly things to her.

The other told her how beautiful and amazing she was.

One saw nothing wrong with hitting her.

The other would have gladly taken every single punch for her.

One she'd loved with all of her heart, only to have it broken time and time again.

The other she hadn't even given a chance.

She absently set the glass down in the sink, still staring at Owen's house. With a nod and a set jaw, she shoved away from the counter and grabbed her phone and keys before walking out of the house and to her truck.

For better or worse, the bandage was about to be ripped off.

CHAPTER TWENTY-THREE

"I'M COMING, I'M COMING! HOLD ON TO YOUR HORSES!" Owen yelled as he set his gloves and safety glasses to the side before turning down the volume on Wade Bowen's "Patch of Bad Weather." Who the hell would be pounding on his door like that at—holy crap, how was it already after three?—on a Friday afternoon.

Muttering to himself, he bounded down the stairs that led up to the loft and made his way to the front door. He swung it open. "Matt, I told you th…" his heart lodged itself somewhere in the vicinity of his throat. "Caridad."

She nodded. "Owen."

"Uh, how are you?"

She licked her lips. "Mind if I come in?"

"I don't think that's a good idea." Not if he wanted to keep his heart intact.

She drew in a sharp breath and closed her eyes. Her head hung and her shoulders slumped, making Owen think of a broken marionette.

Fuck.

Against his better judgment, he asked, "Are you okay?"

Her shoulders and her head shook, her hair curtained her face, and Owen knew for sure that there was no way he could shut her out. Maybe it was stupid of him, maybe it was reckless, but she needed him even if she didn't quite realize it or want to admit it.

He'd never been able to say "no" to a damsel in distress—even if said damsel could probably kick his ass twelve ways to Sunday.

"Come here." His command was gruff, but she stepped willingly into his arms. They stood in the doorway, his hand smoothing her hair as she doused his shirt with tears.

Long moments later she quieted and muttered into his chest, "I'm sorry."

His heart squeezed. "For what?"

She sniffled. "Everything."

"I feel like I should apologize, too, except I'm not sure what I would be apologizing for."

Her chuckle was watery. "You don't need to apologize. I was being stupid and irrational."

"I refuse to believe anyone could be stupid and irrational while facing down a guy hopped up on meth."

Her laugh warmed his heart. She stepped out of his arms and brushed her hair out of her face. Her eyes and nose were red, her lashes spiked together. Tears had dried on her cheeks, and her olive skin looked slightly pale. Just as quickly as his heart had warmed it broke.

She'd obviously had a rough week.

Ya think?

"Sit with me?" she asked before heading towards the rocking chairs on the front porch. He closed the door and followed her.

They both sat, the silence awkward and filled with too many unsaid thoughts and feelings. He waited her out, figuring she would speak when she was ready.

The toe of her Converse pushed against the porch, making her chair rock back and forth.

"It was really crappy of me to be such a bitch to you the other night," she said as she stared straight ahead.

He blew out a breath. "It was a high-stress situation."

She snorted. "No shit. That still doesn't excuse the way I treated you."

He stared at her profile. "Then why did you?"

She looked down at her hands and took a deep breath. "I needed to take care of it myself, Owen. When Eric and I were together, I never stood up to him. I just let him walk all over me and beat me down. For so long I felt hopeless, worthless, weak. I needed to stand up to him. For myself."

Suddenly things clicked into place. "And you saw me trying to help as my way of telling you you weren't capable of standing up to him."

"Kind of. More that I didn't need you to take care of it, but it felt good that you wanted to stand up for me. I was conflicted, and that pissed me off. Plus, I didn't want you getting hurt."

He scoffed. "Did you forget about the whole Army and National Guard thing?"

"That doesn't mean you couldn't have gotten hurt, Owen, and I needed to focus on Eric—not you and Eric."

"Fair enough. You know I wasn't trying to be disrespectful, though, right? I know you're more than capable of defending yourself, but it killed me to see him hit you like that." He took a deep breath. "I haven't felt that helpless since my mom died."

"I'm sorry, Owen," she whispered.

"Me too."

Cari's chair continued to rock, and Owen sat back in his.

"I keep reliving it. Over and over again. I haven't been able to sleep in days. I'm exhausted and feel like I'm walking a razor's edge right now." She laughed humorlessly. "Oh, and to top off the shit sundae that has been this week, I found out that my father was a schizophrenic, manic depressive abusive asshole and that he killed himself after Mom left him."

Owen drew in a sharp breath. "Jesus, Cari."

"Tell me about it." She grew quiet and continued to stare straight ahead. "In a way, though, I'm glad to know that about my father. And it hasn't been all bad; Mom and I finally cleared the air, which is something."

"Definitely something."

Caridad's swallow was audible. "Are we okay, Owen?"

He rubbed his hands over his face. "I honestly don't know, Caridad. I understand where you're coming from now and why you got mad at me, but how is this going to work—how are we going to work—if you shut me out every time I do something that upsets you? Because newsflash—I'm not perfect. I'm going to screw up. I'm going to piss you off. You can't shut me out every time that happens, because that's no way to have a healthy relationship."

She sniffled. "So that's it? You're breaking up with me?"

"Wait a second. First, I'm not saying it's over because I doubt I'll ever be over you. Second, how can this be a break up when we're not even officially together?"

She finally turned her head and looked at him. "Seriously?"

"Yes."

"Seriously? For the love of tits, Owen, I took your virginity!"

"I'm well aware of that fact."

"Argh!" she pulled at her hair and stood. "God, you confuse me!"

Owen shot to his feet. "I confuse you? Jesus, Cari, you just shut me out for almost a week after I watched you shoot your ex-boyfriend. Talk about confusing!"

She turned to him and poked a hand into his chest. "And I apologized for that!"

"And I accepted your apology!" He gently grabbed her hand.

"Why are we fighting right now?"

"I don't really know why."

She looked up at him, those big brown eyes wet with unshed tears, and licked her lips. "I need to forget, Owen. For just a while. I need to forget," she whispered before bringing her lips to his.

Her name was a curse on the wings of a prayer. "Cari."

"Make me forget, Owen. Please," she asked against his mouth.

Even though he felt like his heart was breaking, he couldn't deny her, couldn't say no. She needed him, simple as that.

❧

Caridad clung to Owen as if her life depended on it. In so many ways, she felt like it did, like he was the only thing anchoring her. The calm in the middle of the storm that raged inside of her.

Their tongues tangled, caressed one another, and for the first time in days she felt something *good.* Something whole. Something right.

With a gasp she pulled away. She couldn't do this to Owen. To herself. She couldn't cheapen what was between them.

Despite all her resistance, all her walls, he'd somehow gotten inside of her. This wasn't just a flirtation or an affair.

You knew that from the get-go.

"I can't do this, Owen." She gripped his t-shirt in her hands, unable to meet his gaze.

"Do what, Cari?"

His voice was so kind, so soothing. Understanding. It was the understanding that did it, that made those walls crumble all the way down. *This man.* Despite her behavior over the past week, despite her prickliness and her issues, this man saw her like no one else did. He saw her. The person she was, beneath the gunpowder and lead.

"I can't use you to make myself feel better. It'll only make us both feel worse." She swallowed and met his gaze with her own. "Sex right now would do nothing but cheapen what we have."

"Just a few minutes ago you thought I was breaking up with you."

"I know." She swallowed thickly before continuing, "I

can be an idiot sometimes, Owen. I live in my head too much. I shut people out. I'm no good at asking for help much less accepting help. I'm an anxious, neurotic mess. And yet you're still here."

He tucked a strand of hair behind her ear. "I'm still here."

"Why? Most people would have run by now."

"Because I love you." He shrugged, like it was the easiest, simplest statement in the world.

Caridad's jaw grew slack and her brain cells flew in a million different directions. He...wait...he...holy crap...he *loved her?*

"Breathe, Cari." There was laughter in his voice.

She took a deep breath, and at the sight of his slight smile those million scattered brain cells came back together at the same time she became aware of her wildly thumping heart and the butterflies in her stomach. "Seriously?"

"Absolutely."

"But I'm hard to love."

"Not really."

"Even though I can be bitchy and have random panic attacks and the only time I feel remotely in control of my life is on a gun range?"

"Those things make you who you are."

The butterflies settled and her heart rate slowed, and she felt calm for the first time in...wow, years. She smiled, the movement feeling joyful and carefree. Right. "I don't know what I ever did to deserve you, Owen Daniels, but God I love you. So freaking much."

His answering smile filled up the rest of her broken places. "I know."

She punched him in the arm. "You know? Cocky bastard."

He pulled her to him and kissed her hard. "And you love it."

She smiled up at him. "Yeah, I do," she said before pulling his head down to hers for a kiss.

This one she didn't stop.

***

Keep reading for an excerpt from the book that started it all:
Between the Seams

Enjoy what you read? Please consider leaving a review so
other readers can discover great books, too!

Acknowledgments

First, I want to thank The Randy Rogers Band for writing "Speak of the Devil," which contains the words "hair trigger heart" in the chorus. The very first time I heard that song, I looked at my husband and said, "That's a fantastic book title!" And from there, this story was born. So thank you, Randy Rogers Band. ;-)

Second, I want to give a HUGE thank you to Janna Reeves who was a big help in getting certain things right about Caridad. I had a ton of questions for her, and she answered all of them (and then some!). If this book was your introduction to the shooting sports and you're curious, check out Janna's Facebook page—she posts all kinds of cool stuff, including match videos if you're curious as to what a Three Gun match entails.

Third, thank you to you, the readers, for making all of this possible. I know this book's a few weeks later than I'd originally promised, so THANK YOU for your patience and understanding during what has been a stressful, hectic past few months. I hope it was worth the wait, and that you love Owen and Caridad as much as I do.

As always, I have to thank my husband for his never-ending support not only of my writing but me in general. Thank you, honey, for giving me time to write and not pestering me too much about silly things like cleaning, laundry, dishes, or eating.

To all the survivors out there—this one's for you. Here's to your continued healing and journey to happiness and love.

AUBREY

P.S. Love what you read? Share the love and leave a review and/or rating so other readers can find books to read!

Want to Read more from Aubrey?
Check out the other books in the Devils Ranch
Series: Between the Seams, Baseball and Lessons.,
and Dallas' Most Eligible And be sure to keep an
eye out for the first book in her new series, coming
soon!

Keep reading for an excerpt from the book that
started it all, and that readers are calling "a home
run" and "a grand slam!"

Excerpt: Between the Seams

What happens when life throws you a curveball?

Chase Roberts is the quintessential Good Guy. Attractive, athletic, intelligent and successful, the former college baseball star and one-time major league prospect is the kind of guy any woman would love to take home to Mama. Except there's one small problem: Chase has never really gotten over his former best friend—and first love—Jolene "Jo" Westwood, who broke his heart as a teen. Now, all grown up with two thriving businesses, Chase has enough to worry about.

Jo Westwood just wants to come home to Del Rio, Texas, help nurse her grandmother back to health and go back to her calm-okay, boring and lonely--life in Austin once the summer's over. Unfortunately (fortunately?), her best-laid plans come to a screaming halt the moment she accidentally bumps into her former best friend--and first love--Chase Roberts in the feminine hygiene aisle. The cute boy she once knew has become a HOT man. A hot man who seemingly hates her. Great.

As the long, hot summer drags on, Chase and Jo find themselves spending more and more time together, resurrecting not-so dead feelings and putting the past behind them. Unfortunately, summer only lasts so long, and even love may not be able to survive long-held secrets that threaten to tear them apart.

CHAPTER ONE

"Yo, Chase, did you hear a word of what I just said?"

Chase Roberts snapped out of his reverie and glanced over at Owen Daniels, his best friend, business partner and occasional pain in the ass. "Sure."

Owen snorted. "No, you didn't."

A pretty blonde entered the building across the street, and Chase fought the overwhelming urge to follow her. "Did you see the blonde across the street just now?" He asked instead.

Owen opened the driver's side door of his car. "I thought you'd sworn off women? Called them all second-hand group-ies or something like that."

Chase looked at the building—Mitchell's Drug Store—one more time before climbing into the passenger seat of the low-slung Mustang. "I didn't say they were all second-hand groupies. There just happen to be more than I would like."

"Must be tough, being chased by hot, scantily-clad wom-en all the time."

Owen pulled away from the curb and Chase fought the urge to turn and watch to see if the blonde came out of the drug store.

"It is when the only reason they're chasing after me is because of my brother." Chase's brother, Matt, was Mr. Base-ball. The long-time ace for the Texas Wranglers, Matt was well-loved in their hometown of Del Rio, Texas. So well-loved the high school baseball fields now bore his name. Without a sponsorship. So well-loved that he had his own menu item at Francine's Diner. So well-loved that there was a freaking Matt Roberts Day, complete with a downtown parade. In November. After the World Series and before Winter Ball started. Hell, his brother had been given keys to the damned city.

As much as Chase loved his brother, he got tired of the groupies who decided that if they couldn't have Matt they would just settle for Chase. After one too many stories posted about him on internet message boards and questionable websites, Chase had decided about a year ago that maybe a female hiatus was in order.

Besides, he had a business to run, and even with his last name he still wanted to project the image of responsible, trustworthy businessman—not wannabe playboy.

"Boo-freaking-hoo."

Chase ignored Owen's sarcasm. "Anyway. Did you happen to see her?"

"Who? The curvy blonde going into Mitchell's?"

"Yes. That one. Apparently you did."

Owen shrugged. "She looked like she had a nice ass."

"She looked familiar."

Owen turned into the parking lot of Roberts Ventures, LLC, and swung into the space next to Chase's pickup. "Previous one-night stand?"

Chase snorted. "No. Definitely not one of those." Hell, Chase could count on one hand the number of one-night stands he'd had over his entire lifetime. His brother's groupies just made it sound like he was, well, a player.

They got out of Owen's Mustang and entered the building. Chase's executive assistant and all-around office goddess looked up and smiled at Chase. As soon as Kimberly's gaze landed on Owen, her smile quickly turned to a frown.

Chase didn't know why Kim didn't like Owen, and no amount of gentle prying had managed to get the information out of her. "Good morning, Kim."

"Mornin', Chase. We got the Sutton contract in, and Frank Wimbly called earlier, said he found a spot out by the lake that he would like to take a look at."

Chase nodded. "Thanks. I'll take a look at the Sutton contract and give Frank a call back."

He made his way to his office, shaking his head as the sound of Kim scolding Owen could be heard from down the hall.

Never a dull moment he thought as he got back to work.

Jolene Westwood was usually pretty hard to embarrass. As a high school guidance counselor, she'd heard—and discussed—some of the most embarrassing things human beings experienced. From high school crushes to missed periods to kids grappling with their sexuality, she thought she'd heard—and seen—it all.

But embarrassment was much easier to deal with when it wasn't your own, and unfortunately she was currently knee-deep in it on this lovely evening.

She'd just been standing there, in front of the pads, tampons and Monistat cream that lined the back wall of the Del Rio Walmart, debating small pack versus value pack, when she accidentally backed up into someone.

A solid someone who radiated warmth and *man.*

Slowly, she turned around, her hands still paused mid-air, holding the bright yellow and blue boxes up like some sort of offering.

Or maybe as a big fat red light.

No pun intended.

Her gaze wandered up from the box of Crest toothpaste in one hand to the center of what was definitely a polo-clad male chest and up to a jaw shadowed with dark stubble. Firm lips. Slightly crooked nose. Brown eyes that made her think of warm, cinnamony Mexican chocolate. Dark eyebrows. Dark brown, almost black hair that curled out from under a blue YETI coolers ball cap.

Jo swallowed a gasp—or, more realistically, a longing-filled sigh—and took a quick step back.

Chase Roberts.

Childhood best friend.

Teenage crush.

The boy she'd long ago said goodbye to.

Her stomach flip-flopped as she slowly lowered her hands and her gaze. Mentally drank him in.

Six-one.

Two hundred pounds.

1.87 ERA.

At least, those had been his college stats. If anything, he looked like he might have gained a couple of inches, and whatever he weighed, it sure looked like it was pure muscle.

Realizing she was staring like an idiot, she mentally shook herself and somehow found her voice. "I am so sorry, Chase. I didn't see you behind me."

Stupid, Jolene. Of course you couldn't see him behind you, it isn't like you have eyes in the back of your head.

His melted chocolate gaze traveled up and down her body before settling on her face. "I'm sorry, you seem to have me at a disadvantage—you know my name, but I don't know yours."

Jo smiled, even though she was cringing on the inside, and she fought back the sense of disappointment his words evoked. They'd been friends for years and he didn't remember her? Hell, her mother had tried to end his parents' marriage, until the truth finally came out years later that Chandra Sommers had never slept with Bo Roberts. Ends up Sarah Roberts had known that for far longer than Jo had—Chandra was more than happy to let her daughter believe the worst. And he didn't remember her?

Serves you right, for ending things the way you did.

Her voice tinged with the disappointment she apparently couldn't hide, Jo responded. "Sorry. I've changed some since the last time we saw each other. Jolene Westwood."

Chase's brows drew together over those hot chocolate

eyes. "I feel awful, but I don't remember a Jolene Westwo—wait a second. Jo? Jo Sommers?"

Jo could feel her cheeks warming and knew she was probably beet red by now. Could this be any more awkward? "Sorry. I changed my name a few years back, after my parents died."

"Westwood is your grandma's name, right?"

Jolene nodded and swallowed. "Yeah."

Lame, Jolene, lame.

Chase stood before her, a brown-eyed god with a 92 mile per hour fastball and a nasty curveball, looking for all the world like a pitcher who couldn't understand a single one of the signals the catcher was sending him.

⚭

Jo. Jo Sommers. His childhood friend and teenage crush. The captain of the cheerleading squad and smartest girl in the room (and hell, their class).

He'd known it was her as soon as she'd turned around and allowed that sea glass gaze to travel up his body oh so slowly. He'd never be able to forget those eyes——they'd haunted him for so long they were a permanent part of his psyche at this point.

She may have changed a little bit—her blonde hair was softer, longer and wavier than he remembered, and she'd gained some curves since he'd last seen her when they were in college, but he sure as hell would never be able to forget her.

So why was he playing stupid now?

She'd fueled more than one of his teenage fantasies, even after she'd suddenly stopped talking to him their freshman year of high school. As a teen he wondered if it had to do with the health issues—and eventual scarring—he'd had as a kid and young teen. Had she been embarrassed to be around him?

As an adult, he realized there could have been other reasons, but even a cocky teenage athlete can be felled by one simple brush off from the prettiest girl in school.

"So, uh, what brings you back to town?"

Smooth, Roberts, real smooth.

Worry briefly turned those sea glass eyes stormy, but the expression was gone so fast he wondered if he'd imagined it.

"Gran had a hip replaced. She refused to go to a rehab facility, and pretty much ordered me to come take care of her." A small grin played at the corners of Jo's generous mouth, and for a brief second Chase was reminded of the girl she used to be. The one who'd been his playmate and confidante.

"How's she doing?"

Jo waved her hand, and then blushed as she looked at the box she still held.

"I'm really not trying to accost you with tampons, I swear."

Chase barely managed to choke back the laughter that threatened to escape. "Well, at least they're not used."

Jesus, Roberts, that was awful.

Her blush deepened, and the chuckle that had been threatening to escape somehow managed to rumble out. Jo shook her head, smiled, and tossed the box into her cart. "I'm glad to see you still have a sophomoric sense of humor, Chase."

"At times, yes." Unfortunately.

Their gazes met, held, and then a slow smile bloomed over Jo's face before she, too, was laughing. "How about we try this again?" She held out her hand. "Hey, Chase! Nice to see you again."

Chase wrapped his hand around hers, and he swore he felt tingles shoot up his arm. "Jo, it's good to see you, too."

Unsettled, he dropped her hand and stepped back. A look of confusion flitted across her pretty face before she once again replaced it with an odd, too-placid-to-be-real smile.

Had she felt it, too?

"Well, uh, I better get going." She gestured to her cart, which held a small amount of groceries and toiletries. "Gran's waiting for me to get back so I can cook supper. Can't let her starve."

Chase took another step back, feeling the need to put

some amount of distance between them. He flexed his hand, still feeling slight tingles in his fingertips. "No, can't let her starve."

Jo began to push her cart away, and before he could take the words back he blurted out, "We should do lunch some time. Or supper. Catch up. For old time's sake."

God, he sounded like an effing idiot. Catch up for old time's sake? Yeah, because *that* sounded like a brilliant idea.

An expression Chase couldn't identify clouded Jo's eyes before it, too, was gone almost as quickly as it came. "Um, sure." She nodded her head once, her wavy blonde hair falling over one shoulder. "We'll have to do that."

Chase nodded in ascent and shoved his hands into his pockets. Jo shot him one last glance before turning from him. Chase allowed himself to enjoy the view as she walked away.

Couldn't not appreciate it, really, as it was a damned fine view. The same damned fine view he'd seen just this morning walking into Mitchell's Drug Store.

❧

 "Jolene, is that you?"

Jo set down her grocery bags and blew a strand of hair out of her eyes. "Yes, Gran, it's me."

"Good, that rehab woman just left and I'm starving."

Jo rolled her eyes. "I think that rehab woman has a name."

"Yes, the Devil's Harlot!" Gran shouted back from the living room.

Jo sighed and yelled back. "She's not a harlot, Gran." Who even used the word "harlot" anymore? "She works for Val Verde Regional Medical Center. Last I checked, Satan wasn't on their payroll."

Gran harrumphed from the living room. Jo finished putting up the groceries and walked into the living room. "Did she make you do something new today?"

Her grandmother sat in a big, somewhat comfortable chair. She waved a hand in the air dismissively. "Just a new exercise. Nothing too bad."

"Then why the name-calling, Gran?"

Gran gestured towards the flat screen TV mounted on the wall across from her. "She was lusting after that Roberts boy. Acting like a cat in heat."

"Roberts boy? Chase? Why was Chase on TV?" Jo's mind went back to the embarrassing scene in Walmart, and realized it was a good thing Gran couldn't read her thoughts. Chase Roberts all grown up was definitely worth lusting after.

Gran waved the remote. "No, not the sick one, bless his heart. The older one."

Sick? Was Gran referring to Chase's childhood illness, or did he only look like the picture of health? Hot, hot health.

"And we're back at the top of the eighth inning, and Wranglers ace Matt Roberts is back out on the mound."

Jo looked at the television and saw Chase's older brother, Matt, readying the mound for another inning. The camera zoomed in on his face, and Jo had to admit that he was definitely attractive. Always had been. Problem was, he'd always known it, too.

While Chase had been popular and well-liked in his own right, Matt had always had that "it" factor that just drew people to him. Throw in obnoxiously good looks and talent that had scouts looking at him as a freshman, and you had a combination that was hard for any girl to resist.

"The PT was openly lusting after Matt in front of you?"

Gran pursed her lips. "The shameless hussy wouldn't shut up about him. Went on and on about how 'hot' he is. Cat in heat, I tell you!"

Jo loved her Gran, she truly did, and while Jo was by no means remotely promiscuous, her grandmother's old-fashioned views sometimes came across as a little, well, old-fashioned.

"Well, Gran, in all fairness he's not an unattractive man."

"Don't you start acting like a hussy too, Jolene!"

Jo sighed. "Gran, just because a woman thinks a man is attractive, that doesn't make her a hussy. Come on, you thought Pawpaw was handsome before you married him, didn't you?"

Gran's eyes misted over and a small smile tugged at her lips. "Oh, your Pawpaw was so handsome in his dress blues. He had the most beautiful eyes—that's where you get yours, you know—and the sweetest smile. Curly black hair. Such a fine figure the first time I saw him. I knew right then I was going to marry him."

Jo smiled. "You just proved my point, Gran."

The older woman shrugged and absently massaged her hip. "Always been too smart for you own damned good."

Jo leaned over and kissed her grandmother's wrinkled cheek. "And you know you wouldn't have it any other way, young woman."

Gran couldn't hide her smile. "Don't go getting a big head, young lady. Now what's for supper?"

꧁꧂

Later that night, feeling restless and crampy and border-line maudlin, Jo climbed out of the full size bed in the room that had been her's as a teen and pulled a box from the top shelf of the closet. She set it on the floor, brushed the dust off and opened it.

Inside were high school mementos.

Her Homecoming mum from her senior year, the bells still shiny but missing a glittery letter from her name. A set of royal blue and white pom poms. The corsage Billy Walther gave her for senior prom, the roses dried and in a protective plastic case, the lilac elastic band's color still as vivid as the day he'd slid it on to her wrist. There were other pieces of flotsam and jetsam, memories of years gone by.

A newspaper article talking about how she'd made vale-dictorian. The notecards from her graduation speech. An old report card. Her acceptance letter to Baylor. Notes she and her best friend Jenn McDonnel had passed during algebra.

At the bottom of the box lay her senior memory book and

four yearbooks. She withdrew all of them and returned to the bed, leaving the other items on the floor where she'd left them.

She wasn't sure what had her feeling nostalgic. Maybe it was being back here in Del Rio, sleeping in the same room she'd slept in as a teen far too often when things went downhill at home. Maybe it was seeing Chase tonight. Or maybe Aunt Flo was just a mean bitch who made her do crazy things.

She opened the memory book, smiling at the memories and the thoughts of an eighteen-year-old girl hell-bent on changing the world. Or at least her little corner of it.

10 Years From Now I...
Will be Oprah's go-to psychologist on all of her shows
Will own my own practice
Will be married with two kids—boy and girl—to a gorgeous man who owns his own business, makes a lot of money and will never cheat on me
Will be a great mom who never cheats on her husband or abandons her kids
Will be living somewhere super cool, like New York City or Chicago or San Francisco
Will be making a six-figure salary with no debt, a nice house and driving a BMW
Will no longer feel the need to be perfect
Will know what love really is
Will be a member of the Junior League
Will be gearing up to run for office

Funny how the only one of those things that had happened was number seven.

Jo brushed away a lone tear that rolled down her cheek, hating herself for feeling maudlin but realizing that if she was there was probably a good reason for it.

She hadn't gone on to become Oprah's therapist, and instead of opening her own practice had decided to help out high school kids. God knew as a high school counselor she certainly wasn't making a six-figure salary, her student loan debt was mind-boggling and her dreams of owning a shiny new BMW had been replaced with the reality of driving a Ford Fusion. Mr. Right still hadn't come along, and at thirty-two she was beginning to wonder if he ever would. The only guy she'd loved as an adult had been shipped off to Afghanistan, and he'd ended things before leaving the States. And she certainly wasn't a member of the Junior League or planning on running for office any time soon. As for her current town......well, she sure hadn't pictured herself back in Del Rio taking care of her grandmother, but she supposed her adopted town of Austin was pretty cool. At least that's what people and dozens of weekly Top Ten lists always told her.

Jo continued to flip through the memory book, smiling at the photos and random pieces of high school life she'd glued to the pages. Towards the back, folded up and tucked underneath a photo of her, Jenn and Chase, was a lined piece of notebook paper, which she unfolded.

Dear Chase,

I'm sorry.

I'm sorry I haven't been talking to you much. I think I've hurt your feelings. I never meant to do that.

But I can't. I can't talk to you knowing that my mom has a thing for your dad. It's weird and gross and makes me embarrassed and ashamed.

My dad doesn't care who she sleeps with. I think the whole town knows that by now. He probably doesn't care if I sleep with someone, either.

But I'm not my mom. And I can't be around you because I'm too embarrassed and hurt and afraid you'll hate me.

You're my best friend. You, Jenn and me. We're the Three Amigos. I don't want to hurt you.

I'm so sorry.

Love,

Jo

She folded the paper back up and placed it in the book again, tucked neatly under the photo of her, Jenn and Chase. They'd been going into the ninth grade, the best of friends since elementary school. Until that awful day when Jo had overheard her mom on the phone with Chase's dad. The things her mom had said had made her hot with embarrassment and shame, and even though she didn't think Chase's dad would ever cheat on his wife, Jo still felt awful and as if it was somehow her fault. If she and Chase hadn't been such good friends, her mom might not have ever met his dad. So she'd done what seemed best to a fourteen-year-old girl—she'd distanced herself from her best friend even though it had killed her.

She'd written the note to him to try to explain, but in the end had chickened out. She couldn't. She was too embarrassed and ashamed and didn't want Chase to think she was like her mom.

Instead, she'd folded the note and tucked it into her diary. That night, after eating supper with her parents and being told not to eat so much—that "thinness is perfection!"—by the woman everyone thought of as The Easy Mom, was the first time Jo made herself throw up.

Want to keep reading? Purchase *Between the Seams* now, available at the following retailers:

Amazon | B&N | iBooks | Kobo

About the Author

Aubrey has been reading and writing since she was about two and a half and has been an avid romance reader since she read her first romance novel in the 6th grade. She wrote her first novel in high school. It was an ~~awful~~ imaginative historical romance that involved a cross-country trip via covered wagon, and maybe some Indians. She thinks it's still on a floppy disk somewhere (DOS computer, y'all), but can't be too sure. These days, she writes contemporary romance with a lot of humor and sass and characters that have issues.

She graduated from Seton Hill University's Writing Popular Fiction program with a Master of Arts in 2008. When she's not writing, she can be found with her husband and their two dogs at home in Austin, on their ranch in west Texas, watching a football or baseball game, or with her nose stuck in a (usually virtual) book.

Connect with Aubrey:

Website | Subscribe to Newsletter | Facebook | Twitter | Goodreads